MORE PRAISE FOR
RONDA THOMPSON!

COUGAR'S WOMAN
"Ronda Thompson has a gem here."
—*Romance Communications*

"[Thompson's] warmth and humor breathe life
into the story and keep a reader turning the pages,
long past time to go to sleep! Bravo!"
—*Under the Covers Book Review*

SCANDALOUS
"Ronda Thompson is one of those authors
whom you should have on your author's list. . . .
Scandalous is a wonderfully wry Regency . . . that
makes you want to come back for more."
—*Romance Communications*

"Ronda Thompson is not to be missed.
An innovative writer, she is not afraid to take chances.
Scandalous is a juicy Regency which will have you
smiling over the foibles and fancies of the period.
Wonderful as usual."
—*Affair de Coeur*

"*Scandalous* is a fast-paced romp readers will find
difficult to put down until the last page is read. Strong
characters provide high quality entertainment, while
the chemistry between Christine and Gavin sizzles."
—*Under the Covers Book Reviews*

His Captive's Kiss

The feel of Violet's naked body beneath him brought less than honorable thoughts to mind. Gregory stared down into her lovely face, remembering the kiss they'd shared the last time they'd met.

"Don't even think about it," she warned. "And let me up this instant! I don't want you touching me."

"You didn't mind three days ago," he grumbled. Gregory wasn't used to women growling and snapping at him. Most found him quite charming.

"Let's get something straight," she said. "I only let you kiss me so I could manipulate you into letting me get to my gun. I did not enjoy it, not for one moment."

A man's pride had no chance under the lash of her sharp tongue. "I have enough experience to know when a woman enjoys being kissed, and you did."

Her face turned red. "You are a conceited ass. I can say with all truthfulness that I did not!"

Gregory grimaced. Wooing Violet when she didn't find him attractive would prove bothersome.

"All right. I'll let you up," he finally said. "The sooner we stop this argument, the sooner I can get you home, with Miles, where you belong."

A flash of panic crossed her lovely features. He started to rise, then found the collar of his shirt twisted between her hands. "Don't you want to kiss me again?"

VIOLETS ARE BLUE

Ronda Thompson

LEISURE BOOKS NEW YORK CITY

A LEISURE BOOK®

July 2002

Published by

Dorchester Publishing Co., Inc.
276 Fifth Avenue
New York, NY 10001

ISBN 0-8439-5029-3

Printed in the United States of America.

Visit us on the web at www.dorchesterpub.com.

To Jennifer Archer. We have traveled many roads together. Through the ups and the downs, the laughter and the tears, it has been an amazing journey. A shared love for writing brought us together, but it is the gift of friendship that will forever bind us to one another. Thank you for your support, your wisdom, your willingness to listen, and for getting us back on the right road when we were lost coming home from our last conference.

Violets Are Blue

Chapter One

The gun in Violet Dalton's hand shook. She hoped Henry Blake didn't notice. The bank clerk stared down his nose at the weapon. Beads of sweat dotted his forehead. His hands trembled as he gathered the money into bank bags, then stuffed those bags into her saddle packs.

"Hurry it up," she said gruffly, hoping the deepness of her tone matched the disguise she wore. A bandanna covered her nose and mouth. She'd smeared her face with dirt, braided her hair and wound it around her head beneath her hat, but she worried that Henry might recognize her eyes. She tried to keep them squinted.

She had seethed in helpless rage for too long to let anything or anyone get in the way of her plans. There was a dark side to her that no one in St. Louis knew.

Outlaw blood ran in her veins, vengeance burned in her heart, and it was time to face the ugly truth—the nightmares from her past.

"Don't kill me, Mister," Henry said with a squeak. "I'm hurrying as fast as my hands'll go." The clerk lifted the saddle packs. "That's all there is."

While trying to impress her at social engagements in the past, Henry had often bragged to Violet about the responsibility of keeping watch over large amounts of money. What he'd stuffed into her packs just now wasn't enough to make the law sit up and take notice of her; it couldn't be everything. She cocked her gun.

"Money ain't worth dying over. I want all of it. And you'd best hurry faster!"

The clerk swallowed, his Adam's apple bobbing. He nodded, reached inside the drawer below him and stuffed another bank bag full of larger denominations before placing it, too, into her saddle pack. Violet tapped her foot impatiently. Sheriff Johnson would soon make his rounds, and while she planned to be long gone before he did, and though the man was too old to come after her himself, she knew he would send a posse.

But that was part of Violet's plan—which went farther than simply robbing Henry Blake of the bank's money. After six years of being away from her true family, she was finally going home. And if she didn't kill that sorry, drunken, son-of-a-bitch who'd sired her, she'd make certain he spent the rest of his life behind bars.

"Thank you kindly," she said, hefting her saddle

packs over her shoulder. "I got kin around Coffeyville who'll be right happy to see this loot. Does the name Dalton sound familiar?"

The clerk's face paled. "Dalton?"

"Yeah, that's what I said." The fear that clouded his eyes made her sick. She hated bragging about her relations, those villainous people tied to her nightmares, but it was necessary.

"Don't run out after me calling for help, or I'll shoot you, understand?" she added. She dug the barrel of her "uncle" Miles's gun into Henry's throat.

"I understand," he croaked.

Backing away, Violet chanced a quick glance outside. All looked quiet. She nodded toward Henry, then made her escape.

Her horse stood in the alley. Henry Blake might easily recognize the animal as belonging to Miles Traften, but Violet hoped he would be too frightened to peer out as she raced past. There was no helping the situation; she needed to head in the direction past the bank.

Mounting, she settled her money-packed saddlebags in front of her and dug her heels into her horse's sides. Blaze shot out of the alley. She would shed her disguise at the edge of town. While Violet wanted the law to come after her, she planned to lead them on a merry chase—a string of robberies that would lead straight across Missouri to the miserable shack in Coffeyville where she had grown up. Her father would pay for what he'd done to her.

Of course, if Harold Dalton had harmed one hair on her siblings' heads, he'd pay for that too—only

3

his punishment wouldn't be a lifetime in prison, it would be spitting blood from a bullet. A bullet from her gun.

But the gun in Violet's holster did not belong to her. Neither did the horse she rode or the rations she'd stolen from Miles Traften's pantry. Conscience tugged at her. Miles had been good to her over the past three years. He'd treated her kindly, like a father should treat a daughter. He'd given her fancy clothes, and fancy manners, and a home when she'd had nowhere else to go. The man had taken a stranger under his wing at his daughter's request. He'd never asked Violet about her shameful past, about the screams from her nightmares that woke his household each night. He'd been nothing but wonderful to her, and this was how she would repay him?

Tears came close to filling her eyes. Violet blinked them back. She couldn't be soft and still do what she had to do. She couldn't be the scared, pathetic creature she'd been when she'd first met Miles Traften three years prior. To save her brothers and her sweet sister Rose, Violet had to become as ruthless as those outlaws whose name she carried. She'd waited a long time to seek her revenge—too long. It was now or never.

Miles had been deceived in other ways, as well. He'd given Violet an allowance when she'd come to live with him. He'd said every young girl needed extra coin for bows and hats, flippant necessities. But Violet hadn't used her money for costly silk ribbons and fancy feathered hats; she'd hired herself a detective. For two and a half years the man had been searching for her family. Finally, he'd found them. The rat who'd sired her had at last scurried back to his nest, Violet's younger brothers and her sister Rose in tow.

Violet wondered why they'd left in the first place. Perhaps the law had taken to watching the shack at some point during her long absence. Her father had often allowed his home to serve as a hideout for his ruthless outlaw relations; perhaps that had forced him to flee. Either way, now he'd come home. And Violet's mother, God rest her soul, had not been with him. The detective had already told her about the grave on her old homestead. The tiny cross sticking up out of the barren ground that looked as if it had been fashioned by a young child.

Violet felt a stab of guilt for being relieved at the knowledge one of her younger brothers or her sister didn't rest beneath that cross, but her mother had been long dead, even before she died. She'd had her spirit beaten out of her by her husband. Violet hoped her mother had finally found peace. Now to send her father to hell, and rescue the children Violet had been forced to leave behind six years ago.

Forced. The very word made her ill. Violet had been forced to do many foul and degrading things in her past. She'd be damned if she would let anything like what had happened to her, happen to her younger sister Rose. It was a promise to herself that she must keep.

The vow gave Violet courage and strengthened her resolve. She reined her horse from the main road.

Her manly disguise must be shed quickly, now, the dirt she'd smeared across her face washed off. The law wouldn't be looking for a woman, but a man. A man she hoped they would later believe was her father.

Blaze snorted at the smell of water as Violet steered him toward the Mississippi. She dismounted and tied his reins to a tree branch. All seemed quiet. No steamboats. No sign of anyone. She removed her gun belt, threw it aside and unbuttoned her sturdy cotton shirt. Inside was the stuffing she'd used to make her body look bigger. She pulled it free. The tight binding wrapped around her breasts nearly cut off her breath. Violet glanced around again, slipped off her shirt and unwound the binding.

The cool morning air felt wonderful against her bare skin, but Violet didn't have time for sinful indulgences. She slipped her shirt back on, went to the river, and washed away the dirt she'd smeared over her face. After removing her hat and tugging her fingers through her braid, she shook her long hair free. She returned to the stand of trees where she'd tied Blaze and hefted the valise from the back of his saddle. Inside were female trappings that would transform her into a lady.

As Violet Mallory, no one would question her comings and goings. Even so, Violet wouldn't return to St. Louis to board a train, or a steamboat, or even a stage. That wasn't part of her plan. She'd find another form of transportation farther down the line. But first she had to make it farther down the line.

She removed the dusty men's clothing she wore,

slipped her chemise over her head then grabbed her corset. Her nerves were on edge. She had trouble lacing the contraption.

"Need help?"

Her fingers froze. She glanced up. A man stood before her, and where he'd materialized from she had no idea. "What are you doing here?" she asked.

His gaze drifted over her in a curious manner. "I'm camped not far away." He nodded toward another stand of trees a short distance from where they stood. "I was about to leave for St. Louis. Lucky for you, I'm still here and available to render you aid."

Lucky? This was the worst luck. The stranger would probably comment to someone in St. Louis that he'd encountered a half-dressed woman on the outskirts of town. Violet didn't want Miles to know what she was up to, where she was headed. He might get involved and get hurt. She wasn't certain she'd done a good job of convincing Henry Blake that she was a man, either. If the sheriff started putting two and two together . . .

"How long have you been watching me?" she demanded.

The stranger shoved his hat back on his head, affording her a better view of his face. He was ridiculously handsome. A fancy dude if she'd ever seen one.

"Not long enough to see you in any state but your present one. Which, of course, makes me curious about what you're doing in your present state."

"Curiosity can be dangerous," Violet said, her mind in sudden turmoil over the turn of events.

Should she do something about the man? Shoot him? She wasn't sure she'd embraced her darker side enough to kill a man with whom she had no quarrel. It occurred to her that her gun belt was too far away for her to get to easily. She'd placed herself in a compromising position.

"Have I interrupted a lovers' tryst?" the stranger asked.

She eyed him warily. "A what?"

He eyed her, too, but not warily—more with interest. "When a man finds a beautiful, half-naked woman out in the middle of nowhere, he must naturally assume a half-naked man can be found not far away."

Violet followed his gaze to the men's clothing she'd shed. Not only had the stranger provided her with an excuse for having men's clothing at her feet, but she could pretend she wasn't alone and defenseless.

"You have assumed correctly," she said. "And it would be wise to beat a hasty retreat. My protector has a nasty disposition and may take offense at another man ogling me."

One of his dark brows lifted. "Then he should have the decency to get the two of you a nice room in a hotel. That is, unless he's afraid his wife will find out."

"Wife?" Violet frowned. She suddenly understood what he meant. "Yes, exactly—so as I said, you'd better leave. Otherwise he'll return, see that you've discovered our little secret, and possibly kill you."

The stranger didn't appear particularly concerned.

His gaze swept over her again. "For some reason, you look familiar to me. Have we met before?"

Good Lord, if he kept poking and prying she would definitely have to kill him. Violet studied his face. The man did look vaguely familiar. His hair hung to his collar, seemingly dark unless one looked closely and noticed the chestnut highlights. His eyes were hazel, more green than brown with the nearby vegetation as a backdrop.

The suit he wore didn't hang on him as if cheaply made. He was clearly a gentleman, or at least he wore the disguise of one. Violet supposed she could have met him somewhere—somewhere in her hellish past or during the lie she'd been living in St. Louis for the last three years.

This was all she needed: someone to identify her leaving town on the very morning the bank had been robbed. Someone who'd found men's clothing at her feet, and her half-dressed. The situation called for desperate measures. Maybe this was another test by Fate to see if she'd grown enough spine to really follow through with her plans. It was time to embrace her outlaw side again. She had to get to her gun belt.

"Would you like to stroll along the river and try to recall where we've seen each other?" she asked.

His gaze shifted toward the bank. "I'm thinking no. It seems logical that if your lover's clothes are here on the ground, he must be bathing. You said he shouldn't see us together."

"You a coward?" she goaded.

The man answered without hesitation. "Yes. And I've just changed into this suit for a meeting in St.

Louis. A very overdue meeting, I might add. Bullet holes and blood would ruin my jacket."

She supposed her eyes widened. Bullet holes and blood would more than ruin his clothes. She'd never met a self-confessed coward before. And this one didn't act in the least ashamed about it. Violet grudgingly allowed that she envied anyone who could openly admit to what they were. Anyone who didn't hide behind a false name, the way she'd done.

"I imagine bullets and blood would mess up that pretty face of yours, too," she snapped. He had long lashes for a man, and his mouth—well, it was disturbingly sensual.

He flashed her a bright smile. "Are you flirting with me while your lover lies in wait to riddle me with bullets?"

Violet had never flirted with a man in her life. She didn't even like men. Or, at least, she didn't trust them. Of course, this one had the looks to assume every woman he met couldn't resist him. Better try to kill him and get it over with.

"Could you wait here for a moment while I fetch something I've left unattended?" she asked.

He stepped in front of her. "Something such as your lover? I said I'm a coward, not an idiot. I think we'd better kiss and say good-bye."

If not for the teasing glint in his eyes when he'd said *kiss*, she wouldn't have a single qualm about shooting him. "You must not be a coward, after all. Only a brave man would try to kiss me without my consent."

He looked amused, considered, then said, "I'm

hoping to win your consent. And if you're plotting for your lover to kill me it's a small request."

It *was* a small request, all things considered. And it was true: If she found the courage, he was going to die. Violet felt horrible about that. Perhaps a kiss wasn't much to ask. And maybe it would make killing him easier. If it stirred memories of—

In case the man had any ideas about doing more than kissing her, she'd remind him that she wasn't alone. "Perhaps we should ask for my companion's consent as well."

His smile stretched. "I say we let him get on with his bath and have the good manners not to disturb him." He moved closer.

Violet blanched. Bringing herself to kiss the man might prove more difficult than killing him. Yet it also seemed a good way to distract him to the point she could maneuver close enough to get her gun.

"You may kiss me if you'd like," she said finally. She squeezed her eyes shut and waited. The touch of the stranger's fingers against her jaw line, gentle instead of forceful, startled her. She opened her eyes. He stared straight into them.

"I would like," he assured her; then his mouth brushed against hers.

The repulsion she expected to rise up inside of her failed to appear. Surprisingly, Violet found the experience not totally to her disliking. The stranger teased her, barely touching her lips with his own; then his mouth settled firmly against hers. He gently nudged her lips apart. His tongue dipped into her mouth and gave her a jolt. He pulled her close. Too close. Fear overwhelmed her.

Violet pushed away and stumbled in the direction of her gun belt. She needed it. The stranger stared at her, his eyes bright beneath the warm afternoon sun.

"For an experienced woman, you kiss like an innocent girl," he accused. His husky voice sounded surprised. "Who are you?"

She backed from him. Her bare foot hit against the cold steel of her gun's barrel. "Who are *you*?" she countered.

"I asked you first."

Bending, she swiped up her gun, aiming it at him. "But I clearly have the advantage as to which of us will answer."

His eyes widened. "If you think you have to protect yourself, there's no need. A kiss was all I asked for, and I would never take anything from you without your consent. I am a gentleman and behave accordingly."

He thought she wanted the gun to protect herself. *Poor man.* If she intended to kill him, she had better get his name so she could say it in her prayers for forgiveness. "Your name," she prompted.

"Since you asked so nice," he said dryly, "Gregory Kline."

Her knees nearly buckled. No wonder she looked familiar to him, and he to her. He'd ridden with her and Miles Traften from Texas to St. Louis three years ago. Miles had shortly thereafter sent him to oversee a cattle merger in Wyoming. She hadn't seen Mr.

Kline since, although she had penned letters to him for Miles. She'd scarcely paid him any mind during the journey from Texas.

Gregory Kline? He was a blackmailer, if she recalled correctly; a self-professed gentleman but one who valued money and position over all else. Miles had never trusted him. His schemes had never come to much or truly hurt anyone, but still Gregory Kline had several dark marks against him.

"Go," Violet whispered. There was no way she could kill a man she knew, especially one who'd never done her any harm, even if he wasn't exactly honorable. Good Lord, she'd read this man's letters aloud to her uncle, listened to Miles snicker at his continued requests to return to St. Louis. She didn't recall Miles giving him permission.

"Your name?" he asked. "And where I might find you in the future?"

Violet cocked her gun. "We have no future, Mr. Kline. It would be best for all parties concerned if you forget you ever saw me."

Those dark-fringed eyes roamed her body and face again. "That's a lot to ask of a man. I won't forget you. Not ever."

Her insides fluttered in an unfamiliar way. "I hope you are gentlemanly enough not to mention our encounter."

He smiled, an expression she felt certain in the past had disarmed enemies and women alike. "Only a fool strikes gold then yells for everyone else to come see."

Violet waved her gun at him. "Leave."

13

Kline tipped his hat. "If you grow tired of outdoor meetings with married men, look me up in St. Louis."

She wanted him to just go. "I'll do that," she promised, hoping it would do the trick. As he began to turn away, she didn't know what made her add, "You don't mind used goods?"

His smile faded. He paused, then looked her in the eye. "I don't mind them in my bed, but I don't wear them on my arm."

At least he was honest, even if she no longer found him charming. "Your bed is someplace you will never find me, Mr. Kline. Good day."

The charming smile quickly resurfaced. "I feel certain we will meet again," he said.

Maybe in hell, Violet wanted to retort. She watched him walk away; then a few moments later he cantered out from the far-off trees riding a horse. He didn't look back, which caused a strange twinge of irritation to well up inside of her. As she'd been told, business obviously did count first with him.

Violet knew his business. She knew exactly where Gregory Kline was headed: directly to Miles Traften. The man was going to see her "uncle," the man who had treated her so kindly, only to have her stab him in the back. She hoped Kline kept his mouth shut about their meeting. She hoped allowing him to ride away wouldn't be a mistake she'd live to regret.

Chapter Two

Gregory Kline was in no mood to be sympathetic to Miles Traften's dilemma. He'd returned to St. Louis to confront the man, not hold his hand while he sniveled on about his missing niece. Gregory barely recalled the shy girl who'd traveled with him and Miles from Texas to St. Louis three years prior. He did recall that she'd hardly spoken a word to Miles, much less to him. She'd seemed content to sit quietly with her head bowed during the entire journey. Gregory had wondered at the time if she really was related to Miles at all. She'd acted as if he were a stranger to her rather than a doting uncle.

But since Gregory had been walking a thin line with Traften at the time, he'd refrained from delving too deeply into the girl's history, or what Miles had made plain was none of his business.

"About the partnership," he said again. "You said that if I handled the Wyoming cattle merger for you, you'd consider making me a partner once more. I've more than handled the merger. Hell, I've been stuck in that godforsaken place for three years!"

Miles glanced at the note in his hand, pursed his lips, and mumbled, "What was Violet thinking? Running off? Any number of horrible things might befall a young woman traveling the countryside alone."

Gregory rolled his eyes. "The partnership?" he repeated.

Moving to a window to stare outside, Miles went on, "Of course, my first instinct is to send for my son-in-law, Grady. He'd have Violet safely home in no time. But I don't want to wait on him to arrive, and . . ." His face softened. "Since Lilla is with child, I'd hate to pull him from her side." He glanced at Gregory. "Did I tell you I'll soon be a grandpa?"

"That's nice," Gregory grumbled. He was surprised Miles wasn't a grandpa three times over in the three years that Grady Finch and Lilla had been married. He'd figured with the way those two carried on, Lilla had probably been with child the day she married her cowboy. He guessed saying so wasn't a good idea in front of her father.

"I had my doubts that Lilla would conform to Texas life, but she seems to love being a rancher's wife. She—"

"Could we get back to the subject at hand?" Gregory interrupted. He grew angrier by the moment. After three years of being banished to hell, he'd begun to suspect Miles had no intention of making him a partner in the company again, or in fact, of ever sending for him to return to St. Louis.

"Oh, yes." Miles sighed. "Violet."

Gregory's patience stretched past the breaking point. "To hell with Violet!" He approached his old partner. "I'm tired of you tiptoeing around the subject. Did you or did you not promise me that if I'd handle that cattle merger, you would consider reinstating my partnership in the company?"

The man bristled. "Watch it, boy."

It was too much for Gregory. "Have you ever been to Wyoming? It's worse than Texas! Look at my hands!" He shoved them into Miles's face. "Do these look like the hands of a gentleman?"

Traften blinked. "Good Lord, you've developed calluses."

"You should see the ones on my ass," Gregory spat. "Calluses aren't the worst of it. Scorching heat, blinding sun, freezing winters, nothing but cows for company—and I'm referring to the women in that statement as well as the beasts."

"You seem to have survived," Miles commented wryly. "And from all accounts given to me by the ranchers in the area, even managed to earn their respect. That surprised me."

"Don't pretend you didn't know what I was up against when you sent me out there," Gregory said in a snarl. "You knew those ranchers and cowhands weren't going to be ordered around by a greenhorn. They didn't take me seriously until I rolled up my sleeves and jumped in the middle of everything. I worked right alongside them. I told them what grass-land to fence off, how to move cattle from one pasture to another so the grass didn't all die off. I did everything you asked of me; now I want my due."

"The partnership."

"Respectability," Gregory corrected. "A chance to be considered a gentleman about town again. You took my life away from me four years ago. I want it back."

Lifting a brow, Miles said, "You're the one responsible for your bad fortune, Gregory. You were too greedy. You used blackmail against another partner. You used blackmail against his wife. You tried to woo my daughter, not because you cared for her, but because you wanted my wealth. You even followed her to Texas in hopes of talking her into marrying you, and when that didn't work out, you used her to worm your way back into my good graces. Wyoming was better than you deserved."

If the man expected him to lower his gaze in a show of shame, Gregory wouldn't oblige him. He'd done what he'd been raised to do: rise above, be better, be richer, do whatever it took to get to the top. It was a family tradition. Every man for himself.

"You never planned on giving me the partnership," he accused. "You thought I'd either get killed in Wyoming or tuck my tail between my legs and run. You never counted on me sticking by my word."

"Do you blame me?" Miles walked away. He seated himself behind a desk, carefully placing Violet's farewell note before him. "You've never proven yourself trustworthy. I admit it: I didn't think you had the brawn or the brains to last in Wyoming, much less do a good job of things and earn the ranchers' respect."

Gregory's hands clenched and unclenched at his sides. "But that isn't good enough for you, is it? I haven't suffered enough, in your opinion."

"You haven't changed," Miles countered. "Not on the inside, only on the outside. Life is still about power to you, isn't it, Kline? It's about who has the most money, the most prestige. It's about who is the most envied."

He had trouble seeing the man's point. "So?"

With a sigh, Miles retrieved his letter and stared at it, his eyes misting over. "Life is about so much more than those things. Without love and family, none of it means anything."

Good God, Gregory thought, the man might break down and cry. Who was Violet Mallory? And how had she managed to turn this once-strong, business-smart man into a blubbering old fool?

"So that's it?" he asked. "I work hard for you for three years, and I walk away with nothing but calluses and scars." He swore, then moved toward the door. "I'd like to punch you, Traften—but since you've turned into a blubbering old man, I can't see where I'd find it very satisfying."

Miles glanced up. "Well, at least you've learned to be honest."

Gregory could be honest, all right. His parting remark was two short words—vulgar ones. He almost made it out the door before Traften stopped him.

"Hold on a minute, Kline. Maybe Wyoming has toughened you up." He glanced at the letter he held. "I may have another proposition for you. That is, if you can still conduct yourself like a gentleman when in the company of a lady."

"I haven't been around many ladies for the past three years, and if this proposition is anything like the last one, go to hell. I'm not stupid."

"No, you're not stupid," Miles agreed. "In fact, you can be quite cunning. Which may work to your advantage in this particular venture. I want you to find Violet for me and bring her back."

Gregory laughed. "Why should I?"

"For the partnership." Miles dangled the bait. "If you find Violet for me and bring her back, I'll help you get all that your heart desires—respectability, a place here in the community, a position in my cattle company. Walk away now, and you leave with nothing."

Gregory turned back. "And that's all I have to do? Find a girl and bring her home?"

Miles wouldn't look him in the eye. "There's more that you should know."

Curious in spite of himself, he retraced his steps. "Such as?"

The older man tugged at his collar. "I believe Violet's done something . . . something horrible."

"Go on," Gregory prompted.

The man rose from behind his desk. "She took my best horse and supplies, but that is not any concern to me. This morning someone robbed a bank downtown and made off with a considerable amount of money. Henry Blake said he wasn't sure the man was a man, after he thought about it. Maybe a young boy or a woman. I fear . . . well, Violet didn't take any money from me, and she has a bit of a past."

Gregory lifted a brow. "Your niece has a past?"

Miles frowned. "Nothing you need to worry about. But I fear Violet might have robbed that bank with some grand scheme in mind."

"Robbed a bank?" Gregory laughed again. "That little mouse I met three years ago in Texas? You've got to be joking."

"Violet is much changed since you last saw her," Miles argued. "She's grown into a breathtaking beauty, and I fear something—or someone—has sent her on a journey for vengeance. The rumor has reached me that she was lately seen in a rather . . . unsuitable establishment talking to a man of unscrupulous character."

His accusations were hard for Gregory to believe. He'd barely seen the girl's face, since she'd had her head bowed most of the time along the journey. He did remember thinking her hair was lovely, all different shades of gold and brown. The same color as that of the woman he'd encountered earlier this morning. He suddenly felt uneasy. That woman had claimed to be a man's mistress but kissed like an innocent. She'd looked familiar to him.

"But the bank robber was dressed like a man," he said.

"Yes," Miles agreed. "However, Henry thought that his voice didn't sound deep enough to be that

21

of a man. That's why he later suspected a boy, or possibly a woman."

Gregory remembered the dusty clothes pooled at the woman's feet. They hadn't been fine clothes, now that he thought about it. Not something a wealthy man would wear while entertaining a mistress. He remembered thinking the horse was from good stock, though. And it hadn't occurred to him to wonder why there was only one.

"Describe the horse she took."

"Blaze. A black gelding with four white socks and a blaze down his nose."

It couldn't be. The delicious creature he'd stumbled upon earlier that morning couldn't be the mousy girl he'd traveled to Texas with. But everything he'd just heard since said she was.

"Did she take a weapon?"

Miles nodded. "My Peacemaker is missing."

Gregory swore under his breath.

"Beg your pardon?"

He didn't respond. Thoughts whirled through his head. Violet. Could she really be the woman he'd kissed that morning? The woman he'd had every intention of stealing away from her married lover once he'd settled into his former lifestyle? He'd thought she was a kept woman; instead, she might be Miles Traften's niece. And a bank robber.

Money. Miles had said lots of money had been taken from the bank.

"Why would you trust me?" he asked Traften suspiciously.

Miles looked like a man who'd eaten spoiled meat.

"I don't trust you, but this is your chance to redeem yourself. I'm too old to catch up with her myself. I don't want anyone else around town knowing that Violet has run off. It will cause gossip and scandal. I don't have time to send for my son-in-law. You're my best hope of getting Violet back home quickly and safely."

A thought occurred to Gregory. "I could find her and take the money."

The older man sighed. "Then by all means do. Maybe then the law will be after you instead of Violet. And without money to fund her plans, perhaps she will return home."

"What are her plans?"

Traften shook his head. "I have no idea."

Gregory played his earlier hunch.

"She's not really your niece, is she?"

Miles drew himself up. "Violet is family; make no mistake about that. You are to treat her with respect. "He paused, then sighed." The robber told Henry Blake his destination was Coffeyville, Kansas. If Violet did indeed rob the bank, I have no idea which route she will take—or if she took the horse to sell, or had plans to ride all the way to Coffeyville."

"I know which road she took," Gregory said.

Glancing up, his brow furrowed, Miles asked, "How could you possibly know that?"

Gregory couldn't help but smile at the memory: Violet, her long hair down around her shoulders, her firm breasts pushed up from the corset she'd been trying to lace. If he hadn't been raised a gentleman, he might have tried to do more than kiss her, her

23

lover returning to put a bullet in him or not. "I believe I met Violet on my way into town this morning. I thought at the time she looked familiar."

The older man rose and hobbled to Gregory's side. "Did she seem all right?"

"Oh, she seemed fine."

Miles drew a shaky breath. "Thank heavens for that. The sooner you leave, the sooner you can catch up with her."

"I never said I'd do it," Gregory reminded him.

"You're all I have." Miles's eyes watered again. "You want to earn my respect? A place in my company? You will find Violet and bring her back, or at least do something in character and rob her so she has no choice but to return home."

A desirable woman *and* money? Either alone was tough to turn down. He'd thought to steal her from her lover and set her up as his mistress, but clearly she'd been lying about having a lover. Whoever she was, Miles seemed to dote upon her and considered her family. And if she was a lady, that also made her marriage material. Gregory's options just kept getting better.

"All right," he agreed. "I'll find Violet. I'd rather have the partnership than the money from the robbery. You swear to me that it's mine if I do this for you?"

"I swear," Miles said. "Just bring Violet home safely. I'll give you enough funds to see you comfortably through the journey, although Violet hasn't gotten much of a head start, so that is encouraging."

The fact that Miles asked him to step from the

room while he opened his safe was not encouraging. The man still didn't trust him. Well, hell, Gregory had never considered himself trustworthy, either. When push came to shove, he didn't imagine that too many people were.

Miles shortly reappeared and shoved a large stack of bills into his hand. "That should be sufficient."

Gregory stuffed the bills into his coat pocket and turned to leave.

"One other thing," Miles said, stopping him. "I do expect you to conduct yourself like a gentleman in regard to Violet. She is a lady and . . . uncomfortable with men."

"Really?" Gregory smiled enigmatically. "You could have fooled me."

He liked leaving Miles puzzled. He also liked the options that had suddenly materialized due to Violet Mallory. He could win his partnership with the simple task of fetching her home. He could steal the money from her, or he could seduce her and marry into the Traften family. And the best scenario of all would be to somehow find a way to do all three.

Chapter Three

Bubbles. Violet loved bubbles. She settled deeper into her hotel room's steaming tub, lifted a handful of suds, and blew them from her palm. Changing into lady's clothes the day she'd robbed the bank had proven her plan would work. Not long after she'd left Gregory Kline, a group of mounted men, a posse, had ridden straight past her. None of the men had given her anything but a glance. They were looking for a *male* bank robber.

Once the posse had disappeared ahead, she'd changed back into men's clothes. It was safer to travel that way. Of course, Violet had again changed back into women's finery before she'd entered Boonville and gotten herself these accommodations.

This hotel was the finest money could buy, given her location. She felt somewhat guilty about that. It wasn't her money, after all—but surely the law wouldn't expect to find all of it within her father's possession. She'd been riding for three days and felt she deserved the luxury of a nice room and a hot bath.

Her last thought caused her another stab of guilt. She didn't deserve anything she'd been given during the past three years. Lilla Finch, Miles's daughter, had found her working in a saloon in Langtry Texas, after the girl herself had been sent there to teach charm lessons. Finding upon her arrival that there were no decent young ladies for her to instruct, Lilla had taken the ragtag group of women who worked at Sally's Saloon under her wing. Violet had been one of those girls.

But Miles's daughter had done more than just taken Violet under her wing. She'd given Violet a grand opportunity to start her life afresh. Miles had brought Violet to St. Louis and passed her off as his niece from Boston. But Violet wasn't Miles's spoiled niece from Boston. She wasn't a refined lady like Lilla Finch. She was the daughter of a man who had outlaws for kin. The daughter of a man who'd sold her into a living hell at the age of fourteen. She was a woman living a lie. A woman who must now right the wrongs done to her, and those probably committed against her siblings.

Miles would have understood her decision to rescue her brothers and her sister. He would *not* understand the deeper emotions the past had ignited inside her. He would not comprehend the hate, bitterness, and consuming anger she feared might incite

her to kill—to take the lives of not just one man, but
the lives of both men who had taken her happiness
from her all those years ago.

Had she gone to Miles with her dangerous plans,
he would have tried to talk reason with her. If that
hadn't worked, he would have insisted he accompany her to Kansas. Violet loved him too dearly to
include him in her scheme. Just as she loved him too
much to tell him everything about her past.

Or had she been too afraid to tell him about it?
Afraid he'd no longer love her like a daughter?

No. There was nothing she could say that would
break the old man's love for her. In fact, she still
feared Miles might come after her . . . or might send
someone in his stead.

Leaning her head back against the tub, she closed
her eyes to think. Whom would he send? He
wouldn't want anyone to know she'd run off. It
would cause gossip. She doubted if he'd take the
time to send for his son-in-law, Grady Finch. But
Miles surely wouldn't come himself. He didn't get
around as well as he once did. He'd send someone
younger. Someone faster. Someone—

"Hello, Violet."

She jerked her head up. A man stood in the shadows. Realizing she had nearly exposed herself, she
quickly slumped back down into the bubbles.

"Who are you? How did you get in here?"

When he stepped from the shadows, a little of her
tenseness eased. Only a little.

"I didn't have to do much. I just told the proprietor
I was looking for a woman, and he assumed that I'm

the absent husband you said would be joining you. Seems as if I've developed a habit of finding you in various states of undress."

"Kline," she identified him. She'd told the proprietor of the Ballentine House that story only to keep from causing gossip about herself. A young lady did not travel alone. "What are you doing here?"

He sauntered toward her. "You already know the answer to that question."

The fancy hat and suit were gone. Gregory Kline looked less gentlemanly in cowboy garb. She'd stashed her gun inside the valise sitting on the bed. He strolled in that direction and made himself at home.

"Do you mind?" she asked.

His brows lifted. "Not at all. Go ahead and finish your bath."

The situation was unacceptable. Violet had the disadvantage. The fact that she was naked and had a man in her room made the circumstance doubly intolerable. "I meant, would you mind leaving so I can make myself presentable?"

Kline sighed. He removed his hat and ran a hand through his hair. "Yes, I do. I've been chasing you for three days. I'm not letting you out of my sight until I get you back to St. Louis."

The water grew cooler and the bubbles lost most of their fluff. "Did Miles send you?"

Rather than answer, he picked up her valise. "Is the money you stole from the bank in here?"

A shiver raced up her back, a combination of being uncomfortable with both him and the question.

"Money? I don't know what you're talking about."

"Should I open it and see?"

The money was in the bag, and so was her gun. Violet needed that weapon. She decided to call his bluff. "You told me you were a gentleman. A gentleman would never barge in on a lady's bath, or go through her personal belongings."

Kline frowned. He sat the bag on the floor. "You're right. I did promise Miles I'd act appropriately with you."

Violet couldn't call what she felt relief. Despite his handsomeness, she knew Gregory Kline's ilk. Miles had called him a wolf in sheep's clothing often enough. She'd have to keep her guard up.

"Would you mind scooting my valise toward me, then turning your back so I can slip something on?"

His gaze drifted over her. "You look lovely the way you are."

She tried to sink down lower in the tub. "I would hate to tell my dear Uncle Miles that you were disrespectful toward me."

Rather than act intimidated, he smiled. "You don't mince words, do you?"

Deciding not to, she asked, "What did he offer you?"

His smile faded. "What makes you think he offered me anything? I could have come out of the goodness of my heart. One friend doing another a favor."

She snorted. "I don't believe that for a moment. Your reputation precedes you."

He lowered his gaze. She thought he actually had

the decency to feel embarrassed. "Then you have the advantage. I know nothing about you." He glanced up at her again. "What's in Coffeyville?"

Her skin started to shrivel. The bubbles were almost gone. She had to get rid of him. "None of your business. How much will it take to make you go away?"

"That would depend." He rubbed his chin. "How much did you take from the bank?"

The money from the robbery wasn't going anywhere. Violet needed it, or at least most of it, to frame her father. The banks she planned to rob en route to Coffeyville would have no way of tracing the money except for the bank bags and an estimate of how much was taken. "Why don't you slide my valise over to me, let me dress, and we will discuss the issue of bribes and payment."

"No tricks," he warned.

Violet mimicked her best friend, Lilla Finch, placing what she hoped was an exaggerated expression of offended dignity upon her face. "I would never go back on my word, Mr. Kline. To suggest otherwise is both disrespectful and—"

"All right, all right," he grumbled. He slid the valise on the floor toward the tub, then rose and turned his back. "Hurry up. I haven't eaten since last night and—"

Violet jumped from the tub, grabbed a nightgown, and had her pistol digging into his back before he even completed his sentence.

"You're not very bright, are you, Mr. Kline?"

*   *   *

Violet Mallory was obviously not a woman of her word. He'd assumed that she was a lady, and that a lady would not stoop to telling lies. Due to her actions, he didn't feel honor-bound to play the gentleman. He turned. She backed up a step, holding a thin nightgown pressed against herself. Her wet, creamy skin was clearly visible through the thin fabric of the nightgown. It took him a while to notice the gun in her hand.

"You can't shoot me," he reasoned. "Then a crowd will rush in and you'll have a lot of explaining to do."

"Under the circumstances, I'm sure I could convince them that I had good reason to kill you."

He had to give her credit for having brains. His gaze lowered. That wasn't all he had to give her credit for having. Her lush curves were made to pleasure a man. With difficulty, he forced his gaze back to her face. She might have a body made for sin, but she also had the face an angel. Gregory didn't really think Violet would shoot him. And there wasn't a situation in the world that he couldn't charm his way out of.

"If you plan to shoot me, I might go to my grave more willingly if I got another kiss good-bye."

She didn't smile. Not even a little. "I'm not going to kill you . . . this time. I'll just tie you up so you stay put for a while—and don't come after me again, understand?"

For reasons that escaped him, Gregory felt moved to be truthful. "I can't make that commitment. I told Miles I would bring you back, and that's what I intend to do."

So it wasn't the whole truth. He hadn't decided exactly what he was after yet. The money? The partnership? The woman? The money and the woman? The woman and the partnership? Maybe just the money alone.

"You won't catch me again," she promised, then motioned him toward a chair. "Sit, and no sudden moves."

"Sudden moves?" He furrowed his brow. "Oh, you mean like this?" Gregory lunged forward and grabbed the gun, pointing it upward. She struggled, and harder than he anticipated. For a woman of small stature, she had a great amount of strength. She was also forced to drop the nightgown she'd clutched against her naked flesh.

Gregory was honorable enough not to stare, but his pride wouldn't allow him to be bested by a woman. It was just the sort of thing that would do further damage to his already compromised reputation. He didn't like manhandling her, but he saw no help for it. Gregory pulled her forward, then reversed their positions, forcing her down onto the bed. He squeezed her wrist until she cried out and dropped the weapon.

The feel of her naked body beneath him brought less than honorable thoughts to mind. He stared down into her lovely face, remembering the kiss they'd shared the last time they met.

"Don't even think about it," she warned. "And let me up this instant! I don't want you touching me."

"You didn't mind three days ago," he grumbled. Gregory wasn't used to women growling and snapping at him. Most found him quite charming . . . well, until they got to know him better. The way Violet stared up at him, her eyes narrowed and her teeth clenched, he suspected she might start hissing.

"Let's get something straight," she said. "I only let you kiss me so I could manipulate you into letting me get to my gun, I did not enjoy it, not for one moment."

A man's pride had no chance under the lash of her sharp tongue. Gregory thought back. He recalled the incident clearly, very clearly. There had been a moment there . . . "I have enough experience to know when a woman enjoys being kissed, and you did."

Her face turned red. "You are a conceited ass. I can say with all truthfulness that I did not!"

Gregory grimaced. Wooing Violet when she didn't find him attractive would prove bothersome. He, on the other hand, found her extremely desirable. Her eyes were beautiful, almost the color of her namesake flowers and surrounded by thick, dark lashes. Her lips were full and pink. She had pale, porcelain skin, high cheekbones, a short, straight nose, and a little dimple in her chin. He wanted badly to prove her a liar about not liking the kiss they had shared outside of St. Louis.

"All right. I'll let you up," he finally said. "The sooner we stop this argument, the sooner I can get you home, with Miles, where you belong."

A flash of panic crossed her lovely features. He started to rise, then found the collar of his shirt twisted between her hands. "Don't you want to kiss me again?"

He frowned. Now what was she up to? "You just insisted that you find my kisses distasteful."

"I do," she admitted, then chewed on her tempting lower lip. "I thought you might want to change my mind."

At that moment, Gregory wanted nothing more. He knew he should be thinking about other things: Where she'd hidden the money. How he would convince her to tell him the location. How much there was. If it would be enough to tempt him to steal it from her, rather than return her to Miles. . . .

Actually, all things considered, kissing her wasn't a bad idea. He should do all in his power to win her affections. Since Miles thought of her as family, regardless if she was, he would also have to think of Gregory as family if he married Violet. A partnership and the prestige of being considered family by Miles Traftcn, thc wcalthicst man in St. Louis? Kissing her was tempting. Too tempting. He lowered his mouth to hers.

Violet allowed him to kiss her for one reason and one reason only: The man was obviously easily distracted. He assumed a handsome face and a few winsome words could seduce her. He probably thought that women were mindless creatures made simply for the sake of ordering around and taking advantage of. Of using, humiliating. No man, certainly not this one, would ever use her again. But she would use Gregory, and his conceit, against him.

She had set her path. In order to escape Mr. Kline, and his intentions to return her to Miles, she needed an equalizer. Violet needed the weapon he'd wrested from her hand, and she needed to distract him. It took nearly more willpower than she had to lie beneath him, to allow him to kiss her, but for her siblings' sake, she would suffer his attentions.

The kiss was gentle, as it had been before. She noticed that Kline's cheeks were smooth, not rough with whiskers that rubbed her sensitive skin raw. His breath didn't smell like liquor, either. He didn't grind his mouth painfully against hers, but kissed her as if she had sensibilities he feared he might offend.

Violet's heart speeded up a measure. Fear, she felt certain, caused the response in her. Wasn't it? As he kissed her, she wondered if his long hair would feel as silky beneath her fingertips as she imagined. Then his body pressed against hers and all thoughts fled but escape. Violet groped around for her gun, found it on the edge of the bed and reacted instinctively: She slammed the gun butt against Gregory Kline's head.

He pulled back, staring down at her with a dazed look in his eyes. She hit him again, and he collapsed. She didn't realize how heavy he was until she felt the full weight of his body pressing her down. Glancing sideways at him, she felt the prickle of remorse.

"I'm sorry," she whispered, but allowed herself only that one moment of regret. She had to escape before he regained consciousness. Violet had a feeling that the gentlemanly Gregory Kline might become a lot less charming after having been tricked and knocked senseless. She wouldn't wait around to find out.

*　　*　　*

Gregory had a goose egg the size of Texas on the side of his head. He wasn't sure that he wanted to seduce Violet Mallory anymore, or see her safely returned to Miles Traften—but he did feel fairly certain he wanted to wring her pretty neck! She'd tricked him. Seduced him. Made him feel like a fool. He wasn't sure Violet Mallory was all Miles thought she was—wasn't quite sure what to make of her himself.

He'd never met a woman who could be as cunning as himself. One who could lie without batting a pretty lash; seduce a man when, from all indications, she was an innocent. Beautiful women didn't necessarily have to be smart. But this one was—and mean, too!

With Miles Traften's fortune to aid her, he couldn't see why she'd want to rob a bank, though, or feel as if she needed to. Perhaps that story had been a lie, a lure on Miles's part to tempt Gregory further into going after his niece.

Still, Violet had proven she had the courage to pull off something like a bank robbery, even if Gregory couldn't see where she'd have a motive. He respected that. He found himself wondering if there was any chance left of seriously wooing her. He'd have to consider whether the cost of missing body parts would be worth the effort, though. He could simply return her to Miles. The partnership also held great appeal. Maybe with money in his pockets and the prestige he'd lost in St. Louis regained, he could find a less deadly wife.

Not reassured by his thoughts, he rode onward. He could only assume Violet had gone ahead of him by horseback, since the livery owner had said that was how she'd left, and he followed the route that he assumed she'd take. She wouldn't stick to the main road; he knew that much. A lone woman would be an easy mark for less reputable sorts. Men like him. The types who would take advantage of a female, given the right circumstances. Not that they'd do it if they knew what they'd be getting into . . .

Violet would keep hidden—as far from the road as possible without costing herself too much time. Gregory had to wonder again what was in Coffeyville. Why had she left the safety and protection of Miles Traften's extravagant home to journey there? And why had she stolen that money? If indeed she had.

She was mysterious; he'd say that much for her.

She was also beautiful. The sight of her standing with that thin nightgown pressed against her creamy wet flesh was enough to turn a man's mind to mush. That and the gun butt she'd slammed against his head. Who was she really? And why the hell couldn't he get her out of his thoughts?

Because too much was at stake, he reminded himself. Unless he wanted to return to the wilds of Wyoming and punch cows for the rest of his life, or to give up everything that he'd ever worked for, Violet was the key to his future. Bearing that in mind, he glanced around for a place to break camp. She'd gotten a good lead on him while he'd lain unconscious. He'd followed her for a day, and now his head

38

throbbed and his stomach grumbled. If luck was with him, he'd catch up with her tomorrow.

His spirits lifted. He felt certain he could charm Violet into whatever he wished once he found out all he needed to know about her. Just because things hadn't worked out as he planned up to this point, didn't mean he couldn't turn them around. He pushed away the sudden reminder that his luck with women hadn't been good in the past.

Camile Langtry had certainly turned the tables on him. He'd once believed he could blackmail her into giving him the deed to her ranch. The hellion had ended up not only costing him his position in Miles's cattle company, but also leading to his banishment from St. Louis.

Then there was Miles's daughter, Lilla Traften, now Finch. He'd wooed her mainly for the sake of getting his hands on her father's wealth. He'd also made a fool of himself by trying to rescue her from her cowboy husband, believing she'd been held in Texas against her will. That hadn't turned out well, either.

Any woman seemingly connected to Miles Traften was a curse for him. But Violet, Violet would be different, he assured himself. He'd simply have to outsmart her. The fact that he'd only met Violet twice, and she'd taken the upper hand in both situations, he conveniently chose to ignore.

A scream split the silence surrounding him. His horse jumped. Gregory quickly pulled the gun he'd taken to wearing while on the road. The scream sounded again, but then quickly died, as if it had been muffled. It was really none of his business, whatever might be going on in the trees ahead of him. If some man had decided to take his woman in hand, who was Gregory to interfere? Of course, the woman might be Violet—and he suddenly had the sick suspicion she was. That would fit with his luck.

Gregory dismounted and crept toward where the noise had sounded. The scene he came upon filled him with rage. Two men had Violet tied up on the ground. A gag was stuffed into her mouth, and her shirt had been ripped at the sleeve. He stepped into the clearing, aiming his gun at her assailants.

"Get off of her!"

The men weren't wearing their weapons. He saw their gun belts on the ground where they'd obviously shed them in order to better defile their prey. Gregory stormed over and kicked the weapons from reach, shoving the barrel of his gun into one man's startled face.

"I said, get off of her and get out of here, before I kill you both."

Violet tried to communicate behind her gag. Gregory couldn't lower his guard or the gun long enough to rip the foul-looking bandanna from her mouth. Her lovely eyes were huge, her pale skin even whiter in the fading light of evening. These foul men and their rough intentions sickened him.

"You heard me," he said in a growl. "Mount up and get out."

The men looked at each other, glanced at Violet, then hurried to their horses. Gregory didn't relax until he heard them ride away. Violet squirmed and tried to shout behind her gag. Gregory replaced his gun and bent beside her.

"Do you see what can happen to foolish females who ride all over the countryside alone?" he asked.

Tears glistened in her eyes, and he noticed how badly she shook. Gregory supposed a reprimand could wait until later. He pulled the foul gag from her mouth. She took in deep gulps of air. Since there were guns lying about everywhere, he felt hesitant to untie her. He did help her to a sitting position. Thinking she needed comforting, he placed an arm around her shoulders. She jerked away from him.

Gregory sighed. "You don't have to act as if you think I'm about to beat you, Violet. Even if you did club me over the head with a gun and give me a goose egg the size of Texas. Even if you have tricked me on both occasions we've been in each other's company, and even if—"

"Be quiet," she whispered, her voice shaky. "You don't know what you've just done."

So much for soothing her fears. "I believe I've just saved you from losing your virtue to those scum. A thank-you would be nice, even a—"

"They have the money," she interrupted. "They came across me while I was burying it to keep it safe."

His stomach made a twisting motion. "The money? Would that be the money that you stole from the bank in St. Louis?"

She nodded.

Gregory ran a hand over his face. So she really had stolen the money? It shouldn't surprise him considering what she'd done so far, but it did. The thought of going after the men surfaced. Two against one were not good odds. And they wouldn't be taken off guard the next time he stumbled upon them. It was too dangerous. Besides, "a bird in the hand," as people were always saying.

"Now you have no choice but to let me take you home," he said.

"No choice?" The color returned to Violet's cheeks. "Don't you dare tell me I have no choice. Untie me. I'm going after them."

"Like hell you are," he said. "What you're going to do is stop this foolishness and go home where you belong. You've seen what can happen to you. Are you out of your mind? And just why are you robbing banks in the first place? Are you in some kind of trouble?"

Violet felt on the verge of hysterics at his question. Those men would have defiled her had Gregory not interrupted their foul plans; she would have been raped, humiliated, probably beaten and left to die. But while she felt grateful to him for saving her, now her plans had been messed up. The money the men had stolen wasn't nearly as important as the stamped bank bags. She needed to be held accountable for the St. Louis robbery, or rather, her *father* needed to be held accountable.

Of course she planned on robbing other banks along her route, mentioning Coffeyville and the name Dalton at each stop, being certain all the money would be stuffed into the banks' bags, rather than just loose in her saddle packs, so that the law could trace it. But the St. Louis money was a big part of her plan. It was the only way the law would have of being certain her father was responsible for the whole string of robberies she planned to pull across the state of Missouri. But her reasons for robbing were no one's business but her own.

"I have an idea," she said. "Why don't you go home. I won't drag you into my business. You're liable to get hurt if you stay around."

He frowned, obviously not caring for her suggestion. "You didn't say what your business is, or why you robbed the bank in St. Louis. You leave me with a dilemma: No Violet, no partnership from Miles. I've earned that partnership, and I intend to have it."

So, everything she'd heard concerning Gregory Kline was true: Life was all about money and position for him. Violet suspected even the kiss they had shared in Boonville held a purpose other than the obvious. He had been trying to charm her into doing as he wished. Charm would not work any better than force as far as she was concerned.

If he wanted to play dirty, Violet supposed she could play that way, as well. She'd have to pretend to be exactly what he thought she was. Pretty, impulsive, and a little on the dim side. *Helpless.* Yes, judging from past experience, men liked their women helpless. It made them feel more powerful. Violet easily summoned tears. What had happened earlier was plenty to work with.

"That's all you care about?" she asked. "Some silly partnership? Being Miles's lap dog? I thought, well . . . since you've kissed me twice, I thought that you liked me."

He blinked. "Well, yes, I do like you. I mean, I liked kissing you. Lap dog?" he added more forcefully. "I'm not anyone's lap dog." He looked as if he'd say more, but suddenly his eyes narrowed. "What is this? Another trick to lower my defenses?Playing the helpless female to tug at my heart strings? It won't work," he said flatly. "I know you're not helpless, and since you know so much about my past, you probably have heard I don't have a heart."

Violet wanted to cuss. She also wanted to sob. Her ploy had failed, and she'd truly been terrified when those men had found her burying the money. They'd taken her by surprise—been joyful to see the saddle packs full of money, then turned their lustful eyes upon her. She began to cry.

She'd been foolish to remove her hat and unbind her breasts. Of course, had they mistaken her for a man, they probably would have shot her. Then there wouldn't have been time for Gregory to come to her aid.

"I am grateful to you for coming to my rescue," she admitted quietly. Her nose ran and, with her hands being tied, she had no choice but to try to wipe it on her sleeve. Kline removed a handkerchief from his coat pocket and bent beside her.

"Blow," he said, then politely glanced away.

She did, and noisily. What was she going to do about this man? How was she going to give him the slip? It occurred to her that having him along wouldn't be so bad. This evening, he'd proven he could be very helpful. Maybe he could be bought off.

"If you help me steal the money back from those two men, I'll split *it* with you."

His head jerked toward her. "Are you crazy? Those two are long gone by now. Even if we did manage to catch up with them, they'd be watching for us, waiting to gun us down."

"We have their guns," she reminded.

"Guns are not hard to come by," he scoffed. "That money's gone, Violet. Accept that, and do the smart thing. Let me take you home."

She *was* going home. He didn't realize it, and she couldn't turn back. Her sister had been nine last time Violet had seen her. Rose would now be fourteen. The same age Violet was when her father had sold her to a man for a case of whiskey. She wouldn't take any chances that the same horrible thing might happen again.

Gregory was right, though, she supposed. She doubted if she could catch up with the men and steal the money back, and the possibility of placing herself at their mercy terrified her. There was no help for what she must do next. She only hoped she could be convincing now that Gregory suspected every word from her mouth.

"I see the sense in your suggestion," she lied with a sigh. "You win. I'll let you take me home. We'll leave at daybreak, but I want to return to Boonville and make myself presentable. I think we should pay someone to bring the horses to St. Louis and travel by train."

For a moment he looked relieved; then his eyes

narrowed again. "This isn't another trick, is it?"

Violet widened her tear-filled eyes innocently. "A trick? What sort of trick would it be? As you say, I have lost the money. What is left for me to do but abandon my plans and return to Miles?"

Removing his hat, Gregory Kline ran a hand through his thick chestnut hair. "You still haven't told me what your plans were."

And she didn't intend to. He'd be appalled by the truth. The man might have his own less-than-reputable past to deal with, but her own was much darker. And it was none of his business. "Just a wild oat I had to sow," she answered. "Now, if you'll untie me, I'll fix us something to eat. We can rise before dawn and make it back to Boonville by early afternoon tomorrow."

The mention of food made Kline's stomach grumble, which she supposed aided her cause. "Swear to me on your honor that you will not run away?"

"I swear," Violet readily agreed. Her honor had been stolen from her long ago. She made him dinner and bided her time.

Later, after he'd devoured the simple meal she prepared, Violet and Gregory Kline climbed into bedrolls placed at a proper distance from each other. Violet lay awake, afraid to lower her guard. Kline had looked truly outraged when he'd found those men attacking her, but that didn't mean he wouldn't resort to the same tactics if given half a chance. He was a man, and he *did* have a history of trying to kiss her. And he hadn't earned her trust. Only Miles Traften had done that—over the past three years.

Miles had treated her differently than she had ever been treated by a man before. He'd been generous, kind, and he'd never wanted anything in return. Without Miles's tender care, Violet didn't know what might have become of her. She'd probably still be working in a saloon somewhere, terrified that she'd be called upon to do more than clean up spilled drinks and cook meals.

Yet living in Miles's fine house, wearing pretty clothes, and being taught fancy manners, didn't change who Violet was, or who she had been before Lilla rescued her. Beneath the powder and perfume, she was still Violet Dalton, not Violet Mallory. Nothing would change the truth about her. The best she could hope for was taking her revenge against those responsible for ruining her life.

The sound of Gregory's steady breathing lulled her. She tried to relax, battled the horror of being attacked earlier, and the nightmares she feared the incident would stir in her mind. Violet fought sleep as long as she could, but at last she succumbed. And the past found her again. The demon came to her, stinking of filth and liquor. Violet fought him—cried out in her fear.

Strong hands reached for her, but they did not bruise her flesh, did not slap her or grab her roughly. A voice whispered soothing words into her ear, rich and smooth as fine brandy. Someone brushed the hair clinging to her wet cheeks aside and held her. The nightmare began to fade, but Violet couldn't stop the tears, tears of shame, of hate.

There had never been anyone to hold her after the nightmares visited her, no one to comfort her and tell her everything would be all right. Violet wasn't sure she would have allowed anyone to touch her before, but tonight, for the first time in her life, she took comfort from another to ease her suffering. She found sanctuary in the most unlikely place: within Gregory Kline's arms.

Chapter Four

Boonville came into view, and Gregory breathed a small sigh of relief. Violet had kept her word to him. Maybe she wasn't as untrustworthy as she'd seemed. His mouth watered for a drink. That was just how he intended to pass the time while Violet bathed and changed into attire befitting a young woman of her background. Not that he had a clue as to what exactly her background was.

Last night confused him. He'd fully expected a belated reaction to the attack on her, but when it came, it had surprised him with both its intensity and Violet's vulnerability. She'd cried for hours in his arms, gut-wrenching sobs that tore at a man's heart. Even a man who supposedly didn't have one.

When morning dawned, she'd looked hollow-eyed and confused. He'd done the duty of making breakfast in light of her sleepless night, regardless that he'd gotten little sleep himself. The coffee he'd shoved into her shaking hands helped to revive her, and now they'd ridden for hours barely exchanging a word. She obviously had thoughts on her mind, but didn't care to share them with him.

"I doubt we'll get a train out until morning," he said to make conversation. "You'll sleep better inside a hotel on a real bed tonight."

Her cheeks turned a pretty shade of pink. "I imagine you will, too. I'm sorry about last night. I mean, about keeping you awake."

He didn't want her to feel awkward about that. Assurances that all would be well might brighten her spirits. "Forget about those men. Soon you'll be home and safe. Nothing like that will happen to you again."

She smiled at him, somewhat sadly, he thought. "You were very brave to come rushing to my aid the way you did. A-and last night, you were kind."

Gregory didn't believe *brave* was a word many would associate with him; and he sure as hell knew that *kind* wasn't. He explained: "I didn't think about the danger when I saw what those two bastards intended. Besides, I couldn't bring home soiled goods to your uncle. The agreement was that I return you unmolested—by me or anyone else."

The softness in her eyes faded. "Thank you for making that clear. One can't do a noble deed out of the goodness of one's heart if one doesn't have a heart, now, can one?"

This was not the girl he'd traveled from Texas to

St. Louis with three years ago, the shy, quiet one who looked ready to jump out of her skin if someone spoke to her. He wasn't very good at treading lightly upon others' feelings, but if he meant to court Violet after he returned her to Miles, he would have to pretend.

"I've been insensitive," he said. "Forgive me."

"You're asking the wrong person." Violet stared straight ahead, her posture stiff in her saddle. "I have a problem with forgiveness."

Most people thought he was charming when they met him. He hoped he could be charming now. He wanted to make Violet smile. Not just to make a future courtship possible, but to chase the haunted look from her eyes. "That's strange—so do I. See? We do have something in common."

The slight smile she awarded him gave Gregory great pleasure. Maybe it was because he didn't think she smiled often. Not with heartfelt emotion. Her eyes were beautiful, big and blue, but there was no joy to light them. He wondered why. Maybe she had a case of homesickness and didn't want to admit it. He felt certain they knew people in the same circles, since she'd lived with Miles for the past three years. Perhaps talking about them was a way to show her that they had more in common than holding a grudge.

"Do you know Katherine Sims?" he asked.

Her lip curled. "Unfortunately."

"At one time, she set the standard for most young ladies of St. Louis. What do you think of her?"

Violet shrugged. "Not much. She slurps her soup

and cracks her knuckles when she thinks no one is watching."

Gregory laughed. It felt good to be discussing those he'd been forced to leave behind after his banishment from society—especially in such blunt terms. "I noticed how large her knuckles were once. Now I understand why."

Her gaze cut toward him. "Are you interested in her?"

With some pride at having drawn Violet out of her somber mood, he teased, "Would you be jealous if I were?"

Sober as a judge, she answered, "No. I only wanted to warn you that she's put on some weight since you last saw her."

He wasn't surprised. "She always was one to linger over the dessert table."

"She's nine months with child," Violet corrected dryly. "She married Justin Burns last year."

"Burns?" Gregory frowned. "He sweats like a pig, even in winter."

"He obviously ruts like one, too," Violet commented with distaste. "They haven't been married but nine months and she's about to pop at any moment."

Her comment shouldn't have surprised him, given all the things she had done in the past several days, but it did. "I didn't think ladies talked about rutting, and certainly not in conversations where men are present."

Violet shrugged, then looked at him. "What you've done to me isn't exactly respectable, either."

Gregory tensed. "A couple of stolen kisses. There's no harm in that. And you—"

Her smile returned. "You burst in on me when I was inappropriately dressed—and last night you crawled into my bedroll. I could get you into a lot of trouble were you to return me to Miles."

What was she getting at? And he hadn't missed her wording. "You mean *when* I return you to Miles."

"Isn't that what I said?"

"No," he assured her. "You're not planning something foolish again, are you?"

She turned her attention back to the road. "I promise you, I have nothing foolish planned. If I were planning something, it would be well thought out."

He wasn't sure what that meant, so he said, "Good." He nodded up ahead. "Here we are. I'll escort you to the hotel, then check on the train and see when we can depart for St. Louis."

Violet sighed. "I can't wait for another bath. And this time I would like a private one."

"So you don't have any more to complain about, I'll give you an hour before I come calling."

"An hour should be adequate."

No one paid them any mind as they rode into town. Violet wore men's clothing and had her hair tucked beneath her hat, as Gregory had agreed that while they traveled the road, it would be best if she assumed her manly disguise. They had ridden up to the hotel and hitched their horses to the post when a commotion in front the jail a short distance away drew their attention. Gregory grabbed Violet and pulled her behind his horse. The two men who'd assaulted Violet were being herded inside the jail.

"I'm telling you, it wasn't us who robbed that bank in St. Louis!" he heard one of them shout. "We stole it from—"

A member of the posse cuffed the man on the back of the head. "Shut up and keep moving. You can tell your story to a judge."

A bulging set of saddlebags was also carried inside.

"There goes your money," Gregory said softly. "But at least the law won't be coming after you. Not when they think they have the robbers in hand."

Violet didn't look particularly relieved. "Meddling bastards," she muttered. "We should get out of town as quickly as possible, in case someone decides to listen to their story."

Gregory nodded. "I'll go ahead to the depot and find out when we can leave. You go inside the hotel and transform yourself back into a lady. Afterward, it would be smart if we both stay out of sight until time to board the train."

He fumbled in his pockets and gave her some money. He'd have to do something about their horses, but first he'd check on the way out of town. The thought of a posse here and the outlaws who could identify the couple in original possession of the stolen money, made him nervous. The sooner he and Violet got on their way, the better he'd feel about the situation.

After watching Violet go inside of the hotel, he

remounted and reined his horse toward the train depot. He learned that the next train to St. Louis wouldn't be leaving until the morning. He purchased two tickets. The saloon sang a siren's song to him as he passed. He could use a good stiff drink, but the less he was seen around town the better. He reluctantly kept riding. A moment later he glanced ahead to find a strange sight: Violet, still dressed in men's garb, riding full-out toward him.

"Hey!" he shouted when she flew by.

"Look out!" she shouted over her shoulder.

"What?"

"Stop those men!" came a voice behind her.

His head jerked back toward the street in front of him. A man stood in the center of the rutted road.

"They've robbed the bank!" the man shouted.

"Damn," Gregory cussed. He turned his horse in the opposite direction, after the woman he would strangle when he caught up with her. *If* he caught up with her. That damn horse she'd stolen from Miles was faster than anything he'd ever seen on four legs.

Violet hung low over Blaze's neck. Her heart beat in time with the thundering of her horse's hooves. This life of crime obviously came naturally to her. Too naturally. Pulling a stunt like that with a posse no more than ten feet away wasn't wise, but she'd had no choice. The two men who had robbed her, and intended worse, had messed up her plans, and she had to right her path. Plus, she'd figured, no one would ever expect a bank robbery at a time like that.

The holdup had gone easy as pie—And she'd made sure the money went in stamped bags, and she'd again mentioned the name Dalton.

She glanced over her shoulder. Gregory ate her dust, but she had to give him credit for keeping up. She imagined he was furious with her. Now the law would be looking for both of them. It would have been better had he not been seen with her, but she supposed there was some good to be had from it. Being attacked by the men who'd stumbled upon her had taught Violet a quick lesson: She could use someone to ride along with her. Thieves and such would think twice about confronting two men rather than one. And Violet intended to keep her gender hidden for the rest of the journey. Except with Gregory. Then she could be herself.

Well, not entirely herself.

Blaze had plenty of stamina, and she pushed him onward, hoping Gregory's horse could withstand the grueling pace. It couldn't. She lost him in a thicket. But that was okay. Maybe, as Gregory rode, he would have time to cool down. She had little fear that he wouldn't be able to track her.

She'd found a place to camp, buried the money, and had a quick sponge bath in the stream before he caught up. She'd started a fire by which she sat brushing the tangles from her hair as he drew his lathered horse up next to Blaze. He dismounted and stormed toward her.

"What in the hell are you doing?"

She pretended to ponder his question. "Brushing my hair?"

He removed his dusty hat, threw it on the ground, and ran a hand through his dark, sweaty locks. "You know what I'm talking about. Don't play innocent with me."

"You know what I did, so why ask?"

"Yes, I know what you did! But *why* did you do it?"

Violet laid her brush aside and stirred the fire. "I've told you. It's none of your business."

Gregory scooped his hat off the ground and crammed it back on his head. "I think you just made it my business! You can't just go around robbing banks anytime the notion strikes you."

"I obviously can," she countered. "And don't play innocent with me. I know your reputation. Don't tell me you've never done anything on the wrong side of the law."

He looked offended. "My reputation may not be spotless, but blackmail is a far cry from bank robbery."

"You would steal from me," she argued. "You intended to. For all I know, you still do."

He began unfastening his shirt, panting slightly from his exertions. "That's different."

Her gaze dropped to his long, slender fingers. "How is it different?"

"If you steal money that's already been stolen, it's not the same thing."

She laughed. "That's just lazy stealing. You don't have the courage to do the real stealing, so you steal from someone who does."

"Well, now you've gotten the law on my tail, too.

They think we're together. The reason I'm so late catching up is because I had to make a false trail and cover up yours. The one you left would have led a posse straight to us."

Violet frowned. "Oh, I went back and—"

"*I* managed to find you, didn't I?" he interrupted. He glanced around the area. "Where is the money, *partner?*"

Violet walked to her packs and removed supplies to prepare a meal. "I buried it again. And no, I won't tell you where. I know that in your case, you are not a partner I should trust. Are you staying for supper?"

Tugging his shirttail from his pants, he said, "That would depend. Do you plan to poison me, or is robbing a bank in broad daylight with a posse gathered down the street enough excitement for you in one day?"

She squatted before the fire and sighed. "I suppose I've had enough excitement for one day."

"Good, I'm taking a bath. I'm covered in dust."

While she fussed with her supplies, Violet watched him from beneath her lashes. Gregory walked to his horse and removed his blanket from behind the saddle. His shirt was open and, as he moved back toward her, she couldn't help but notice his bare chest. He had more muscle on him than his lanky form suggested.

And he wasn't covered in thick furry hair. Gregory's stomach was flat and hard, too, not flabby and hanging over his belt. Violet glanced away from him and tried to concentrate on the meal, and on her next move.

She had no doubt Kline would follow her wherever she chose to go. Her uncle's partnership and the temptation of the stolen money would make sure of that. But what would she do with him during the other robberies she planned . . . and what about once she reached Coffeyville? Violet didn't know, but in the meantime, she needed to come up with a story regarding the purpose of her robberies. Something to pacify him. Something besides the truth. But what?

"Violet?"

"Yes?" she called.

"Do you have a bar of soap I can borrow?"

After spooning lard into the skillet, she dug in her packs again, removed a bar of perfumed soap, and smiled at the thought of Gregory smelling so sweet. Once she reached the stream, she drew up short. Kline stood, seemingly naked, in waist-high water. His broad back glistened in the fading sunlight. Violet swallowed hard.

"Kline?" she called, but her voice came out soft and husky, and she had to clear her throat. He turned to look at her. She hadn't known that his arms would be muscled too. She hadn't known until that moment that a man could be beautiful.

"The soap," he reminded her.

Violet's gaze shot up to his face. Her cheeks blazed. "Oh. Do you want me to throw it to you?"

"Unless you want me to come get it."

"No," she blurted. "I meant—should I toss it to you or leave it here on the ground for you to fetch when I leave?"

He held out his hands. "Just throw it to me."

Although he wasn't that far away, Violet's toss fell short of its mark. The soap sank a few feet in front of him. He waded toward her. The closer he came, the more the water receded. He smiled up at her. Violet quickly turned away. She had no desire to see him naked. This, alone was more intimate than she cared to be with any man.

She returned to the campsite, and the lard was sizzling in the pan. Violet removed slabs of salted pork and a small bag of flour to make gravy. She'd already put coffee on to boil. Gregory appeared shortly. He strung a small rope between two trees and hung his blanket to dry. He'd dried himself off with it.

"I'm surprised you thought to do that," she said. "I didn't think *gentlemen* knew much about making do outdoors. Or how to hide trails," she added thoughtfully.

He joined her next to the fire. "We had a rustling problem in Wyoming. That's how I learned about trails, and how a man could hide his tracks. I caught those responsible." He looked almost proud of himself, maybe a little wistful, before he frowned. "I learned a lot of things I didn't care to know about in Wyoming."

A smile tugged at her lips. "So I read in your letters."

His hand paused halfway to the coffeepot. "You read my letters?"

"For Miles," she explained. "His eyesight is failing."

He cast her a dark glance. "I'm sure you both found them very amusing."

"We did," she stated honestly. "I sometimes laughed upon simply receiving one in the mail, before I even opened it for Miles and read it." It felt good to see his discomposure.

"You've made your point." He snatched the coffeepot and poured himself a cup.

They sat in silence for a moment. Violet lifted the bacon from the pan with a fork and placed it on a clean cloth. She sifted small amounts of flour into the grease.

"So how long was it before I started bellyaching to come home? A year, two?"

"Two," she answered, and fought a laugh. "Two months."

He looked crossly at her, but said nothing.

Suddenly Violet realized it was Gregory who had brought her and Miles together in those difficult beginning months. She'd felt lost, even though she'd also felt safe for the first time in her life. Miles hadn't known what to do with her, and she hadn't known what to do with herself. She'd been used to hard labor: scrubbing the dirty floors of the saloon, washing the windows, cooking for the women. Suddenly she'd had nothing to do. Nothing but pick out clothes, read books about manners, and wait for those secret meetings with the detective who was investigating her family. Miles had seen her wandering about the house one afternoon and asked her to read his mail for him. He said he needed spectacles but was too vain to get them. Soon it became a special time of the day for them. They would sit and have hot chocolate, eat iced cakes, and she would read Miles his correspondence.

The first time they had laughed together was over one of Gregory's pathetic cries for rescue. She supposed she owed Gregory Kline something for that, for bringing her and Miles close. And, in a way, for showing her how kind and caring a man could be. Not Gregory, of course, but Miles.

"I don't guess you think much of me, then."

She couldn't say otherwise. "Why did you do it? I mean, blackmail Wade Langtry into going after Camile Cordell's deed?"

"We needed her property," Gregory snapped. "The river ran through her land. She could have dammed it up and run everyone in the territory out if she'd wanted. If we didn't have her ranch, it made all the other land we'd acquired in the area useless."

Violet said nothing. She stirred the gravy until it became too thick, then thinned it with water from her canteen.

"I tried to reason with Camile. I went to Texas with every intention of offering her father a fair price for the ranch in representation of the company."

"And?" she asked when he didn't continue.

"Camile ran me off with a bullwhip. I swear she took a strip off my hide."

Violet's lips twitched again. "Where?"

"I don't think you'd care to see it," Kline commented, then took another sip of his coffee.

After giving the gravy another stir, Violet removed

the skillet from the fire. "Do you regret it?" she asked softly.

He laughed. "Of course I regret it."

She cocked a brow. "No, I don't mean do you regret getting caught. I mean, do you regret your actions?"

His coffee cup suddenly became of interest to him. "I have a few regrets."

As Violet filled Gregory Kline's plate with thick slabs of bacon and gravy over hardened bread, she waited for him to continue. He didn't.

"Are you going to tell me which parts?"

He reached for his plate, but she withheld it from him. Instead of reaching again, he withdrew his hand and tugged at his collar.

"I behaved badly with Camile Cordell . . . Langtry, as you know her."

Violet felt a prickle of alarm. "Badly in what way?"

His gaze drifted to some distant spot, rather than to her. "I said some less than gentlemanly things to her. Made some less than gentlemanly suggestions."

Her wariness increased. "Did you attack her?" she asked. Maybe she shouldn't have chosen this man as a riding partner after all.

Gregory's gaze snapped back to her. "Of course not." He reached for his plate, but again she held it beyond his reach.

"Why did you treat her disrespectfully?"

"Because I didn't think she was a lady," he answered impatiently.

A sudden rage washed over Violet. "And you think

it's all right to behave badly with a woman who is not what you consider a lady?"

"I said I regret it," he said in a hiss. "And you're a fine one to cast stones: a woman who robs banks at the drop of a hat. One who stole a horse and supplies from a man who obviously dotes upon her—for whatever reason I sure as hell haven't figured out yet. You should have seen him, blubbering on about poor you, and what was he to do, and what if something happened to—"

Violet shoved Gregory's plate into his hands and cut him off. Her eyes stung. Rather than embarrass herself by showing emotion in front of him, she jumped up and ran toward the stream. She felt horrible for causing Miles even one minute of pain. What must he think of her? And Lilla—what if she learned that Violet had run off, taken to robbing banks, was being chased by lawmen? Violet let the tears flow, suddenly homesick for her adoptive family.

"Hey."

She jerked when Gregory touched her shoulder, and she wheeled around to face him. "Don't," she warned.

He held his hands up in the air. "I didn't mean to make you cry. You know I'm an insensitive ass, only out for myself, so why do you take anything I say seriously?"

His honesty slipped past her defenses. It elicited from her some grain of truth in return: "Because you're right. And because I have to hurt Miles to do what I must do, and that's the worst part of it. Hurting Miles and Lilla."

"I don't understand what it is you think you have to do. Can't you just tell me?"

She shook her head, scattering her tears. "You wouldn't understand."

Gregory's brows knit. "You're right. I don't understand. Why would you need the money? And why steal it from a bank when—"

"I could have stolen it from Miles?" she cut in angrily. "What sort of person do you think I am?"

He placed his fingers against his forehead and rubbed. "Obviously a crazy one!" He turned from her then; and headed back to his supper. " 'Just find her and bring her back safely,' " she heard him mutter. " 'It should be simple for a man of your talents.' Easy, my foot!"

Violet wiped her face on her shirtsleeve. As horrible as she felt, she almost smiled through her tears. Gregory's banging around at the campsite lifted her spirits. For some reason she took a certain amount of pleasure from eliciting such a reaction from him. And though he was clearly frustrated, he hadn't gotten violent. She appreciated that, for she had seen only one other man be able to control himself like that—Miles.

Speaking of her uncle, she had to harden her heart against him, even though she loved the man dearly. What she planned to do would be hard enough without letting her conscience get in the way. Her father had had no conscience. Neither had the man to whom he'd sold her for whiskey. To deal with them in the way she intended, she'd have to shed all decency and become like them.

Too, she still needed to come up with a story that would pacify Gregory about why she needed money from the bank robberies; otherwise, he'd just keep hassling her. She pondered her possibilities for a while. She needed a reason that might keep him at her side, but keep him at a distance at the same time. An answer came to her and she smiled.

Violet wasn't smiling a short time later when Gregory suggested they sleep together.

Chapter Five

"Only because it will throw suspicion off of us if we're discovered," he explained. "You were still dressed as a man when you robbed the bank. I'm assuming the posse is looking for two men, not a man and a woman."

"I say we take turns keeping watch instead," Violet argued, although she was exhausted from her lack of sleep the night before, and clearly saw that Gregory wasn't in much better shape.

"Neither of us can be trusted to stay awake. If we're stumbled across by members of the posse, we'll say we're newly married and on our way to visit your kin in Kansas."

He didn't know how close to the truth that would be. The last part of it anyway. "I'm not comfortable with your suggestion."

Kline sighed. His eyes fused with hers. "Hell, Violet, I'm too tired to do anything to you even if you asked me nicely. You hid the money. As long as it's not in our possession and they think that we're newlyweds, they won't have any reason to think we're connected to the robbery in Boonville. We could both use a good night's sleep."

Trust didn't come easily to Violet. She'd learned to trust Miles; of course she trusted his daughter, Lilla, and even Lilla's husband, Grady . . . but this was different. Kline was a young, virile, unmarried man. She felt that difference to her very core. Yet, to his credit, he'd held her the night before when she'd been awakened and terrified by the nightmares, and he hadn't taken advantage of that situation.

"Don't try anything," she warned him, then snatched her bedroll off the ground and joined him across the fire. Gregory removed his boots and stretched out on his blanket, making room for her. They used her blanket to cover them. Violet kept her body rigid, determined not to touch him or be touched by him.

A few moments later she realized there was no need to be on her guard. The sound of his steady breathing told her he'd already fallen asleep. She turned to face him, studying his features in the moonlight. A lock of hair fell across his forehead and over his eyes. For a second she felt tempted to brush it back into place. His scent, which was her scent, the lilac fragrance of her soap, drifted to her and made her smile. Her gaze lowered to his chest.

She remembered his body, and what he'd looked like naked—at least from the waist up. Also, she remembered her strange reaction to the sight of his smooth, muscled flesh. She had thought him beautiful. It intrigued her that she could react so differently to him than she had to other men. She hadn't met any gentleman in St. Louis she would have let kiss her, certainly none whom she would have wanted to see unclothed.

What made Gregory different? Maybe it was the fact that she'd come to know him on some level through his letters. Earlier she'd made fun of him, but in truth, he'd stopped his bellyaching after a while and became quite professional about his duty. He'd see to it that the cattle company merger went smoothly in Wyoming. Miles had even received letters from the local ranchers praising Kline's intelligence and grit. Those letters hadn't been nearly as fun to read as the earlier ones—those threatening an end to the merger if Miles didn't get the arrogant ass he'd sent the hell away from them—but Violet had felt a certain surprise that Gregory had managed to win their respect.

Miles had refused to soften toward him, though. He'd told Violet that Gregory never did anything unless he hoped to gain by it. She had almost felt sorry for Gregory when Miles admitted he had no intention of ever sending for him, or in fact, of ever making him a partner again in the business. Once a wolf, always a wolf, Miles had said. It must have greatly upset her uncle to depend on the one man he considered untrustworthy to find her and bring her back to him safely. But Violet wasn't going to think about that, or imagine Miles pacing in worry over her whereabouts.

Turning back would be easy if she let her heart lead her. She must go forward, rescue her siblings, deal with her past, or she could never go back, never feel safe, never feel clean. Gregory assumed she was a lady because Miles looked upon her as family. He'd be repulsed to know the truth about her. Any gentleman would.

All hope of a decent future had been taken from her at an early age. She had not been allowed to dream of a love she might find someday. She'd been ripped from her home, thrust into the care of a man who had introduced her quickly and savagely to the real world.

Having conjured the demon into her thoughts, Violet was afraid to go to sleep. Afraid to open that world he so easily penetrated—that world of pain and degradation, that dark place where she lay whimpering, beaten, bleeding and abused. She shuddered and stared at Gregory. His chest rose and fell steadily. She noticed that his lashes were long and dark, his jaw square and masculine.

For a moment, she was almost tempted to trace his cheek with her finger. But she didn't dare. If he woke while she touched him, he would assume she wanted something from him she didn't. All she wanted was to look at him. And she did, until her eyes grew heavy and she drifted off to sleep.

* * *

Nightmares didn't wake her, but the stifling feel of someone's weight did. Dawn streaked the sky when she opened her eyes. Gregory was on top of her. His lips nuzzled her ear, and she nearly screamed.

"We have company," he whispered. "Play along."

Company? Play along? Who . . . What? His mouth captured hers before she had a chance to ask the questions tumbling through her mind.

"Pretend you like it," he said against her lips. "Put your arms around me. Two men are watching us. They're both wearing badges."

Her heart skipped another beat. *Oh, God!* She couldn't be captured! Not now, not this far from Kansas. What was their plan last night if members of the posse discovered them? Gregory had said they would pretend to be newly married and on the way to visit her kin in Kansas. As much as it upset her, she threw her arms around his neck. She giggled, although it sounded more hysterical than like a woman enjoying herself.

Gregory continued to kiss her. Violet had to admit that he knew how to be convincing. She didn't think the lawmen could see his tongue dip into her mouth from where they sat mounted. One of the men cleared his throat loudly.

"Ah, excuse me."

As if he hadn't heard the man, Gregory kept kissing her. Violet had no choice but to allow him the liberty. And she wasn't certain a few minutes later if his kiss or the fear of capture made her feel weak and shaky inside.

71

"Sir, ah, ma'am, excuse me!" the man on the horse practically yelled.

Violet's head spun as Gregory ended the kiss and glanced up. He stumbled off of her and up, as if he'd been taken unawares. She had to admire his acting abilities, even if her heart did pound at a frantic pace over their predicament. A look of alarm crossed his face, then relief when he purposely noticed the tin badges pinned to the men's chests.

"I thought you might not be friendly," he said, then nodded toward their badges. "Gave me quite a scare for a minute. Thought I might have to fight you in order to defend my woman's honor."

"We'd like to ask some questions," the first man spoke up. "Mind if we come into your camp?"

Gregory glanced at Violet, then back at the men, and grinned. "We were in the middle of something. Could you come back later?"

The man's face reddened. "This won't take long."

Sighing, as if he were put out by the interruption, Gregory said, "Fine, I'll have the little woman put on some coffee."

Little woman? She cast him a dark glance, then realized the mounted men's focus had turned to her. She supposed she could act as well as Gregory if the need arose. "I'd be happy to rustle you both up some grub." She scrambled upright, and kicked the blankets aside. "Don't have much, but you're welcome to it."

"Don't go to no trouble," the lawman said. "In fact, I'd like it if neither of you made any sudden moves."

72

"Sudden moves?" Gregory wrinkled his brow in confusion.

Violet hoped he wasn't about to rush the men the way he'd done with her that morning he'd caught up with her in Boonville. He'd get shot. Luckily, he remained where he stood.

Both lawmen nudged their horses in closer. "Seems we have some bank robbers roaming the area," the same one who'd done all the talking continued.

Violet gasped. She placed a hand against her pounding heart. "Bank robbers? You mean outlaws are roaming these woods?"

The man nodded. "Me and Tim here just found out about it over the telegraph and rode in from Cobb. I'm the sheriff there now, and new to the territory. Thought I'd come over and introduce myself to the law in Boonville, lend a hand along with my deputy here."

"We haven't seen any bank robbers," Gregory said. "Not much of anyone."

The man's gaze strayed to their tethered horses. "Got a description of the horses the robbers rode. It matches the description of those two tied over yonder."

Violet's head swung toward their horses. She had to think of something, and fast. A second later she swatted Gregory on the arm. "You fool. I told you there was something strange about two men who'd want to trade those nice horses for our sorry broken-down wagon."

He stared at her blankly for a moment; then his

eyes widened. "Hell, honey, what fool in his right mind would have said no to that arrangement? And I told you about hitting me," he warned.

"I should slap you clear into next Sunday," she muttered. "You don't have chicken-scratch for brains. Now it looks like *we* did the robbing!"

"It does?" Gregory glanced toward the mounted men. "Is that what it looks like to you men?"

Both nodded.

"Well, shoot." Gregory kicked the dirt. "Now your ma and pa are for sure gonna think you've married yourself a melon-head."

"I done told them that in my letters I sent before we set out for Kansas," she complained. "Dumb and broke. I don't know what I was thinking."

She received an annoyed sidelong glance from Gregory before the sheriff asked, "So, what you're saying is, that two men approached you and offered to trade their horses for your wagon?"

"I reckon so." Gregory indicated a large piece of driftwood he'd pulled up next to the fire for them to sit. "One of them was kind of scrawny. Ugly as the day is long."

Violet added, "And the other had a long nose. Real long. And he had beady little eyes and a weak chin." She glanced at Gregory, waiting for him to continue their made-up descriptions and hoping they could manage to be convincing.

"The scrawny one had a birthmark on his cheek."

When that's all he offered, Violet quickly continued: "And he also had rotten teeth and—"

"Hold on," the sheriff interrupted. "I'm trying to

keep up with what you're saying. Maybe you two could come back to town with us so we can write it all down. Tim and me need to check in with the sheriff of Boonville, anyway. We need to introduce ourselves and tell him we've joined the posse."

They couldn't go back to town. Violet had a suspicion the lawmen didn't believe their story for a minute. "What's so hard about remembering beady eyes, birthmark, rotten teeth and a big nose?"

"I thought you said a long nose, not a big nose," the so-far silent deputy pointed out.

"It *was* long," Violet said—and she knew she had to do something, even if it was something she didn't want to do. "But it was big, too. Like it'd been broken. Like this."

She swiped her pan up and hit the deputy in the face. Before the sheriff could react, she clubbed him over the head. While one man howled with pain and the other fell to the ground stunned, she grabbed her gun. Gregory, she noted, wasn't much help concerning the situation. His mouth hung open.

Violet aimed her gun at the lawmen. "Put your hands in the air!"

They both obeyed her, although one man's hand was covered with blood from his broken nose.

"Get their guns," she ordered Gregory.

"What in the hell are you doing, ah, Pumpkin?" he asked.

"Get their guns!" she repeated.

He scrambled up and took the men's guns from their holsters. "She's really set on seeing her folks," he said, then shrugged as if that were an excuse.

"Go toss their weapons in the stream," Violet instructed.

Gregory stood with his back to the men. "Do you know what you're doing?" he asked softly.

Violet wasn't certain. She only knew she couldn't be arrested and accused of the robberies she'd intended to pin on her father. "Yes," she whispered back, then narrowed her gaze on the lawmen. "I'm sorry it had to come down to this," she said. "We ain't taking no jail time for someone else's wrongdoings, and I could tell you had it in your head to blame this business on us."

She watched Gregory walk the short distance to the stream and throw the men's weapons into the water. "Let those horses the robbers were riding loose," she called to Gregory, then turned to the men. "Now, you two. Strip down."

Chapter Six

Gregory shined the tin star pinned to his shirt with his sleeve. He had to give Violet credit for courage, if he couldn't give her much for sense. He'd started to suspect that the lawmen weren't buying their act, and he hadn't been sure what he'd have to do about it. He couldn't let the men take them to jail. The concern hadn't materialized. Violet hadn't waited around to see if worst came to worst; she'd simply taken matters into her own hands.

Of course, she would get the both of them killed if she kept robbing banks and bashing men over the heads with hard objects. Gregory wasn't a saint, but he sure as hell wasn't an outlaw! As soon as Violet lowered her guard enough, he should just take the money from the last robbery, count them even, and quit—get the hell away from her. He still didn't know what drove her to rob banks, to take the chances she took, both with her life and his.

"How does your new horse ride?" she asked.

Casting a dark glance at her men's garb, he answered, "He's fine. I still don't understand why you get to wear the sheriff's badge, and I have to be the deputy."

She glared back at him. "Because I did all the work to get us out of that predicament. All you did was stand around with your mouth hanging open."

"You did all the work to get us into it, too," he reminded her. "I'm a blackmailer, remember? I never agreed to risk being arrested and hanged when I told Miles I'd bring you home. You *do* realize those lawmen are going to take stealing their clothes and horses personal?"

"Yes," she admitted. "But I left them in their drawers with no horses; I figured the posse from Boonville would come across them. It'll take the sheriff and the deputy a little while to convince the posse they aren't the robbers. The sheriff said they were from out of town; he was probably unknown by those guys from Boonville. At least that's what I'm hoping."

Although it was a good plan, there were several holes in her reasoning. "It won't take a posse long to figure out that the sheriff and his deputy are not the robbers. For one thing, they don't have the stolen money on them and neither do the horses I let loose."

Violet nodded and chewed her lower lip. "Yes, we're going to have to get rid of the money."

Gregory hoped she had not just said what he

thought she'd said. He pulled up on the reins, stopping his horse. "What?"

Violet reined up beside him. She shrugged. "You said yourself that it won't take the posse long to figure out those two are not responsible. I can't have the sheriff and his deputy believing that we are. We've got to get rid of the money so that it will take the suspicion off of us."

Gregory's head suddenly felt like it might explode. "Why bother stealing money if you just keep giving it away?" He saw Violet flinch at his harsh words and tried to calm himself. "I thought you needed the money."

"I do," she assured him. "But I also need to get to Kansas, and I can't do that if I'm in jail."

"What in the hell is in Kansas?" he demanded. "And why do you need the money in the first place?"

As if she had a secret, and they weren't alone, Violet glanced around then leaned toward him. "I need the money to ransom someone. Someone who's in Kansas."

"Ransom?" Gregory was surprised. "Who? What?"

"Let's take a short rest. I'll explain everything while we have lunch."

Gregory glanced at the road behind them. They weren't being pursued, therefore he had to believe Violet's plan had worked to some extent. He was hungry, and it was about time he knew what was going on. They rounded a bend and came across a man relieving himself in the middle of the road. As if that weren't bad enough, the man held the reins to Blaze, Miles Traften's once-prized gelding.

Gregory heard Violet gasp. He didn't know if it was over the sight of Blaze or the man's limp member hanging out of his pants. His annoyance level was unusually high given what they'd been through that morning, and then Violet telling him they had to get rid of the money.

"Hey!" he shouted. "Put that back in your pants."

The man's head swung toward him, he cussed, then fumbled for his gun. Instinctively, Gregory drew first. The man dropped his weapon in the dirt.

"Aw, hell," the man cussed. He held up his hands. "All right. You got me. No need to shoot. I'll come back to Boonville with you peaceful. But I didn't steal this horse. I swear, found him running loose."

Gregory glanced at Violet. She had her head turned away. He noticed how the sun glinted off of her badge, and his too, he imagined. "Get your pants up," he said to the man, moving his horse in closer. "I believe you about the horse."

The stranger scrambled to do his bidding. He turned his beady eyes up to stare at Gregory. "Then you know about the other, huh? Hell, she was just a whore anyway. So what if I cut her up a little? So what if I knocked her around some? It ain't like them kind of gals ain't used to that sort of thing. Ain't nothing worth being locked up about, or hell, paying some damn fine over. I mean, it ain't like I robbed a bank or nothin'."

When the man grinned, as if trying to convince Gregory that the situation wasn't serious, Gregory noticed his rotten teeth. "You're both men," the idiot continued. "Why you gonna take *her* side? Why do you give a damn about what happens to some diseased ridden, fat-assed—"

"Hey," Gregory interrupted. "Watch your mouth." He started to say there was a lady present, then remembered Violet wasn't supposed to be a lady. Not on the road. The other man reached down and scratched himself. Gregory sighed in disgust. "What should we do with him, Sheriff?" he asked Violet dryly.

Her eyes cut toward him, then she looked at the stranger. "Have you got any money?" she asked, her voice gruff.

"Hell, no." The stranger kicked the dirt. "That's why I ran when she said she'd get the law on me for what I'd done to her. Said she wanted to be paid extra and she'd keep quiet. Then I found this nice animal just grazing by the side of the rode. I turned my old plug loose and took this one."

"I think we should give him some money to settle with the woman before she turns him in to the Federal Marshal," she offered. "But he's going to have to turn that horse in, too. I imagine someone is looking for an animal that nice."

Gregory sighed again. Violet had an idea. They had to get the posse off of their trail, and now they'd been given the perfect opportunity. "If we give you some money to appease the lady, do you swear that you'll return to Boonville and do the right thing?"

The man readily agreed, looking surprised. "What're you two, some kind of whore lovers?" At Violet's nasty glare he added, "Hell, don't want to be watching my back just cause I roughed up some woman. I'll give her your money. Though there shouldn't be no crime in what I done. Truth is, I was hoping to find work in Boonville. Now this mess—"

Gregory dismounted. "I'm taking your gun," he interrupted, swiping it off the ground. He slapped the man hard on the back and steered him away from Blaze. "You know," he said. "It doesn't pay not to be nice to the ladies. If you don't go back to Boonville and do as you've promised, I'll come after you myself. And that's a promise from a lawman."

Swallowing loudly, the man nodded. "I swear I'll go back." From the corner of his eye, Gregory saw Violet trade her saddle packs for the empty ones behind the saddle on Blaze. She stared at the horse and he thought for a minute she might cry. Well, at least they'd know where the horse was and might be able to pick him up on the way back to St. Louis . . . if they ever made it back to St. Louis.

Digging a wad of bills from his pocket, Gregory shoved them into the man's hand. "That's enough to pay the lady and get you liquored up. Go on now, and don't forget what I told you."

The man walked to Blaze and saddled up. Violet said something to him. The man nodded, then swung Blaze toward the direction of Boonville. Gregory knew the law would hear conflicting stories, and of course the man would tell them about the two lawmen who'd sent him to settle his debt with a prostitute, but the sheriff would have the bank's money back, and Gregory figured that's all he'd care about.

As he watched Blaze and the stranger move off,

he kind of wanted to cry, too. All that money. Gone again. His stomach grumbled, and he remembered they were going to have lunch—but more importantly, Violet would at last reveal her secret to him.

They moved farther down the road, then found a wooded area and dismounted. Violet dug the supply sack from the back of his saddle. She brought out jerky and hard bread.

"All right, we took care of the money problem. Tell me who you have to ransom?" Gregory asked after she handed him the food.

Her cheeks turned red. "My beloved."

He nearly choked. "Your what?"

She sighed. "The man I intend to marry."

Those words held an ominous ring. The money from the last robbery was gone. His options were once again limited. He couldn't marry Violet and become part of the Traften stronghold if she already had a husband. He didn't suppose it would be proper to even court her if she were already spoken for . . . of course, that had never stopped him in the past.

"And why would you have to ransom this man?"

Glancing down, she nibbled at her full lower lip. Gregory wouldn't mind nibbling on it himself. Her mouth was a constant temptation to him.

"Miles doesn't approve of him," she admitted. "That's why I couldn't ask him for the money. He would leave poor . . . T-Tip to his fate and be thankful he was out of my life."

Tip? He hadn't missed how she'd stumbled over the name. What sort of man had the name Tip? It sounded more like a dog's name, or maybe a horse.

"Who do you have to ransom, ah, Tip from?"

"Outlaws."

He sat up straight. "Outlaws? What would your intended be doing with outlaws?"

Violet's lashes lifted and she looked at him. "I'm afraid he ran with bad company before he met me in St. Louis. He traveled to Kansas to tell his gang members that he wanted to settle down and turn respectable. He told them about me, and of course he made the mistake of telling them that my uncle is wealthy. Now they're holding him for ransom. If I fail to bring them the money, they have threatened to kill him."

Was this the unsavory past Miles had hinted about concerning his niece? Was this the unscrupulous man Miles had heard Violet was meeting? Had Gregory been risking life and limb to save some outlaw who'd found himself a nice comfortable nest and a very desirable bird with which to settle down?

"Miles is right," he said. "You have no business marrying this unsuitable man."

"I love him," Violet declared—rather too passionately, in his opinion. "I'll do *anything* to save his life. I knew Miles wouldn't lift a finger to help Tip. And besides, I love Miles too dearly to drag him into this dreadful business."

Something about the whole conversation seemed suspicious to him. "Miles told me that you didn't like men. He said you were uncomfortable around them." Certainly she acted like that around him.

"I don't like the men he'd have me choose for a husband," she explained. "I-I like my men wild."

She raised her chin as if she expected him to dispute her claim. He couldn't see her with an outlaw. A man without manners. Her kisses, although sweet, were also innocent, as if she'd never been kissed before, at least with any amount of thoroughness.

Suddenly he thought he'd figured it all out. She'd developed an infatuation for a man beneath her social station. This was a rebellion of some sort against the restraints society placed upon her. He'd seen it before: Lilla, Miles's daughter, had married beneath her station too.

Of course, Grady Finch wasn't an outlaw, just a cowboy. Why did nice girls desire bad men?

Gregory could be bad. He *had* been bad. And it occurred to him that next to an outlaw, he'd look pretty good in Miles's eyes for a relation.

"I'm taking you home. You will forget this Tip character and marry someone Miles approves of, and you will later realize how fortunate you were that I came along to set you straight."

Violet stood. Her cheeks blazed with color again, only he didn't think it was embarrassment.

"Set me straight?" she huffed. "Let me set you straight, *Mr.* Kline. No one—not you, not Miles, not any man—will tell me what I will or will not do! Not ever again! So just leave me alone and go back to St. Louis!"

She stormed to her horse, stuffed the supplies back into the packs, and mounted up. Then she rode away. Gregory sat for a moment, weighing his options. There was no money left to steal. Violet claimed to love another man, an outlaw. Which left him with only the original agreement of getting her home safely. But she didn't want to go home, and what was he supposed to do—drag her back kicking and screaming? The woman wasn't one who'd put up with manhandling. She'd probably shoot him if he tried.

Of course, Miles had made no stipulations to their agreement except finding Violet and bringing her home safely. There were no time constraints thrown into the bargain. And while Gregory had promised to act like a gentleman with her, all the gentlemen he knew would seduce a beautiful young woman in a second if given the opportunity. So maybe that was his course of action. Maybe he'd been too nice with Violet. He'd be doing Miles a favor if he stole her away from this outlaw she planned to rescue.

She liked her men wild? Gregory could be wild. And he could be very bad. But he'd have to show it to her subtly.

Violet fought the urge to turn and look behind her. She couldn't tell Gregory the real reason why she needed the money. Then she'd have to tell him everything. Then he'd surely abandon her. As long as he believed she was marriageable material, as long as he held out hope that he could woo his way into her good graces, and Miles's pockets, he would stick around.

She'd decided upon having an outlaw lover for two reasons: one, men always seemed to chase after what was unavailable to them, and she figured women were probably the same; and two, she might disguise the uneasiness she felt when Gregory got too close as devotion to someone else.

He had to stop kissing her, though. His kisses confused her. She knew she should be frightened, but she couldn't honestly say she feared Gregory Kline. Or that fear had anything to do with the emotions his kisses stirred. Which frightened her even more.

The sound of hoofbeats made her sigh in relief. A moment later Gregory rode up beside her.

"So what's the plan now?" he asked.

"You're not going to like it," she assured him.

"Let me guess. You're going to rob another bank?"

"Without the ransom, Tip is a dead man."

"Maybe he'd be better off that way," Gregory muttered.

She glanced at him. "You don't really mean that, do you? You're a schemer, a man who places wealth and position above all else, but you're not a cold-blooded killer."

He lifted a brow. "I might be. I'm a very bad man."

Laughter came close to bubbling up and spilling out of her throat. Violet swallowed it down. Gregory might not be a very good man, but she doubted that he was a very bad one.

"Tell me about this man you claim to love. Tip."

She inwardly groaned. Why couldn't she have thought of a real man's name? Violet supposed that, besides Miles, she hadn't loved any men. She'd tried to think of something she had loved—a small kitten that had wandered to their cabin when she was a little girl, all black except for a white tip on his tail.

"He's playful," she answered slowly.

"Playful?" Gregory repeated.

She waved a hand. "I don't really want to discuss him with you. In fact, I must insist that you return to St. Louis. This is dangerous business. You might get hurt."

He straightened in the saddle. "As I've proven more than once, I can take care of myself."

She looked over at him. "I thought you were a coward, and seemingly proud of the fact."

There was silence for a moment; then he turned to her and smiled. "You know what they say—the right woman can change even the most hopeless of men."

His smile disarmed her—but only for a moment. She knew his game. "I hope you find her."

The smile he wore faded. He glanced back at the road ahead of them. "Has this outlaw you plan to marry seduced you?"

It was her turn to stiffen in the saddle. "That is none of your business!"

"Judging by your lack of experience, I'm thinking he hasn't. I find that strange."

Violet thought about her kin, the scruffy men who sometimes came to hide out at her father's cabin, and gave her father part of whatever they'd stolen to do so. They weren't the types to treat a woman with respect. None of them had manners. They had leered at her mother, said things that made her blush, and her drunken father had never put any of them in their place.

"He's different from what I suppose most outlaws

88

must be like," she said. "He's always treated me with respect."

"A gentleman outlaw?" Gregory laughed. "You're naive, Violet. And he's obviously wise enough to hide his true nature from you. He's pulled the wool over your eyes. You're not in love with him; you're merely infatuated with what he represents: danger, a man society would frown upon. All the things nice girls find appealing in their harmless little dreams."

Her dreams were not harmless or appealing. The conversation soured her mood. Gregory was the innocent. He believed she was a lady, that she was virtuous simply because she'd lived beneath Miles's roof—simply because the man doted upon her as if she had worth. Gregory had made himself clear enough during their first meeting. He didn't mind used goods in his bed, but he didn't wear them upon his sleeve. No one would.

"You won't change my mind about what I must do," she told him. "But I might agree to come back to St. Louis with you afterward."

"You and your outlaw?"

"Yes."

"And you really think these men can be trusted to keep their word to you? That you'll just hand over the money and they will release him, allowing you both to go on your merry way?"

Her story obviously had flaws she hadn't thought through. To distract him until she had time to patch the tale up, she decided to prick his male sensibilities again. "I *said* it would be dangerous. Not an undertaking for cowards."

"There's a difference between cowardice and stupidity," he snapped. "I will try to change your mind about rescuing the outlaw."

"Is that a warning?"

"It's a promise," he answered.

"And I promise you, you won't. You're wasting your time to try."

"I haven't got anything better to do."

Anything that might prove more lucrative, she thought. Only the fact that she knew Gregory was the type who'd lie, cheat, and do anything he must to get what he wanted, kept her from having a guilty conscience about lying to him. But she didn't want him to get hurt on her account. She needed him only until she reached the outskirts of Coffeyville. The next bank that she robbed, she'd make certain he was out of the way. And if the law caught them, she'd take full blame for her actions, and he'd be released.

It occurred to her that wanting Gregory around for safety purposes might be a mistake. He had saved her once already, she reminded herself, but if he took a notion to seduce her, believing that to do so would be to his advantage, and if he used any amount of force, the situation could get dangerous . . . for both of them.

His words later that night proved her right. He suggested they bed down together again. She couldn't see his logic. Now they were traveling under the guise of two lawmen. She didn't honestly believe two lawmen would care to find themselves wrapped around each other come morning. Since she'd prepared their meal, she made Gregory take first watch. Violet settled into her bedroll, tired from riding all day but wary of trusting him. Kline sat across the fire, staring at her. She swore she heard the wheels turning in his head.

Gregory watched Violet until her breathing deepened and sleep claimed her. She didn't trust him. Which only proved what he already knew about Violet Mallory: she was smart. Too smart, he'd been thinking, to get mixed up with an outlaw. He had a suspicion she had lied to him about the real reason she wanted money. Her story didn't add up.

But nothing about Violet Mallory added up. Miles hadn't said she wasn't his niece; nor had he sworn that she was. He'd instead said that he considered her family, and to make no mistake upon that issue. She claimed to like her men wild, but he knew she was uncomfortable any time he even touched her. And there was an outlaw named Tip who'd had the manners to keep his hands off a desirable young woman like Violet?

She was hiding something from him. The truth. How bad could the truth be? he wondered. And why did a young woman with Miles's wealth at her disposal really need to race around the country robbing banks? But if her relationship with an outlaw wasn't what Miles had referred to as her past indiscretions, what were? And now that he thought about it, hadn't Miles mentioned revenge?

Who would Violet be seeking vengeance against? And where did the money come into play? He should have asked more questions—no, demanded more answers—from Miles before he'd agreed to chase after the man's niece. But he'd gotten the impression Miles didn't know exactly what Violet planned either. Perhaps something had happened to her, something she was too ashamed to tell Miles Traften about.

Violet moaned in her sleep. The firelight flickered over her long hair. It shimmered and shone with streaks of blond. He wanted to run his fingers through it. She sighed, forcing his eyes to her lips. They were full, ripe . . . tempting. She jerked, flipping onto her back. The rise of her breasts stretched the cotton shirt she wore tight across her womanly curves. Gregory had met many beautiful women, had courted more than a few, but Violet . . . she got to him on some deeper level.

Her sudden whimper made him jump. She tossed restlessly upon the blankets. She twitched again and he rushed to her side. Her body was tense, and her face was a mask of anguish. He bent beside her and gave her a nudge.

"Violet, wake up. You're dreaming."

Her hands shot up, her fingers curled into claws. He captured her wrists to keep her from cutting his face.

"Violet! It's me, Gregory. Calm down."

Her eyes opened. She stared blankly at him for a moment, shuddered, then started to weep. He released her wrists, but didn't know what to do.

It had helped soothe her when he'd held her the last time the nightmares woke her, so he took her in his arms. She fought him for a moment, but he spoke softly to her. After a few minutes, she relaxed.

He was confused again. The two men who attacked her hadn't gotten far, only ripped her shirt and probably scared her. These horrible nightmares seemed too strong to stem from something like that.

"Violet, we have to talk." He pulled away from her. "What are these nightmares about?"

Violet wiped the tears from her face. She couldn't tell Gregory that her nightmares stemmed from her past. She couldn't tell him that in her dreams, she relived the horrible things done to her by a disgusting, abusive man. Shame washed over her. What would he think if he knew the truth? What would anyone who knew her in St. Louis think? Shy Violet. Quiet Violet. Sweet Violet. Lies. All lies.

The truth was too horrible—too awful for even her mind to handle. She'd been beaten, bruised, battered, but that wasn't the worst. *Defiled*. She'd been degraded in the vilest sense—her young body forced to accept the probing, painful intrusion of a man's hateful weapon. Not once, but many times.

Her hands shook as she brushed her hair from her face. She wanted badly to let it hang down in her eyes as she'd done when she first met Lilla in Sally's Saloon: a veil to hide her from the cruel world. But she would not hide any longer. The past had scarred her, she knew that, but she'd once promised Lilla that she wouldn't allow the past to control her, and she would try to keep her word.

"The dreams are nothing," she finally said. "I'm all

right now. I'll just go back to sleep, or I can take over watch if you—"

"They are not nothing," he interrupted. "Do they have to do with those two men attacking you?"

She couldn't look at him. "I guess so."

"What did they do to you? I saw that your shirt was torn, but—"

"I don't want to talk about it," she snapped. "Just leave it alone. I told you that I'm all right."

"You're not all right or you wouldn't wake up screaming and fighting in your sleep," he argued. "I think it will help you to deal with what happened if you talk about it."

"I can't talk about it. Not to you."

He reached out and gently cupped her chin, turning her face toward his. "Yes, you can. Did they touch you?"

"No," she whispered then decided to be a little truthful. Gregory had to go on believing that her dreams stemmed from the other incident, not the real one "I mean, yes. They grabbed me roughly."

Fury rose up in Gregory. "Grabbed you where?" he demanded, then *wished* he hadn't spoken so harshly, because she looked like she would shut him out. "A man isn't always rough, Violet, and he shouldn't touch a woman anywhere unless she's given him permission."

"T-they said things," she whispered. "Things about what they would do to me. How they would hurt me."

His anger increased, but he held it in check because he didn't want to further frighten her. But he found himself overcome with a need to explain that all men weren't cruel. "Those men were scum, Violet. They don't know how to treat a lady or how to be gentle. A man can be with a woman without hurting her. He can give her pleasure, just as she gives him pleasure."

She glanced up at him, her expression skeptical. "Have you?"

He wasn't positive what she was asking, but he was very certain this wasn't a proper conversation to be having with her. "Have I what?"

"Been with a woman?"

That was what he'd thought she was asking. Gregory tugged at his collar. "I don't think that's something we should discuss."

"You said you wanted to talk," she said stiffly. "How am I supposed to take anything you say seriously if you don't know what you're talking about?"

"I know what I'm talking about," he assured her.

"Then you have been with a woman before."

They'd come this far, a long way past decency regarding conversations between gentlemen and ladies; he guessed they might as well go farther. "Yes."

"More than one?"

"What does that have to do with anything?"

She shrugged. "Maybe if it was just one, she didn't tell you the truth."

"It was more than one," he said—a bit defensively, he realized. "Don't ask me anything else, because Miles would skin me alive if he knew we were having this conversation."

"You do realize he'd skin you alive if he knew you'd so much as kissed me. I hope you remember that and don't get any other ideas."

It was time to set her straight. "Violet, you're very desirable. Even so, it doesn't mean I'm going to throw you on the ground and have my way with you. Being with you, intimately, would have to be of mutual consent."

"That will never happen," she said.

She looked as if she sincerely believed her words, as if she didn't want to be with anyone, ever. Again, Gregory couldn't imagine her with an outlaw. She was not attracted to dangerous men; he didn't care what she claimed. "Because of Tip?" he asked.

For a moment, she looked confused. Then she quickly agreed: "Oh, yes, because of Tip. My heart, along with the rest of me, is spoken for."

He felt very tempted to prove otherwise, but instead he said, "Go back to sleep."

"I'm not sure I can. I could take over your watch."

He saw that Violet had dark circles beneath her eyes from lack of sleep. "How about a compromise?"

She lifted a brow.

"I'll settle next to this tree, and you settle up next to me. If I see that you're starting to have a nightmare again, I'll wake you."

She looked as if she'd refuse, then she nodded. "Promise you'll wake me if I start dreaming?"

Gregory leaned against the tree and motioned her toward him. "I promise."

*　　*　　*

Violet reluctantly settled next to him. She still wasn't sure she could trust him, but she was tired, and she needed rest. When she leaned against him, she heard the steady beat of his heart beneath her ear. His arms went around her, and she fought to keep still. He didn't try to touch her anywhere he shouldn't. After a few minutes, she relaxed. His shirt smelled like dust and wood smoke. She imagined hers did, too.

What she wouldn't give for a tub full of bubbles and a good long soak. Her life with Miles had spoiled her, but it hadn't erased her past, the way she'd foolishly hoped it might. She'd heard of people who lost their memory—couldn't remember who they were or what had happened to them. She'd like to be one of those people. But the nightmares were always there to remind her, lest she forgot, even for a little while.

Gregory's body heat warmed her through his clothes. He'd said he'd been with women before. Women who'd found pleasure with him. Violet had trouble associating pleasure of any kind with what she knew of . . . of that. Still, some of the women she'd worked with at Sally's Saloon hadn't seemed to mind spending time with men in the back rooms. Violet had used to stuff cotton in her ears when she went to bed so she wouldn't hear all the moaning and groaning that took place. She had never known whether to associate those noises with pain or with pleasure.

Gregory's touch startled her. He lifted a few strands of her hair and let them slide through his fingers. When he seemed content to only fondle them, she let her body relax again. She found it soothing, the feel of her hair sliding through his fingers. She supposed if she could admit the truth, she'd found his kisses pleasant, too.

As her eyes grew heavy, Violet realized that there were women who could be with a man and find it pleasurable, although she wasn't sure how. She knew she would never be one of them. How could she enjoy anything that would hurt that much, or that made her feel so worthless and dirty?

Answers remained just beyond her reach. The feel of her hair sliding through Gregory's fingers made her feel relaxed and oddly content. She needed sleep, needed her strength. Tomorrow she had to convince Gregory to go into the next town with her. She needed money, needed the law to keep chasing after her—needed to find another bank to rob.

Chapter Seven

As it turned out, convincing Gregory wasn't difficult. The next morning Violet merely had to show Gregory her pack of dwindling supplies, and comment on the filth that covered both of them, and he agreed they could both use a bath and their supplies restocked. Now she walked the streets of Lawrence, again dressed like a lady. She'd bathed, put on her women's trappings, and left the room so Gregory could clean up as well.

The bank was next to the sheriff's office which didn't please Violet. She had hoped the jail would be farther down the street. The bank was busy this afternoon, too; people hustled in and out. Morning would be a better time to pull off a robbery, which meant that she and Gregory would have to spend the night at the hotel.

Ronda Thompson

She couldn't risk a robbery in midafternoon. Not with the bank crowded and the sheriff up and about next door. She shouldn't risk it at all, an inner voice added. But Violet ignored the uneasy feeling that washed over her. She'd have to think of a good excuse to tell Gregory about wanting to stay in town. Her gaze scanned the street and lit upon the stage depot station. Then she smiled and rushed off to make the arrangements.

A short time later, the idea of knocking didn't even occur to Violet. She burst into their room at the hotel, waving stage tickets.

"I've decided I want to go home," she cried.

Gregory sat in a tub of steamy water, smoking a thin cigar. He stared at her through a haze of steam and smoke. "What did you say?"

She had trouble remembering what she'd said. His hair was wet and slicked back from his handsome face. He'd shaved. His upper body glistened with steamy moisture from his bath. His legs were drawn up due to the smallness of the tub. From what she could see of them, they were long and muscular.

"I-I said I've decided I want to go home," she repeated, her gaze roaming his smooth, wet skin.

"Would you mind closing the door?"

While she was at it, she decided she should close her mouth. She suspected it might be hanging open. Gregory Kline's body held some magical fascination for her. She had no idea what it was, or why; she just knew she liked looking at it. After she closed the door, she moved to the other side of the room.

"I thought you would be finished with your bath,"

she said. "Otherwise I would have never burst in the way I did."

"I like my water steaming hot," he said. Settling back in the tub, he added, "It was worth the wait. Now, what's this about deciding you want to go home?"

Violet fussed about, picking up the room. Her gaze kept straying to the tub. "I should leave and come back when you've finished. Then we'll discuss my decision."

"I'm not all that modest," he admitted. "I'd rather discuss it now. I find it hard to believe you've just suddenly changed your mind." He gave her a hard look.

Being convincing might prove difficult under the circumstances. She thought it would be easier to fool him if she made eye contact and tried to appear sincere. The problem was, she didn't know if she could keep her eyes on his face and off of the rest of him.

"And I find it hard to converse with a man who isn't properly dressed," she countered. "I'll meet you downstairs, and we can discuss it over dinner."

"If you plan on going home, why did you buy supplies?"

Violet paused. "I bought the supplies first . . . before I made the decision," she said, moving toward the door. She heard the slosh of water, and the next thing she knew, Gregory blocked the doorway.

"I think you're up to something," he accused.

Her mouth fell open again. "Good grief, Gregory. Have you no shame?"

He glanced down. "I'm covered."

He'd as good as invited her to see for herself. She did. Quickly. He had a towel wrapped around his middle. Even so, his chest was bare and still damp, and she could see his legs sticking out from beneath the towel. She'd been right—they were long and muscular.

"I cannot stand here and have a conversation with you while you're half-undressed."

"Then wait, and I'll put some clothes on."

As if she'd agreed, he turned and moved to where he'd laid a rumpled suit over a chair. Her gaze roamed him from the top of his head to the backs of his bare heels.

"How is it that your skin is that sun-kissed color all over?" She'd meant only to think the question, not ask it out loud. He turned.

"What?"

Her face blazed. "Your skin. Why is it so dark? I mean, everywhere?"

Gregory shrugged. "In Wyoming the summers are hot. If a man finds a puddle of water while out riding cattle, he strips down and jumps in it."

"Oh." Her face flushed hotter at the vision that entered her mind. "I should wait for you downstairs."

Gathering up his clothes, Kline said, "It isn't decent for a young woman to enter the dining hall alone."

It was more indecent for a young woman to stand and watch a man move around half-naked!

And decency shouldn't even be an issue. Violet wasn't a sheltered, innocent miss, though Gregory made her feel like one at times. Why was he able to do that? Maybe because she'd been given adequate opportunities to stare at naked men in the past but never found herself wanting to.

"Why this sudden change of heart?" he asked.

She'd forgotten the original conversation, and, for a second, thought he had read her mind. He meant about going back to St. Louis, though. He looked as if he might take his towel off and proceed to dress.

"You *are* going to move behind the dressing screen?"

Gregory glanced over his shoulder at her. "Of course." A moment later he draped his suit over the top of the screen. He'd obviously moved it earlier, because Violet had placed the screen in front of the tub when she'd bathed. The new location was not good. The thin cotton barrier sat before the window, and the fading sunlight outlined Gregory Kline's body to perfection. He might as well have been standing before her naked.

There was a slight difference. She could see him, but he couldn't see her.

"You were saying?"

Saying? What *had* she been saying? He removed the towel and was now drying his body. She had trouble concentrating.

"I said, I have decided I want to go back to St. Louis. Strolling the shops, wearing my fine clothes again, has made me homesick. Maybe I should have told Miles about T-Tip . . ."

Her voice trailed off when Gregory turned sideways. He obviously had a tip, too, only his didn't look small, harmless, and cuddly. She quickly averted her gaze.

"I mean about his dilemma," she continued, sitting on the bed. "I naturally assumed Miles wouldn't help Tip because of his prejudice regarding outlaws. But maybe if I beg and plead with Miles, he will see Tip rescued from his outlaw gang."

Gregory didn't respond, but Violet heard rustling sounds and assumed he was proceeding to dress. He appeared a moment later, shrugging into his suit jacket.

"And you've just now had the good sense to consider asking Miles for help rather than running around all over the countryside robbing banks?"

Her story sounded suspicious, she realized. "I told you that I didn't want to get Miles mixed up in this dangerous business, but what am I to do?" She made her bottom lip quiver. "I'm only a woman. This racing around, camping out-of-doors, it's not what I'm accustomed to. It's made me realize a life with Tip won't be what I'm accustomed to, either."

His gaze narrowed. "So you're abandoning Tip to his own fate the way you should have done to begin with?"

The way you *would have done,* she wanted to say, but didn't. "I'm not abandoning him," she clarified. "Just my plan to rescue him without Miles's help. And if I know that at least Tip is safe, I may be able to take a harder look at my decision to marry." She figured that last statement might help convince him.

"What about revenge?"

His question startled her. She'd never mentioned

revenge to him. "What are you talking about?"

He moved toward her, fixing his tie. "Miles told me he feared you had some grand scheme in mind. A plan that included revenge against someone."

She'd told Miles little about her past, and he had been kind enough never to push her for details. But that didn't mean Lilla hadn't given him what Violet suspected was a watered-down version of how Violet had come to be working in the saloon where she and Lilla met. Lilla had probably told him that Violet's father had sold her to a man for a case of whiskey, and Miles, being highly intelligent, had filled in the rest.

"I did plan on revenge," she admitted. "Revenge against the gang members who are holding Tip hostage. I feared that once I rescued him, they might try something unscrupulous. I thought they might even try to kidnap me to get more money from Miles."

"That would make sense," Gregory agreed, but still stared at her suspiciously, as if waiting to find a hole in her story.

"Why do you think I told Henry Blake where I was headed when I robbed the bank in St. Louis?" she asked. "Why do you think I robbed a bank with a posse gathered down the street in Boonville? Why do you think I purposely humiliated those two lawmen by making them strip, then stole their horses?"

His brow furrowed. "Because you're crazy?"

She rose from her position on the bed, tired of staring up at him. "Because I *wanted* the law to follow me to Kansas. Once I exchanged the money for Tip, I planned on turning the gang in. They would be caught with the money, thus making the law believe members of the gang were robbing the banks. And I'd probably collect myself a nice reward in the bargain."

Kline's eyes lit with amused admiration. "That's pretty smart. But how did you think you were going to exchange the money for the outlaw without being captured by the gang?"

Violet moved past him and fussed with her hair before the dresser mirror. "I hadn't worked that out yet, but planned to before I reached Coffeyville."

"But now you want to go home?"

Her gaze met his in the mirror. She had no trouble saying it, because her answer was the truth. "Yes, I want to go *home.*"

His wary expression didn't relax the way she had hoped, but he did glance at the stage tickets she'd left on the bed. It was as if he were trying to reassure himself.

"Shall we go to dinner?" she asked enthusiastically.

"Yes," he agreed, then walked over and offered her his arm. "Because until I make sure you're telling the truth, I'm not letting you out of my sight."

Violet was a better cook than whoever prepared their meal, but Gregory enjoyed the simple pleasure of dining with a roof over his head. The company wasn't bad, either. Even without frills, Violet was a beautiful woman; when she dressed like a lady, her thick hair arranged attractively in loose curls atop her head, she was a vision.

A dangerous vision, he reminded himself. A woman who looked like an angel but lied like the devil. Violet couldn't be trusted; she'd proven that to him more than once. Her earlier story had sounded valid. She'd had an answer for every question he hoped to trip her up with, but he still found it hard to believe she wasn't leading him down another false trail.

An outlaw named Tip she planned to rescue from his own gang members; he just couldn't imagine it being true. The more time he spent with her, the less he believed she'd get mixed up with such a man. Maybe with any man. If he touched her, or tried to hold her, if anything that went on between them wasn't another trick she'd instigated to throw him off guard, she seemed physically terrified of him. And he didn't have a good reputation, but he wasn't that bad!

"Tell me about Wyoming," she suggested, cutting into his thoughts.

"You read my letters. You already know about Wyoming."

"Tell me something *nice* about Wyoming," she amended.

"I'm no longer there," he supplied. Although there were times he actually missed chasing down rustlers and punching cows. It was certainly simpler than *this*. "Why don't we talk about you."

She fiddled with her napkin, then pushed a stray curl from her forehead. "I'd rather not."

He wouldn't be put off again. "Are you really from Boston? Is Lilla in truth your cousin? What were you doing in Texas three years ago? Why—"

"Why don't we retire?" she interrupted. She placed a hand against her temple. "We're finished here, and I have a horrible headache."

It was the oldest trick in the book. A man didn't press a woman about anything if she claimed to have a headache. Gregory threw his napkin on his plate, rose, and pulled out her chair. He attended to the bill, then followed her upstairs. The swish of her skirts, the sway of her hips, caught his attention and held it until they reached their room.

Once inside, he locked the door. Violet immediately began plucking pins from her hair. Gregory removed his suit jacket and the tie that felt as if it had been choking him all evening. Violet muttered something. She struggled with a stubborn pin.

"Would you like my help?"

Her gaze found his in the mirror. "I'm sure I'll get it in a minute," she answered.

Amused, he watched her as she continued to dig and, if he wasn't mistaken, curse beneath her breath. He walked over and removed her hands. The pin was stubborn, but he managed to retrieve it; then he slid his fingers through the long strands of her hair. He loved the silken feel. His gaze met hers in the mirror again. Her cheeks were flushed, her full lips slightly parted. Had he seen fear staring back at him, he wouldn't have been as forward. He didn't. Pushing her hair over one shoulder, he placed a soft kiss at the place where her neck and shoulder met. She shivered.

"Gregory," she warned, but her voice sounded soft, breathless, not frightened.

"Did that hurt you?" he asked.

"No. But I didn't ask you to kiss me or touch me, and you said a gentleman should always ask."

He decided then and there that he wouldn't give her further advice on what a man should or should not do to a woman. He stepped away from her. They were returning to St. Louis in the morning. He should conduct himself like a gentleman. There would be other days—and nights too—to win Violet Mallory. He walked to the bed and stared at the tickets.

"Don't think you're sharing that bed with me, either," Violet warned as she grabbed up her valise and moved behind the dressing screen.

"I plan to sleep on the floor," he assured her. "In front of the door."

She stuck her head out from behind the screen. "What?"

He smiled. "I don't want anyone sneaking in during the night. Or out," he added meaningfully.

Her eyes widened. "Don't you trust me?"

"About as much as you trust me," he said. He walked to the bed and grabbed a blanket and pillow, then tossed them on the floor. He figured it wouldn't be much different from the hard ground he'd been sleeping on. He shrugged out of his suit and wrapped the blanket around himself.

"Turn down the lamps, please," Violet instructed him from behind the dressing screen. "I'm sleeping

109

in nightclothes for a change, and it wouldn't be decent for you to see me."

He'd seen her in less than nightclothes, but he did as she asked. It occurred to him that she could crawl from the window behind the dressing screen . . . but she'd break her pretty neck if she tried, because they were on the second floor of the hotel, and it was straight down to the street below. He glanced at the screen, thinking he should have moved it, but the view that greeted him chased that thought from his mind.

Moonlight spilled through the window and silhouetted Violet behind the screen. He saw her shape clearly as she undressed. The voice of decency told him he shouldn't look, but he ignored it. Her dress slid down her body and landed in a heap. She stepped out of the garment. Next, he watched her unfasten her corset. She removed the contraption and stuffed it into her valise. When she straightened and pulled her shift over her head, he swallowed the lump in his throat. She stood sideways, affording him a torturous view of her body from a side angle.

Her breasts were full, high; he even saw the buds of her nipples standing erect, which caused a similar response from him, only in a different area. He groaned softly when she slid her drawers over her hips and stepped out of them. Her legs were long and slender. Her hips flared slightly from her slim waist. She was perfection, and it had been too long since he'd been with a woman, even an imperfect one.

"Gregory?" she whispered softly from behind the screen.

"Yes," he answered, then cleared his throat because his voice sounded as though he'd just swallowed a sip of rotgut.

"I've been thinking."

So had he, and she wouldn't like what he'd been thinking.

"Maybe we should the share the bed tonight after all."

Chapter Eight

Gregory was sure she hadn't said what he thought she'd just said; it was some cruel trick his imagination had played upon him. He wouldn't even dignify it with an answer.

"I-I'm suddenly afraid I might have nightmares again," she continued. "I wouldn't want to wake the patrons of the hotel with my screaming. If you hear me tossing around and moaning, you could wake me before I disgrace myself."

And if she tossed about on the bed and moaned, he wasn't certain he wouldn't disgrace himself. "Under the circumstances, I don't think that would be a good idea."

He watched her pull a nightgown over her head. "What wouldn't be a good idea? Us sharing the bed, or me screaming in the night and waking the patrons?"

"Either," he answered.

"The circumstances aren't any different than they have been," she pointed out. "We've shared a bedroll on more than one occasion."

The circumstances were *very* different. He'd known she had a nice figure the day he met her standing in her underclothes outside of St. Louis, but he hadn't seen such an erotic display as her undressing herself. The blanket he had wrapped around himself resembled a tent. He couldn't be trusted with her, not tonight.

"All right, then. If you're certain you prefer a hard floor to a nice feather mattress," she said, moving from behind the screen. "The stage will be hot and uncomfortable tomorrow. I thought you might want a good night's sleep before we embark for St. Louis."

What he desired had nothing to do with sleep. "I'll sleep fine here on the floor," he lied. He heard her settle into the bed.

"Gregory?"

"Yes?"

She didn't say anything for a moment, then continued, "I don't know how to ask this without giving you the wrong impression."

He propped himself up on one elbow. "Every impression I've had about you has been wrong. What do you want, Violet?"

Silence for a moment again. "I want . . . I want to touch you."

Before her words even fully registered, he was off the floor and climbing into the bed beside her. "What?"

"You heard me correctly," she answered, and in his mind he saw her tilting her chin defiantly as she spoke. He couldn't see her face in the dark.

"Why?" He thought he should clarify.

"I . . . I'm curious."

He laughed. "Curiosity can get a person into trouble."

"I know," she admitted. "I shouldn't have asked. I'm totally appalled with myself. It's just that today when I barged in on your bath, I wanted to touch you. To see if your skin felt as smooth as it looked."

He bit back a groan and refrained from telling her what he'd been thinking when he saw her silhouette against the dressing screen. His thoughts had included a lot more than touching.

"I couldn't ask another man, but you . . . you're a gentleman, and I know you would allow me to satisfy my curiosity without taking liberties."

His first response was to laugh. He held it in check. God, she was innocent. "Where exactly do you want to touch me?"

"Nowhere indecent," she assured him. "I know I shouldn't have asked, but tomorrow we'll be going back to St. Louis, where society's rules must be strictly abided by. Miles doesn't approve of you, and even if he does agree to rescue poor Tip, I'm certain he'll insist I choose someone more suitable than either him or you to court me. After tonight, I may never be alone with you again."

Although he was relieved she had agreed to go home, Gregory hadn't considered all the obstacles Miles would throw in his path to keep him from courting Violet. Miles would give him the partnership; he'd sworn to it. But believing Traften would encourage—or even allow—Gregory to see Violet might be expecting too much of the old man. And that was in addition to whatever objections Violet might raise. Still, if this Tip character did exist, and Violet had really become infatuated with him so easily, given time, provided Gregory gave her all that she desired, the girl might transfer her obsession for the outlaw to him. To stay on her good side, he felt it would be a good move to humor her. No matter how much being touched by her would arouse him.

"All right. Go ahead."

"You do understand that only I will do the touching," she specified. "You are not to touch me in return."

He could manage. He could be a gentleman a little while longer. "I understand," he said, and hoped his body would cooperate. He waited, and waited, then said: "You've changed your mind. It's just as well. I'll return to the floor." He started to rise, but a trembling hand touched his shoulder.

"Don't go," Violet whispered.

Her hand moved tentatively down his chest. Fingertips brushed his skin, sending a surge of pleasure through him. He fought his first impulse—the one to pull her into his arms, kiss her, touch her. His lack of aggression obviously fueled her courage. She splayed her hand against his chest.

"Your skin is so warm," she said. "So hard."

If her hand strayed lower, she would find out how hard he really was. Her fingernail grazed his nipple. He jerked.

"I-I'm sorry. Did I hurt you?"

"No," he managed, trying to keep his voice even. "Have you satisfied your curiosity?"

"Not entirely." Her hand moved lower, over his stomach. "Your skin is smooth, but it's not soft, the way mine feels."

He was itching to make comparisons. Instead he balled his fists at his sides. "Men are hard; women are soft. Any other differences you're curious about?"

"No," she answered.

That seemed strange to him. He assumed she'd be curious about the most obvious difference between men and women. Of course, he couldn't just lie there and take it if she did want to explore all of him. Despite rumors to the contrary, he wasn't made of ice. And despite what he wanted society to believe, he wasn't *that* much of a gentleman.

"I should return to the floor."

Her hand moved back up to his chest, pushing as if she meant to keep him in place. "I wish you'd stay. I've already grown accustomed to having you here."

That wasn't such a bad thing, Gregory decided. But he wasn't sure how Miles would react when he brought Violet home and she insisted on sleeping with him every night. "You do realize telling Miles we've slept together during our journey is not a wise idea?"

"I'm not a fool," she assured him. "I'll keep our secret if you will."

Secret? Every secret was a future opportunity for blackmail in his book—or at least in his old book. But this feather-down mattress felt a hell of a lot better than the floor. . . .

"Good night, Violet."

"Good night." She sighed, then snuggled up next to him.

He wanted to put his arms around her and hold her, but he'd promised to allow only her to do the touching. It was a promise he regretted making when he woke the next morning, reaching for her, only to find her gone.

Violet had a bad feeling about the robbery. A real bad feeling. The teller stuffed money into her packs as she'd ordered, but he kept staring at her, as if making a mental description in his mind. She didn't know if the dirt she'd smeared across her face was thick enough to hide her feminine features. There'd been no time to stuff her clothing, although she'd quickly bound her breasts and made sure her hair was tucked beneath her hat. She even wore a bandanna around her nose and mouth.

"Hurry!" she ordered. "And stop staring at me!"

Most of the town hadn't stirred. A quick peek inside the sheriff's window next door had shown the man asleep in his chair. She'd followed the teller and the bank manager inside when they'd unlocked the doors. The bank manager stood next to the teller, and he kept staring at her, too.

"You, help him," she instructed the older man. "I want to see your hands busy. You shouldn't mess with us Daltons."

The manager helped stuff her saddlebags, but he kept glancing up, as if waiting for an opportunity to try something. The bell over the door jingled. Violet glanced over her shoulder. A man with a bandanna tied around his nose and mouth stood there, a gun drawn.

"Best hurry," he said. "The town's waking up."

If it wasn't the gentlemanly Gregory Kline! His gaze met hers, then returned to the bank teller and the manager; then his eyes widened.

"Look out!"

Violet spun around to see the manager with a gun in his hand. But it wasn't pointed at her. When Gregory shouted, the gun had swung toward him.

"No!" Violet lunged at the manager. His gun went off.

She felt a horrible stinging in her left shoulder. Another shot was fired. The manager stumbled back, clutching his arm. Violet wheeled around. The barrel of Gregory's gun smoked.

"Are you all right?" he shouted.

She nodded.

"Let's get the hell out of here!"

Violet grabbed her saddlebags, trying to ignore the horrible burning in her shoulder. Afraid she'd drop them, she tossed the bags to Gregory. He caught them and slung them over one shoulder, never lowering his guard.

"Go," he ordered, kicking the bank's front door open with his boot.

Violet scrambled outside. She heard a creak and saw the door to the sheriff's office beside the bank open. Raising her gun, she fired a shot that splintered the frame. The door slammed closed. She quickly untied both her horse and Gregory's. He was outside and mounted in another second.

"Hurry," he yelled, his horse rearing in the excitement.

Violet pulled herself up into her saddle, which wasn't easy with her shoulder causing her such pain. She dug her heels into her horse's sides and the animal lunged forward. Shots rang out behind her. One whizzed past her cheek. If a bullet found Gregory because of her, she would never forgive herself. She should have given him the slip days ago and made sure he never caught up with her. This wasn't his fight.

"Kick him out!" he shouted beside her.

Violet leaned over her horse's neck and let him have his head. They thundered down the road. She didn't think they'd ridden fast and hard enough when she realized Gregory was slowing his mount.

She had no choice but to do likewise. "Why are you stopping?" she asked. "We have to keep riding!"

"You're bleeding, Violet!"

Glancing at her shoulder, she saw that her shirt-sleeve was soaked in blood—her blood. Suddenly she felt light-headed. She might have fallen from her horse had Gregory not reached out and grabbed her, pulling her in front of him on his horse. Her vision

119

blurred; everything around her, even his face, became fuzzy; then blackness descended upon her.

Pain roused her. She heard the ripping sound of material, then jumped when something cold touched her shoulder.

"Easy, Violet. I want to take a look."

Gregory had spoken the soft words. She opened her eyes to see his face staring down at her. Above him, rotted boards made a canopy. Sunlight filtered through the wide cracks between them.

"Where are we?"

"I found an abandoned cabin. The place looks like it might fall down at any minute, but I have to take a look at your shoulder."

"We should be riding." She tried to sit up.

He pushed her back down. "I've hidden the horses. I think we'll be safe here long enough for me to see how badly you're hurt."

Recollections of the blood staining her shirt made her feel light-headed again. "Do I have a bullet in me?"

"That's what I'm trying see."

The cold she'd felt against her skin was a bandanna he'd soaked in water. He dabbed gently, but even so, her shoulder stung. She winced as he probed.

"I don't see a bullet hole," he finally said. "You have a nasty gash and it bled a lot, but I won't have to dig any lead out of you."

She breathed a sigh of relief, then remembered

that the law was probably on their tails. "We should go."

"You're not going anywhere. Not yet. You need rest and food. Lie still, and I'll fix you something. Then I'll go out and take a look around."

When she realized he'd placed her on a dirty mattress on a broken-down cot, she wanted to scramble up. She didn't have the strength. Instead she closed her eyes. Maybe a little sleep and something to eat would see her back on her feet.

She thought she'd lain there for only a moment, but when she opened her eyes again, the sunlight above had disappeared. Violet heard shuffling noises.

"Gregory?"

"I'm here." He settled beside her. "I can't make a fire or light a lantern. I went out and scouted around. The posse saw me and gave chase. I led them away and backtracked, but I don't how long that will give us. I brought you some jerky and water. Sorry, that's all I can do without a fire."

He'd been out being chased by a posse? Placing his life in jeopardy? Over her? He helped her to sit. Violet realized she only wore her shift tucked into her pants, and he'd tied something around the top of her arm.

"That shirt was ruined anyway," he explained. "I think most of the bleeding has stopped."

How he'd managed to remove her shirt and tie a bandage around her arm without stirring her, she couldn't imagine. He handed her the jerky and the canteen. In the moonlight slipping past the cracks overhead, she saw him clearly. His handsome face looked worried. She tried to eat, but moving her arm hurt. She also felt like she had an inch of dirt covering her face.

"I don't suppose there's a stream nearby where I can bathe?" she asked.

Gregory shook his head. "No. But there's plenty of water in our canteens, and you can use strips from your ruined shirt to wash off after you eat."

The jerky was so tough Violet could barely chew and swallow it, but she knew she needed her strength. Once she finished Gregory rose, returning a moment later with her ruined shirt. She never realized how strong he was until he easily tore her old shirt into strips with his bare hands.

Wetting a strip with water, he took the cloth to the dirt on her face. Violet started to take over the task, but even the thought of protesting took too much effort. She allowed him to wash her, and he did so with a gentleness that belied the strength in his hands.

"Why'd you do it, Violet?"

Her gaze met his. A wave of guilt hit, and it almost drowned her. "I shouldn't have tricked you. I shouldn't have lied. I—"

"I'm not talking about that." He didn't look angry. He looked confused.

"I still need the money. I—"

"I'm not talking about that, either. At least not at the moment."

"What are you talking about?"

His fingers brushed the bandage wrapped around

her arm. "Why did you throw yourself in front of a bullet meant for me?"

She had no idea why she had reacted the way she had. It wasn't anything she'd even thought about at the time. She'd never intended for anyone but those deserving to get hurt, but . . . Violet couldn't say whether or not she would have done the same for anyone else. She knew she might not have. All she'd thought of since she met Gregory was trying to get away from him, or using him, or lying to him.

"I guess I owed you," she said softly. "I mean you'd have done the same for me, right?"

Violet's question wasn't one Gregory wanted to answer. He'd never thought about anyone in his life but himself. His parents had believed a man's measure was taken by what he managed to acquire. They had taught their son manners—how to fool society into believing that because he had them, he was a gentleman. Their idea of sacrifice was tossing scraps to Gregory and his brothers from the food the boys worked like dogs to bring home. Their idea of compassion had been throwing their boys out to make it on their own as soon as they reached manhood.

Yes, his parents had taught him to survive—that to be successful, others must pay. He'd had to work to put himself through college, even though his parents had plenty of money to pay for his education. The reason they had so much, he'd figured out, was because they never spent a cent except on what was necessary to create an illusion of wealth for the benefit of others.

His father had also told him a man had no use for a wife unless she brought something to the marriage, either wealth or prestige. Gregory had always judged women by what they could give him, whether it was pleasure or a hand up the ladder. Even Violet, as much as he desired her, was only a pawn to further future plans. He'd never expected her to be anything else. But suddenly she *had* become more. She'd treated him as if he were worth something, worth saving.

"Your actions were foolish," he said instead. "You could have been injured worse than you are, or even killed."

She straightened, her posture stiff. "And you wouldn't have gotten to collect your reward for returning me safe and sound to Miles."

"Damn right," he snapped. But a minute ago he hadn't been thinking about Miles, or the partnership. He'd been wondering how this one woman, a woman who'd lie to him, who'd use any trick to throw him off guard, had touched him, not just on the surface, but somewhere deeper.

"I should have let him shoot you," she muttered. "What were you doing at that bank in the first place?"

He dipped his cloth in the water again and wrung it out. "I had to cover your back and guard my investment, remember?" After taking the rag to her neck, he continued, "I shot a man, Violet. Sure, it was only in the arm and he'll probably be all right— but this is lower than even I usually stoop! I deserve answers! Why did you lie to me about going home?

Has everything you've told me been a lie? I don't believe you're doing all of this for some outlaw named Tip. He doesn't even exist, does he?"

"He certainly does," she huffed, shoving her face into his. "And if you knew anything at all about love, you wouldn't have to ask why I'm doing it! But you don't know how to care about anyone but yourself. You don't know the first thing about—"

"I know something about this," he interrupted, angry that she kept insisting Tip was a flesh-and-blood man whom she'd risk life and limb to save. Gregory grabbed the back of her neck and kissed her. He forgot to be gentlemanly about it, too.

Chapter Nine

His passion took her by surprise. Violet started to struggle, but he sparked something deep inside of her. Maybe he'd fired her bad blood, because her heart leaped, but not with fear—with excitement. Her response was a reminder that she wasn't good or sweet, and that if Gregory didn't know the first thing about loving unconditionally, she didn't either. Her mission wasn't about love, it was about hate. It wasn't about sacrifice; it was about revenge.

He nudged her lips apart, and she allowed him inside. His fingertips barely brushed her shoulders, sending a shiver down her back. Again, she could not identify the reaction as fear. He didn't hurt her. The slight sting in her shoulder when his hand brushed over her reminded her of how far she'd come from St. Louis. She wasn't at all proud of robbing the bank in Lawrence. Or of getting Gregory involved.

Being bad came easily to her, she guessed. It was in her blood. She deserved to be punished, maybe deserved every horrible thing that had happened in her life. That's why she didn't stop Gregory when his kiss deepened and his hands became bolder. He didn't grope, or grab, but explored the place where her shoulder bones jutted slightly from beneath her skin. His hands moved lower. He traced the top swell of her breasts.

When he cupped her breasts, she felt a moment of alarm. The moment was short-lived. He didn't squeeze her painfully, but teased her nipples through the thin fabric of her shift. They hardened in response. She moaned, and for the first time in her life, felt a spark of true desire rising up inside of her.

"You are beautiful, Violet," he whispered. "So perfect."

His words cut into her. She was *not* perfect. She was flawed, ruined, dirty. As she'd once told Lilla, she was a bad apple, all pretty and shiny on the outside, eaten up with worms on the inside. "Stop." She pulled away from him. Tears misted her eyes.

"I'm sorry," he said. "I got carried away. I wanted to prove to you that you don't feel all you claim to feel for this outlaw. I wanted—"

"Is that what you were doing?" She cut him off. "Trying to make a mockery of my feelings for someone else?" Violet thought he'd kissed her and touched her because he wanted to, because he desired her—because he cared about her.

127

"That's what I intended at the start, but—"

"You are everything Miles told me you are," she broke in. "You can't do anything unless it's to your advantage."

"And you're the sweet innocent that he thinks you are?" he scoffed. "I've figured out why you wanted me in your bed last night. Good God, Violet, would you whore yourself for this Tip as well as rob for him?"

Her reaction came swiftly. Before she had time to think, she slapped him. "Don't ever call me that!"

His gaze, full of light, either from anger or from the intimacy they had shared, banked to a soft glow. "I apologize." He rose. "Do you think you can ride?"

They should be moving on, getting as far from Lawrence as quickly as possible. "I'm sure I can."

"I'll get the horses. Your valise is next to the cot. I knew you'd need another shirt."

"Thank you," she said.

He didn't reply, just stormed from the cabin.

Gregory, you sure have a way with the ladies, he thought sarcastically. They'd ridden hard for three days to put distance between them and the last robbery, and Violet had said all of five words to him during the trip. She hadn't asked him to bed down with her at night again, either. Instead of sleeping with him, she slept with the saddlebags full of money. He could steal the money from her. He had no doubts about that, but he doubted if it would make her see reason. She'd just find another bank to rob. She'd probably get worse than that nasty scratch on her arm in the bargain.

If he took the money and ran, however, what happened to Violet shouldn't matter to him. His agreement with Miles would be off. He'd only have to worry about himself. That arrangement had suited him fine through the years. Alone and penniless, Violet might come to her senses and go back to Miles. . . .

Who was he kidding? She hadn't been rational about anything since he'd met her.

Besides, Gregory didn't think a life on the run was one for him. Things would be much simpler if Violet would come to her senses, go back to St. Louis with him, allow him to collect his partnership from Miles, act like she was supposed to act, and marry him once he'd gotten back into Miles's good graces. But Violet obviously didn't want the life she should have.

"This outlaw of yours," he said while they ate a simple meal. "What's he planning to do once he turns respectable? Become a lawyer? Write dime novels? Maybe he'll open a school and teach other outlaws how to reform?"

She glanced up from her plate, cast him a dirty look, and went back to her meal.

"I can see where he'd have plenty of options," he continued. "And won't you be the envied woman about town? All the spoiled socialites wherever you settle will rush out to find an outlaw of their own. They'll all want to live in broken-down shacks and wear old clothes. They'll all want a horde of dirty, hungry children clinging to their worn skirts—"

"Be quiet," she snapped. "You're not going to change my mind about what I plan to do, so you might as well save your breath."

"I thought maybe I could save your pretty hide. Didn't what happened in Lawrence teach you anything?"

"Yes, it did," she readily agreed. "A gun in each hand works better—one trained on the people I'm robbing and one trained on the door. I should just shoot whoever happens inside the next time."

He lifted a brow. "Will there be a next time?"

She glanced up at him again. "That will depend on you, won't it, Mr. Kline?"

"Mr. Kline?" He laughed. "After all we've been through, all we've done together, you're back to that." His gaze moved over her. "And I have no idea what you mean by that remark."

"I know you'd like to get your hands on the money."

While her words were true enough, he wasn't sure he wouldn't like even more to get his hands on her. Besides the obvious reason—the one he had trouble keeping from being obvious when she got within touching distance—Violet would be the smarter investment in the long run. That was, if he managed to keep his life and his sanity while chasing her around on this fool's errand.

"Tell me about your family," she said suddenly.

Her suggestion took him off guard. "Why?"

She shrugged. "Just curious."

"I liked what you were curious about the other night better," he retorted, trying to make her uncomfortable. The memory of her hands on him brought him to a full sweat. "But I forgot, that was just a game to get me from in front of the door so that you could escape."

Her cheeks blazed with color, but she refused to lower her gaze. "It worked, didn't it?"

"Yes," he answered. "Scheming, teasing, thieving, lying. Now, those are qualities a man looks for in a wife."

"As if your qualities are any better," she pointed out.

"You haven't seen all of them," he countered. He smiled meaningfully at her.

She obviously didn't get his drift, at least not for a moment. Her cheeks darkened another shade. "You're avoiding the subject."

"I've forgotten the subject."

"Your family. What are they like?"

He couldn't say that he was proud of his family, but then he wasn't really ashamed of them either. "Typical. Well-to-do. Self-absorbed. I haven't seen any of them for years. Not since I left for college." She'd given him a good opening to learn more about her. "And yours?"

The color in her cheeks faded. She glanced away. "I guess mine are as typical as yours."

"Do you miss Boston?"

She tugged at the collar of her shirt. "No."

"Funny, but I don't notice an accent."

"I've been in St. Louis for the past three years. I guess I've lost it."

"And were you lost three years ago when you decided to travel to St. Louis by way of Texas?"

"I-I wanted to see Lilla. I knew she was in Texas. I thought we would travel home together."

"Why would—"

"We aren't discussing me," she snapped. "I simply asked you about your family. Why is it so difficult for you to answer?"

He'd put her on the defensive. "I could ask you the same thing."

"I had a falling-out with my father," she said quietly. "That's how I ended up staying with Miles."

Now he was getting somewhere. "Let me guess. A man was somehow involved?"

Her smile was both amused and sad. "You might say that."

Gregory had been firmly entrenched within polite society since birth. He knew the story. "Your father wanted you to marry a man you weren't interested in. You rebelled and ran away."

She rose and gathered the supper dishes. "Yes. I ran away."

He took his empty plate and followed her. "Then when Miles tried to sway you in the same manner, you rebelled again. You chose someone he would consider inappropriate."

They'd camped near a stream this time, both envisioning a later bath—of course not together, or at least he didn't think she'd invite him to join her . . . unless it was another trick. She bent beside the stream with her dishes.

"If I'd wanted to stir Miles up more than I have, I

would have chosen you," she informed him pee-vishly.

He met her challenge: "It's not too late. I could take you home, and you could have the pleasure of really upsetting him."

That got a smile from her. She sobered a moment later. "And you would marry me, even with all I've done?"

Her eyes were bluer than the sky behind them. Violet wore her hair tucked beneath her hat when they took to the road, but now it hung in a silken cloud around her shoulders. The fading sunlight brought out the gold. He couldn't resist the urge to lift a lock and let it slide through his fingers.

"Whatever you've done, you've done it with me, right?" he asked quietly.

She glanced away. "Whatever I've done with you, I've done because of someone else, remember?"

He lifted another lock of her hair. "Not the other night. That had nothing to do with anyone else. That was just you and me."

Blushing, she snatched her hair from his grasp. "If I recall correctly, that was just you trying to make a point."

Honesty wasn't anything he was overly familiar with, but he found himself admitting the truth. "You know I want you, Violet. I want you more than I've ever wanted any woman in my life."

Violet knew what he wanted. He wanted an illusion. He wanted to marry into what he believed was Miles's family. He wanted what he thought was a good girl gone bad over a silly infatuation with an outlaw. She was none of the things he believed she was . . . none of the things he would truly want . . . at least, not for long.

Her body responded to the heat in his eyes, but she wasn't certain whether her reaction was the flush of alarm or of pleasure. "What you want isn't proper," she said, shaken by the warmth flooding through her.

"It is if my intentions toward you are honorable," he countered, his gaze lowering to her mouth and causing her pulse to leap again.

She had to stop this before it went farther—before he kissed her, before she allowed him to. "From what I know about you, you've never had an honorable intention in your life."

Her words delivered the blow she'd intended. He backed off. Staring across the stream for a moment, Gregory ran an impatient hand through his hair. "Who am I being measured against? An outlaw? A man who'd drag you into this danger and expect you to rob banks and risk getting killed over him?"

"I never said he expected me to do anything." She rose with her clean dishes. "I'm doing what I feel is right in my heart. What I feel I must do, what I am driven to do."

"Well, I sure as hell don't understand what is driving you," he muttered.

"No, you wouldn't." She walked back toward camp.

Gregory, she suspected, knew plenty about greed and blackmail. About doing the right thing for the wrong reason. Or was it the wrong thing for what he thought was the right reason? Either way, he didn't know about shame, humiliation, feeling worthless, used, discarded. He didn't know how a thirst for vengeance could kill everything good and kind inside of a person.

He didn't have brothers and a sister he had to be ashamed of abandoning. For all she knew, her brothers were now part of an outlaw gang, and her sister had been sold off for more liquor. He and Violet were worlds apart, linked only by one common association with Miles Traften. Gregory might think he wanted her, but he wouldn't want the baggage that came with her; Violet knew that as sure as she knew tomorrow would take her one step closer to Kansas.

"Do you have any idea where we are?" she called over her shoulder.

"As near as I can guess, a few days' ride from Independence," he responded testily.

The dishes Violet held crashed to the ground. Independence? The place the demon lived. The place where he'd held her prisoner inside his stinking, run-down whorehouse. Violet had known all along that she would come to this fork in the road . . . but she hadn't imagined it would come so soon.

Reason said to leave her vengeance on the man until she'd rescued her brothers and sister. But reason was hard to maintain in the face of blind rage.

"Violet, are you all right?" Gregory appeared beside her, staring at the dishes on the ground.

"It's my arm," she whispered. "I still have some pain shooting through it."

He looked worried. "Maybe I'd better take a look at that scratch, make sure it isn't infected."

She bent to retrieve the dishes. "No. I've been watching it. The scratch is healing nicely."

He stooped, helping her gather the dishes. Then he asked, "Do you want to take your bath first?"

"No, you go ahead."

She needed to think, to reason with herself. Her head told her she should steer clear of Independence until she'd dealt with more important issues—but her heart screamed otherwise. Vengeance was so close at hand. Could she resist it?

If Miles's daughter, Lilla, hadn't found Violet working at Sally's Saloon in Texas, she might still believe she was somehow to blame for what had happened to her. She might still believe she'd done something to deserve the hell she'd suffered. But she wasn't to blame. She'd been only a girl, uncertain of her fate, unknowing that there were worse monsters in the world than her father.

Violet was no longer a girl. She was a woman, and a very angry one. The wounds inflicted upon her hadn't healed; they'd only been festering. She thought she could run, hide from the truth, hide it from others. She'd been fooling herself. If she did the sensible thing and married someday, the man would know. He'd realize she wasn't pure.

Her gaze strayed to Gregory as he pulled his blanket, razor, and soap from his packs. What would he think if he knew another man had touched her—and in far more intimate places than she had allowed him to do? Because of that bastard in Independence, Violet couldn't even bring herself to look at a man's naked body, at least not all of it. That bastard had forced her to look at him, as if he expected her to like what she saw, as if he expected her to feel desire for the part of him that hurt her.

Violet tried to shake the memories from her mind. Lilla had warned her once that if she didn't stand up for herself, didn't move on with her life, she would be allowing the past to control her. Perhaps Lilla had been right.

Violet had let two men shape her opinion of the entire sex for far too long: the father who beat and sold her, and the man who took her innocence in one swift, violent act that had sealed her future. Neither man had felt remorse. She knew that with certainty. Just as she promised herself she would feel none, either, when it was her turn to make them pay.

"Are you sure you're all right?"

Her nails cut into her palms. Violet relaxed her hands. She hoped the rage she felt inside wasn't visible upon her face. "I'm fine. Go ahead with your bath."

Gregory stared at her for a moment longer, then moved off toward the river. She watched his retreating back. Her gaze slid over him. Gregory wasn't a saint, but he wasn't a monster. She could look at him without cringing in fear, look at all of him if she wanted. She'd touched him, given in to the feeling of curiosity within her; why couldn't she sneak down to the water and watch him bathe? Why couldn't she use him to satisfy her curiosity?

Brave thoughts, she admitted to herself. She knew she wouldn't be able to do it. She'd do just what she had done the last time. If she walked down to the river to watch him bathe, she'd panic and run away before she saw everything that intrigued her. Again the past would smother what she supposed might be a healthy dose of interest in a normal young woman.

But there was nothing normal about a woman robbing banks to frame her father or plotting to kill a man—even if both rightfully deserved to be punished, Violet reminded herself. There was nothing normal about a young woman being pulled from the bowels of hell, landing in the lap of luxury, only to run away and cause pain to the one man who had treated her kindly.

Her gaze strayed toward the path Gregory had taken. Suddenly Violet was in the mood to do something normal. And she would, if it killed her.

Chapter Ten

Violet was killing him. Gregory had spotted her, hidden among the bushes, watching him bathe. She didn't know he knew, and he could only assume she was there because she was curious again. The feel of her eyes sliding over his flesh was exciting. Her curiosity was a stepping-stone—one he hoped would lead to Violet's hand in marriage.

He wasn't particularly modest, but he wasn't lewd, either. He'd give her plenty of opportunities to sneak away if she didn't want her curiosity entirely sated. If she did stay . . . well, then he supposed he might ruin her for other men. She was an innocent and wouldn't know her spying had aroused him. When he turned and walked out of the water, she'd believe all men should be as generously endowed—and at all times.

The thought wasn't too unappealing.

Wyoming had put muscles on his lean body. For her education, he made sure his movements showed their contours to full advantage. He lifted his arms and soaped beneath his armpits, slid the soap over his chest and down the flat expanse of his stomach. He dunked himself, came up, and slicked the wet hair from his face. That was when he noticed his fingertips were beginning to wrinkle; he'd stayed in the water too long. He moved toward the bank, careful to only glance quickly at the spot where he'd seen her hidden. She was gone.

In some ways that didn't really surprise him, but in others it did. Violet wasn't short on courage. She'd robbed three banks, thrown herself in front of a bullet, and tricked him by using unscrupulous methods on several occasions. In all honesty, if she wanted to see something she'd never seen before, he'd be less surprised if she marched up and asked to see it. But she wouldn't.

Everything about her was a contradiction. Gregory left the water, reached for his blanket, and dried off. His clothes needed washing, but he was too tired to do it now. He supposed Violet wouldn't mind if he returned wearing the blanket and nothing else.

She proved him wrong a moment later. She had gathered her own personal items for a bath and sat waiting at their camp. Her eyes widened when he approached.

"It isn't decent for you to be traipsing around like that in front of me," she said.

He decided to call her out. "It's also not decent

140

for proper young ladies to watch men bathe."

"Well, I never," she huffed.

"I assumed that much," he replied. "And I guess it's only natural for a young woman who hasn't seen every part of a man to want to."

She looked properly outraged. "I have no desire to see your . . . part."

"Then what were you doing watching me?"

Pink crept into her cheeks. "I . . . just wanted to be sure you weren't finished yet and that I had ample time to hide the money."

So she'd taken to hiding the money again? He didn't blame her. He wasn't trustworthy—had never been and probably never would be. "If you say so." He shrugged.

"I do say so," she snapped. She rose and walked toward the river, then stopped and glanced over her shoulder. "You will mind your manners and stay put?"

"If that's what you want me to do."

Violet didn't see where he'd think she would want otherwise. She wouldn't want him staring at her the way she'd stared at him, his eyes moving hungrily over her body. Her skin tingled beneath her clothes. She ignored the sensation. So what if she'd received a great deal of pleasure from watching Gregory bathe? His outer self was very appealing. It was his inner self she had to be wary of. She was disappointed that she hadn't stayed and forced herself to see him entirely naked.

She guessed she wasn't ready yet. But she was a

lot closer than she thought she'd ever be. She was attracted to Gregory; she had to admit that. She liked the way he looked, the feel of his skin beneath her fingertips, the heat of his kisses. But she didn't like liking it, not one bit.

Why Gregory Kline of all men? Somehow she had thought that for a man to change her mind about touching and kissing, he would have to be extraordinary. Someone heroic. Someone honest. Someone trustworthy. Kline was none of those things. Miles would have a conniption if he knew she'd been kissing this man. Doing more than kissing him. Her "uncle" thought about as much of Gregory as he did of a snake in the grass. But Gregory was a very pretty snake. Violet would give him that.

She bathed in a hurry, fearful Gregory wouldn't keep his word to her, but when she returned, she found him starting supper. He didn't look guilty of anything. Of course, his beautiful, honest face was a contradiction of his true nature. She suspected it had tricked many a sucker into parting with his money, and seduced many a woman into parting with her virtue. No matter how he looked, Gregory Kline was a schemer, always looking for a way to line his pockets or climb the social ladder. When Violet felt these bouts of weakness for him, she must remind herself who he really was—and she had to remember who *she* really was, as well.

After they ate, they retired to their bedrolls on opposite sides of the fire again. Violet lay awake, tossing and turning. But the images that plagued her were of a warming kind. Visions of sleek, muscled flesh and warm, wet kisses. Of Gregory Kline holding her close. She fell asleep thinking of Gregory.

Unfortunately, he was not strong enough to ward off her nightmares. As always, her dreams brought back the demon. He stood over her, leering. Violet curled herself into a ball, trying to disappear. She smelled the liquor on the demon's breath, the stench of his sweat.

"You think you can hide from me, *puta?*" He grabbed her shoulder. His long, dirty fingernails cut into her skin. "Do not fight me this time, and I will not have to bruise that pretty face of yours."

Violet gritted her teeth. He would not make her scream. Not this time. He would not make her beg. The demon forced her over onto her back.

"Always, it is this way with you," he rasped in her ear. "That is all right. I like it this way best."

She tried to scratch his face. He captured her wrists in his steely grip, pulled back his other hand, and slapped her. Blood filled her mouth, but it tasted better than his foul breath when he ground his lips against hers.

Violet gagged, then tried to bite him. He cursed and slapped her again.

"I gave you a choice, little one. Now I must hurt you."

A moan welled up in her throat. She tried to hold it back, but it escaped. The demon chuckled at the sound of her defeat. His dirty hand clutched her breast through her thin gown. He squeezed hard, forcing another scream from her. A moment later his weight crushed her down into the mattress where she'd hoped to sleep undisturbed.

She tried to clamp her legs together. He nudged them apart, settling between her thighs. Then she felt him probing, trying to shove his disgusting member into a place too tight and too dry to receive him.

That shattered her control. She fought him. Maybe this time she would get lucky and he would kill her.

"Violet! Violet, wake up!"

She bolted awake, her nails curled into claws. But the face staring into hers was not that of Victor Vega, the man her father had sold her to for a mere case of whiskey. It was not the man who had raped her, not once, but on many occasions during the two years he'd kept her a prisoner. It was Gregory's face that stared back at her. Violet drew in deep breaths of air, her heart racing. The dream still held her, refused to give her up, just as Vega had refused to tire of her and let her be.

Gregory's arms went around her. He pulled her close. She allowed herself the comfort of his touch. His warm breath stirred the tendrils of her hair clinging to her damp face.

"It was just a dream," Gregory said softly. "It can't hurt you now."

He was wrong. The same dream had haunted her for years. She woke screaming, her body bathed in a cold sweat; wherever she went, no matter how she tried to hide, Vega always found her in the dark of night.

"Make him go away," she whispered brokenly,

burying her face against the warmth of Gregory's neck.

"Make who go away?"

Rather than answer, she pressed her lips to the pulse beating at the base of his throat. It leaped.

"Violet? Make who go away?"

She couldn't tell him. Whatever Gregory's past sins, they could never compare to Vega's. They could never hold a candle to her own. If she were decent, she would have killed herself before allowing Vega to use her, or at least would have done so after he'd ruined her. But she hadn't had the courage. Instead she'd chosen to live, to continue to suffer Vega's degradation over and over in her dreams.

"Tell me," Gregory urged, his voice gentle.

Violet was tempted. She'd never told anyone, not even her best friend, Lilla, all the horrible details of her defilement. Maybe if she told Gregory, the nightmares would go away. But then, so would he. Gregory would be disgusted by what had happened to her. Disgusted that he himself had kissed her in the past. She was dirty, used, unworthy.

But even as she thought the things Victor had led her to believe, she fought them. Her father and Victor still held power over her. But she could fight that. She was the victim, not the accused. But making herself believe that was almost impossible.

Gregory's chest was warm, and with her face pressed against it Violet came to a realization: there was only way to loosen Vega's power over her. She must give it to someone else. A man she knew could be tender. The only man besides Miles Traften who had penetrated her fears and made her feel more than hate.

Her lips found his in the darkness. He didn't respond for a moment; then his arms tightened around her. There was no storming of her defenses, no sudden fire that leaped to life between them, only softness, the gentle brush of his lips against hers. She touched his tongue with hers, explored his mouth the way he'd done when he kissed her. Heat built between them, a slow burn, until she had to do more. Her hand slid inside his shirt. His heart pounded wildly beneath her fingertips. She felt the questions on his lips, but she refused to let him ask them.

Bravely, she took his hand and moved it to the front of her shirt. He traced the shape of her breast. His thumb brushed her nipple through the fabric.

"Can I kiss you there, Violet?" he asked.

Vega had never put his mouth against her breast. He'd squeezed her painfully. She couldn't imagine what Gregory wanted to do, but he didn't wait for an answer. He trailed a path of kisses down her throat, unfastened her shirt, then loosened the tie at the neck of her chemise. His mouth traveled, lower, sending shivers of pleasure up her spine.

She wasn't prepared for the jolt that shot through her when his mouth closed over her nipple. He suckled softly, forcing a gasp of pleasure from her lips. She slid her fingers into his thick hair and closed her eyes. His tongue teased her, caused the muscles in her stomach to clench. She ached for him, but couldn't understand how she could, and in that place she believed she'd never want another man to venture.

"I feel so strange," she whispered. "What are you doing to me?" This was everything she'd been afraid of, and yet everything she had wanted since Gregory Kline had first kissed her on the bank of the Mississippi.

He moved back up to her lips. "Do you want to touch me the way I'm touching you?"

She did, but she was frightened. Vega had made her fear the male body—but tonight she meant to exorcise him from her mind.

"Yes," she answered.

He pulled his shirt from his pants and removed it. Violet slid her hands over his smooth, warm flesh. He had only a light dusting of hair across his chest. She liked the way his nipples stood erect when her nails lightly scraped them. She liked the soft intake of his breath. He leaned forward and shoved her shirt from her shoulders, kissing the place where her neck and shoulder met. He removed her shirt, then her chemise.

"I want to feel your skin against mine," he said huskily.

She went willingly into his arms. The fire leaped to life between them again. He eased her back onto the blankets. She had trouble catching a normal breath, trouble thinking beyond the taste of his kisses and the feel of his hot, firm flesh pressed against hers.

Then something else pressed against her. Fear threatened to engulf her desire. Gregory was a man.

He had the same lust Vega had, the same power to hurt her with it. But he was not Vega. And when he kissed her again—a slow, wet, melting fusion of mouths, tongues, and breaths—she forgot to be afraid. She forgot everything.

He cupped her breasts, nipped at her ear. He whispered, "You're making me crazy, Violet. Stop me before I forget who we are. Who you are."

"I want to forget," she said under her breath.

His mouth claimed hers again. He slid his hand down between them, reaching for the fastenings of her pants. She felt a moment of panic, but choked it back, determined to let herself do this, hoping it would end her nightmares.

Then Gregory froze. The next thing she knew, he was up and off of her. He sat beside her, his chest rising and falling as if he couldn't breathe.

"I can't, Violet."

She scrambled up on her elbows. "You can't?"

He shook his head. "No, believe me, I can, but I won't."

"You can, but you won't?" She didn't understand. Some nights Vega hadn't raped her, but usually it was because he was too drunk. A few times he'd stumbled to her mattress reeking of liquor, and she'd learned that at times a drunk man's body would not cooperate with his wishes.

"I gave Miles my word that I'd behave appropriately with you."

She couldn't help the slight laugh that escaped her. It was bitter. "Since when does Gregory Kline's word count?"

In the flickering firelight, she saw the wounded look he cast her. "I guess since now."

Men were strange. When she didn't want one, they forced themselves on her. When she did, they refused to cooperate.

"Is it me?" Maybe men behaved strangely only with her.

"No, Violet." Gregory reached out and touched her face. "You can't know how much I want you. How desirable you are to me. But . . ."

"But what?" she demanded.

He glanced away, looking pained. "Seems I've developed a conscience."

Tonight she might have rid herself of Victor's control over her. She might have proven to herself that matters between men and women didn't have to be ugly and painful. But it didn't look like that was going to happen. "You picked a bad time to do it."

Gregory ran a hand through his hair, as apparently baffled by the turn of events as Violet. "It just popped up," he muttered. "Like everything else."

"Can't you ignore it?" she asked hopefully.

"I'd like to," he admitted. "But you're a nice girl, Violet." He laughed. "I mean, besides the bank robbing and the head bashing. Only the most dishonorable sort would take advantage of your innocence."

To add insult to injury, he reminded her of exactly who she was: a woman living a lie. Violet wished he hadn't stopped touching her. Then he would know. He would have asked her why she wasn't pure, and maybe she would have found the courage to tell him.

"Who do you want to forget, Violet?"

She didn't answer, refused to look at him.

"Your outlaw," he said—rather smugly, she thought. "Tip. The voice of reason is finally getting through to you."

Angry, she assured him, "I won't abandon my plans."

"Even after you're willing to kiss me like this?" Gregory looked both annoyed and impressed. "How noble."

She took some amusement from his frustration—and from his assumption. Her mission was not noble. True, she planned to rescue her sister and brothers from her father. But that was really only an excuse to do what she really wanted: to see Vega dead and make sure her father spent the rest of his life in prison.

"I'm tired. I'd like to get some sleep now."

His hand brushed her shoulder. "You haven't told me about the nightmares."

She hadn't told him a lot of things. "I've had them since I was a child," she said. "They're nothing."

"They don't sound like nothing. Do you want me to sleep next to you tonight? Hold you?"

The moment had passed. Violet's desire had fled with the absence of his body heat. She felt certain he could stir the ashes back to life, but she had to respect his wishes, too. Gregory wanted to do the right thing. He wanted his word to count for something. She couldn't see herself pushing him to lose a conscience it had obviously taken some time to develop. "No, I'll be fine."

He rose and grabbed his shirt off the ground. "Good night, then."

She watched him walk away. "Where are you going?"

He sounded annoyed. "My newfound conscience needs a chilly dip in the river to make sure I stay in my own bedroll for the rest of the night."

As he disappeared, Violet settled back against her blankets and stared up at the stars. At times, it seemed as if she and Gregory were the only two people in the world. They never followed the road, but stayed to areas that provided cover. She hadn't seen another soul since they'd left Lawrence. If she'd stayed in St. Louis, she'd be snug in her comfortable bed beneath Miles's comfortable roof right now. Maybe she would be thinking of a party they had attended, or worried that a particular gentleman would press his suit to call upon her.

She couldn't imagine her whole life being the way it had been for the past three years. If that had truly been her life, she would probably be a married woman by now. Though she wouldn't have children. Since Victor Vega had never planted any seeds in her that took root, Violet assumed she was barren.

Vega. She had to decide what she intended to do about him. Would she have the strength to let him be until she'd taken care of her siblings and her father? Or would the temptation to make him pay prove too great for her to pass Independence without confronting the bastard?

Chapter Eleven

Gregory watched Violet from the corner of his eye as they rode. She seemed more tightly wound than usual, and had been for the past three days. He couldn't say he felt any more relaxed, himself. Damn his conscience. He and Violet could have been doing a lot more than sleeping next to each other for the past few nights. . . .

If he wanted to rationalize seducing her, he supposed he could say he was going to do it to sway her from completing the foolish mission she seemed dead set on; this Tip character would surely find his own way out of this mess. But somehow that sounded just like something people would expect him to do. Underhanded.

Why that bothered him, he wasn't sure. He'd

never listened to his conscience before. It got a man nowhere.

"Independence must be just up ahead," he said. "We'd better skirt out farther, or we'll run into people coming and going."

"We need to go into Independence," Violet surprised him by saying. "Our supplies are running low, and we should trade these horses in for new ones."

"I don't think we should risk it. There might be a posse waiting for us in Independence."

"I need whiskey," she persisted.

He raised a brow. "Have you taken to drinking now along with bank robbing?"

She shook her head. "No. For my arm. You could be right. That scratch could be infected. It's been bothering me."

He'd hardly noticed it the night he'd peeled her shirt and chemise off. She'd told him afterward that it didn't bother her. "Are you sure?"

Her gaze slid away from him. "Why would I take the risk if I wasn't?"

Violet had done some foolish things since he caught up with her in Boonville, but she was smart. Smart enough to outwit him on more than one occasion. She had money, so she wouldn't be robbing any banks . . . at least he didn't think so.

"All right. But we'll only go in under the cover of darkness."

"The mercantile will be closed if it's dark," she reminded him.

"Early evening then. That's probably about the

time we'll reach Independence anyway, unless we ride hard."

"Early evening will be fine."

Something about her looked different. Her beautiful blue eyes had a steely glint to them he hadn't noticed before. The closer they got to Independence, the more nervous she became. Of course, that was understandable. He also felt nervous.

"I think we should leave the money hidden on the outskirts of town and pick it up on the way out," he suggested.

"Good idea," she agreed.

"We'll find a safe place for it."

Her gaze fell upon him. She smiled slightly. "I'll find a safe place for it."

She had every right to be mistrustful of him. In fact, she should be. He figured this new Gregory wouldn't stick around long; then the real one would rear his ugly head.

Her smile faded, and she turned her attention back to the road. "I'm going in as a man. Don't look at me all pie-eyed or try to help me dismount."

He laughed and said, "I'll act accordingly." Then he added, "Although remembering you're a man when I know very well that you're not will be a challenge."

"Not for you," she muttered. "That newfound conscience you've developed should help keep matters straight in your head."

Gregory blinked. He didn't think she meant her words as a compliment. Violet was a strange woman: She claimed to love an outlaw, then nearly let Gregory take her innocence. She was brave and outspoken. He sensed in her a passion unrivaled by any other woman he had ever known. And he wasn't sure exactly what it was she wanted.

Independence was not the busy trade town it had once been. The missionaries had long since been run out, and the town had fallen to lawlessness and lewdness. The dingy saloons lining the streets and the dilapidated buildings were not a welcome sight to a man starved for civilization, but at least they were a step in the right direction. The livery owner tried to cheat them on the trade for horses, but Gregory had learned a thing or two about livestock during his stay in Wyoming. He ended up with a stocky roan gelding, and Violet chose a gray mare.

Her behavior became stranger the longer they stayed in the city. Her gaze kept straying down the street toward the saloon section of town. She could hardly pay attention inside the mercantile while he purchased the supplies they needed. He felt edgy himself. He didn't see signs of a posse, but when they'd passed the sheriff strolling the streets, the man had given them both a good once-over.

Thank God, Violet had smeared her face and clothes with dirt, and had made Gregory do the same. They looked like a couple of saddle tramps. He'd breathe easier once they got out of town, though. They left the mercantile and headed for their horses.

"The whiskey," Violet reminded him. "There's a place just there."

The place she indicated didn't look like much but

a run-down whorehouse. A couple of women stood outside, dressed in ragged, skimpy clothing. A moment later he realized they weren't really *women*; they were young girls.

"You stay here," he ordered Violet. "You're not going into a place like that."

She looked like she'd argue, but then nodded. "I'll wait with the horses."

Gregory crossed the street and stepped up onto the sidewalk. One of the girls eyed him warily.

"Care to spend some private time with me, mister?"

"No," he assured her, and thought she looked relieved by his answer. He walked into the establishment. The sour smell of body odor and smoke hung heavy in the air. A Mexican man stood behind the bar.

"What can I get you?"

"Whiskey, a bottle," Gregory answered, wanting to get his purchase and get out.

The man lifted a brow. "You do not care to spend time with one of my women?"

When the man stepped closer, whiskey bottle in hand, Gregory noticed he smelled worse than his poor excuse for a watering hole itself. "I didn't see any women outside. I saw a couple of girls who look like they belong in a schoolroom, not a whorehouse."

Grinning, the man bragged, "Some men like them young. They are more easily trained. My girls will do anything I tell them. Anything *you* tell them, if the price is right."

Gregory felt his stomach turn. "I'm not interested

in little girls. How much for the bottle?"

With a sigh, the Mexican gave him a ridiculous price. If he weren't in a hurry to get out of town, Gregory would have told him to keep the damn liquor. He dug the amount requested from his pocket, slammed it down on the bar, and walked away.

"You are sure you do not want one of my girls?" the man persisted. "I have a new one in the back. A virgin. Well . . . nearly a virgin." He laughed, a hoarse, grating sound. "I must break them in, of course—to see if they have promise."

"You make me sick," Gregory said in a growl over his shoulder. He made it outside, where the second girl tried her luck with him.

"If my friend's not to your taste, maybe I am," she said bravely. "Victor doesn't like it when we let a man get past us. I'd rather spend time on a mattress with you than with him. What do you say, Mister?"

He stared into her eyes and thought he saw something vaguely familiar there. "How old are you?"

"Old enough," she assured him.

"Not for me." He dug into his pockets and pulled out a few bills. "Get yourself something decent to wear—or better still, get the hell out of this place."

She took the money he shoved into her hand. "I ain't got nowhere else to go, mister, but thank you for the money. Although I reckon Victor will beat me black and blue if he finds out I kept it."

Gregory lowered his gaze and moved on. Violet stood watching him from across the street. She shouldn't be subjected to such vulgarity. Hell, no one should, especially these young girls who worked for the Mexican. But there was nothing he could do about the situation.

"Let's go," he said upon reaching her. "That place is like something out of hell itself."

"Yes, it is," she whispered.

Gregory stuffed the bottle in their packs and mounted up. Violet still stood, staring at the girls across the street. One of them took notice.

"Hey, mister!" the brave one called to her. "Your friend's too good for the likes of us, but maybe you're not. Why don't you come on over here?"

"Stop gawking at them," Gregory snapped. "You're calling attention to us."

Violet seemed to snap out of whatever held her spellbound. Her face turned red beneath the dirt, and she quickly mounted her horse. Gregory was never so glad to leave somewhere behind, except maybe Wyoming.

They'd barely made it out of town when Violet asked, "Those girls. What did they say to you?"

"Nothing fit for your ears," he muttered. "They were, ah—"

"I know what they were," she interrupted. "I'm not that naive, you know."

Gregory shuddered. "I imagine a lot more so than they are—despite the fact that they're a lot younger. It made me sick. And the man inside the place, he should be horsewhipped for putting girls that age to work."

"More than horsewhipped," she agreed. "What kind of man was he?"

"Foul," he answered, feeling a fresh wave of disgust. "I gave one of the girls some money so she could buy herself something decent to wear, and she said the Mexican who owns the place—Victor, I think she said his name was—would beat her for keeping it. He offered me a young girl when I was inside. A new one."

When Violet didn't respond, Gregory glanced at her. Beneath the dirt, her face had paled. The reins in her hands trembled.

"Sorry," he apologized. "Like I said, nothing about that place is fit for your ears. He and his girls would be run out of St. Louis in a second. Seems to me the law should intervene. It's not right, girls that young."

"Maybe he pays the law to look the other way," Violet said.

Gregory felt bad for upsetting her. Bad that he'd even allowed her to witness the exchange between him and the Mexican's girls. He should have made her wait down the street.

"It's not our problem, Violet. Don't give them a second thought. They could run away if they wanted. Those pathetic girls made their beds; now they'll have to sleep in them."

Her eyes were as hard as flint when she glanced at him. He thought she meant to say something, but instead she turned her attention back to the road. "It's getting dark. We should camp where I buried the money."

"I think we should get farther from town."

"And I think you should just go back to St. Louis," she snapped. "I don't need you."

She was still upset by what she'd seen in town, he

suspected. "But I need you." His words held a ring of truth with which he wasn't comfortable. "Because of the partnership," he reminded both her and himself.

"I'll write you a note. I'll tell Miles that you did your best. You behaved properly but I wouldn't listen to reason. I'll tell him to give you your silly partnership."

When Violet got a bee in her bonnet, she wasn't very pleasant to be around. "You know I can't accept that very gracious offer," he said.

She laughed. "I suppose this newfound conscience of yours won't let you? You want your word to mean something."

He could give as good as he got. "I'd think you'd want it to mean something, too. But then, if your highest aspiration is some silly outlaw named Tip, who will most likely put a baby in your belly, then run off to rejoin his outlaw friends—"

"My aspirations are not silly!" Her glare burned him with its intensity.

Gregory wouldn't back down, though. "Neither are mine. This partnership is my future, Violet. But of course, stability is obviously something that doesn't overly concern you. Is being poor also something you'd enjoy?"

Her chin lifted. "I wouldn't mind being poor. Not if I was happy."

She really was innocent at times. "Do you personally know any poor people who are happy?" he asked.

That ended the conversation. It stayed ended for

the rest of the evening. They made camp. Gregory cooked and he cleaned their weapons for lack of anything else to do. Not that Violet seemed to notice what he was doing, or care. She acted angry with him, preoccupied with other thoughts. She would get over being mad, though, he figured.

He also figured she'd realized it was safer to have him around than to be riding alone. That's the reason he didn't protest when, just before it was time to turn in, she said she planned to go dig up the money. A good while later, he realized she wasn't coming back. He also noticed that her gun was missing. Which wouldn't have alarmed him quite so much had she bothered to reload the damn thing. The bullets were still resting on the stump where he'd emptied her gun in order to clean it.

Chapter Twelve

Violet's stomach churned. Just the smell alone in Vega's place sent her reeling back in time. Luckily there were only a handful of patrons inside the saloon. A young girl stood behind the bar serving drinks. She was the brave one Violet had seen outside.

Violet hadn't needed much of an excuse to deal with Vega, but when Gregory said Victor offered him a new girl, she'd had to make certain her sister hadn't ended up in the same place she'd been at the age of fourteen.

"Get you something, mister?" the girl asked.

"I'm looking for a girl," she said as gruffly as her voice would allow.

The one at the bar squinted at her. "I remember seeing you outside earlier. I'll get one of the others to take over for me here and we'll slip into the back for a while."

Violet glanced around. "Do you run this place?"

"No," she answered. "Victor Vega does. He's . . . in the back at the moment."

Violet thought she might retch. She swallowed the bile in her throat. "I'd like to speak with him. Hear he has a new whore."

The girl sighed. "Yeah. Brought her in just last week. She's not even too bruised up yet. He wants more for her, 'cause she's new and all."

"I'd like to see her," Violet said. "In fact, I'd like to see all the girls."

That brought a spark of interest to the child's dull eyes. "Victor will have to show you them. He keeps us all locked up. Only has three of us out at a time. Had one run away on him a few years back, and he ain't never forgot it."

"I don't imagine she has, either. Will you get him for me?"

"You can wait in the hall for him. It's—"

"I know the way." Violet moved toward a place she'd seen many times in her nightmares, past the small, dark rooms, each with only a washbasin and a dirty mattress on the floor. The sounds that greeted her in the hallway were also familiar: that of a fist hitting flesh, and sorry moans.

Violet couldn't stand still and let Victor finish his beating. She followed the sound through the thin doors, pausing before the one where another noise froze her blood: Vega's voice raised in anger.

"I told you that if you ever tried to run from me

with that boy again, I would beat you! You are not his. You are mine! Mine until you are old and used up!"

Another loud slap followed. Violet pounded on the door. She heard cursing; then the door flew open. A scream rose in her throat. The demon stood before her.

"What do you want? I am busy!"

For a moment she couldn't get her mouth to work. "I-I have business with you."

Vega took a deep breath and let it out slowly. "You want a girl?"

She nodded. "The new one."

His eyes lit with greed. "She will cost you."

Violet dug a wad of bills from her jacket pocket. "I can pay."

He held out his hand.

"Not until I see her," Violet said. "I might want a different one."

"But this one is special," he insisted. "I went all the way to Mexico to get her. I traded a few guns to some renegade Apaches for her. She was taken as a small child and raised among them. She is wild." His brows rose and fell suggestively.

"Then she's Apache?"

"No, she is Mexican, but as good as an Apache, since she knows no other life."

"She's a Mexican?" Violet didn't realize she'd been holding her breath until it left her lungs in a relieved sigh.

"You have something against Mexicans?" His eyes narrowed to dangerous slits.

"No," she answered. And it was the truth. She had something against Victor Vega, who was a disgrace to his race, just as there were white men who disgraced their race, and obviously Apaches who disgraced their race, as well. "I like light-colored hair and blue eyes."

He winked. "So do I. There is one here who might interest you."

She followed him to a room at the end of the hallway. He pulled out a set of keys and unlocked the door. The whimper of alarm that followed broke her heart. A girl, thin and bruised, sat huddled in a corner. For a moment Violet thought the girl might be her sister; then she recognized her as one of the two from the street earlier.

"This is Mary. Do you like her?"

Violet's sister's name was Rose. "I can't see her. Have her step into the hallway, where the light is better."

"You heard the man," Vega said in a growl. "Get up and move into the hallway!"

By the way the girl moved, Violet could tell she'd taken a good beating. Probably that and more. She hobbled into the hallway. Her stringy hair hung down in her face, and she kept her head bowed. She reminded Violet of herself all those years ago: beaten, raped, cowed.

"What do you think?" Victor asked.

In a flash, Violet drew the gun strapped to her hip. "I think you should give me your keys."

His eyes widened. "What is going on? Who are you?"

165

"We'll discuss that later." She stuck her gun in his face. "Give me your keys!"

He handed them to her.

"Now step back into that room."

For a moment she thought he might give her the pleasure of shooting him then and there, but he stepped back into the room.

"Close the door, and don't try to open it while I have this young woman lock it, or you'll be eating wood and bullets, understand?"

Vega nodded. His face was bright red. She knew he was angry beyond words. For once, that suited her fine. He shut the door.

"Lock it," she said to the girl.

Used to following orders, the child quickly obeyed. Violet started down the hall.

"Unlock all the girls and have everyone come out front. Gather whatever you can get your hands on in the way of clothes."

Once she reached the drinking part of the establishment, she aimed her gun at the few men seated there. "Get out. All of you," she threatened.

Luckily, no one called her bluff. The men scrambled up and out. The girl behind the bar stared at her curiously.

"What are you doing?"

"Giving you a choice."

The girls from the back rooms entered, their arms loaded with thin shawls and skimpy, threadbare clothing. There wasn't one among the lot who looked over fourteen.

"Who here wants to stay?" Violet asked.

None of them responded.

"Who among you is here of your own free will?"

Again, no response.

"Who would like to leave?"

"We'd all like to leave," the girl behind the bar said, moving around to join the group. "Problem is, we ain't got nowhere to go. We're here because we either ain't got no kin, or the kin we got sold us for something."

Violet had been in each girl's predicament before. She'd been rescued by an angel. Considering her past, Violet didn't suppose she could pass herself off as a saint, but there was one thing she could do for them, a small sacrifice compared to what they had endured.

"I'm going to draw you a map. If you dig in the spot I draw an X, you'll find two saddlebags full of money. It's yours. Not just one of you. All of you, understand?"

"He's crazy," the girl who'd been tending bar said. "Why would the likes of you give the likes of us money, and want nothing in return for it?"

Violet removed her hat. Her hair fell down around her shoulders. "Because I *am* the likes of you."

Silence penetrated the room.

"Who are you?" Mary, the girl who'd reminded her of herself, whispered.

"Vengeance," Violet answered. She moved to a table, picked up a scrap of paper one of the saloon's patrons had left behind, stuck her finger in a pile of cigar ashes, and drew the map. There were plenty of banks between Independence and Coffeyville; she could rob another.

"You swear there's money? You swear we're not leaving only to find we have nothing and nowhere to go?" The girl who'd tended bar asked the questions.

"I give you my word." She recalled how Gregory thought a man's word was a valuable commodity. She had to agree with him.

"What about Vega?" one of them worried. "Or his friends. Won't they come after us?"

"Not if I have my way." She walked a line, staring each girl in the face. "Now, I'd better never see any of you working in another whorehouse. If I do, I'll burn it down, understand?"

"What are we supposed to do?"

Violet reached out and gently touched the bruised cheek of the girl named Mary. "I want you to fly. Is there anyone in this town any of you can trust?"

One of the girls, the one with fresh bruises along with the tears on her face said, "There's a boy. He's decent. I meant to run away with him, but Vega caught me. He'll take me away from this place, and he'll see that the others get away, too."

Vega pounded on the door, causing all of them to jump. Violet handed the map to the girl who'd tended bar. She seemed the most confident.

"Find that young man and get out of town as fast as you can." She walked the line of girls again. "And all of you." A lump formed in her throat. "Don't ever look back."

"But—" the brave girl began.

"Go," Violet urged. "That door isn't going to hold him for long."

The girl nodded, motioned for the others to follow, and started for the front entrance. Then she ran back and kissed Violet on the cheek.

"You are an angel, whoever you are," the girl whispered, then hurried after her companions.

Tears filled Violet's eyes. Angels didn't kill men, and that was exactly what she planned to do. She also remembered where Vega kept his money. She'd take it. Violet moved behind the bar, bent and pried a piece of wood up from the floor. Her eyes widened. There were several large bundles of cash. It shouldn't surprise her. Vega probably had the first dollar he'd ever made. That was why the place was falling down and he dressed his girls in rags.

She glanced around, spotted an old burlap flour sack, and snatched it up. She'd barely managed to pack all the money into the sack when she heard the sound of splintering wood. Vega had kicked the door down.

Violet rose from behind the bar, her gun aimed and ready. Vega stormed into the front, cursing loudly in Spanish. He drew up short when he saw her. His eyes narrowed; then after staring at her for a moment, they widened in surprise.

"You!"

"Violet is my name," she said, her voice low.

"I know your name," he assured her. "I took you in. I clothed you. I fed you. I did not share you with other men, and you repaid me by running away!"

She cocked the pistol in her hand. "You bought

me for a case of whiskey. You beat me. Raped me. Starved me. You made me wear rags for clothes. I haven't repaid you yet. But I'm getting ready to."

He glanced at the gun in her hand, and wet his thick lips. "You do not have the courage to kill me," he said. "If you did, you would have come for me before now."

His words stung. She *had* been a coward. Had been afraid of her own shadow because Vega had made her that way. One of the girls at Sally's Saloon had called her Mouse. She had hidden her beauty, thinking it was a curse. Vega had made her feel useless, ashamed, and unworthy of even being alive. But she had been a child then, and now she was a woman. A woman who longed for the sweet taste of revenge.

"I'm not a little girl anymore."

Slowly his gaze drifted over her. "No. You are not a little girl, but I desire you anyway. Tell me, am I still the only man to have had you?"

"No," she lied. "I've had a real man since you. One who doesn't stink of liquor and filth. One who is gentle with me. One whose belly doesn't hang over his pants, and who makes your sorry little stick look like a twig."

Vega's face darkened. "Where are my girls?"

She smiled. "They aren't yours any longer. I've set your doves free." Lifting his heavy burlap sack, she added, "And I'm stealing your money."

"I will kill you for this," Vega said in a growl, moving toward her.

"No. I'll kill you."

Violet pulled the trigger. Nothing happened. She tried again and again, but nothing but a hollow click sounded. *Damn!* She recalled now Gregory cleaning the weapon. She'd been so preoccupied with her revenge against Vega, she hadn't even checked it. This was a mistake that would probably cost her her life . . . or worse.

A smile broke out on Victor's unattractive features. "Now we will dance again, *sí?* I will make you forget this other man." His smile faded. "Then I will kill you and feed your sweet flesh to the dogs."

Violet spun her gun around, intending to use the butt as a weapon. Vega reached down inside of his boot and pulled a knife. She figured his blade could do more damage than her empty gun. Her greed for vengeance might cost her the chance of rescuing her brothers and sister. Revenge might end up costing her everything.

If she'd only told Gregory the truth, he might have made certain justice was done—or at least that her siblings were rescued. Then again, even if she'd told him, he might have believed—as he had about Vega's girls—that her family was none of his concern.

Vega advanced toward her. Violet threw the sack of money over the bar in hopes of distracting him. Without a weapon to kill him, running would be the wiser move. There was a door at the back that led to the alley. It was her best shot. As she expected, his gaze darted toward the money. He paused. Violet made a dash from behind the bar. She got halfway down the hall before she felt a jerk and a stinging in her scalp. Vega had grabbed her hair.

She turned and lashed out with the gun. The steel barrel connected with his nose. Momentarily stunned, he released her and clamped his hands over his face. She ran in the opposite direction toward the front, where her horse waited outside, tied to the hitching post. She scooped up the sack of money as she ran past. She knew Vega would recover in a minute. Her heart racing, she ran outside. Gregory was there, mounted, staring at her horse.

"Gregory!"

He glanced up. "What in the hell are you doing here, Violet?"

She didn't answer, but tossed the money at him. "Hold that."

"Hey! You, down there!"

A group of men were headed toward Vega's place. Even in the darkness, Violet saw the shine of a tin star. The men she'd run off had probably gone to get the sheriff. Violet started for her horse. Suddenly an arm clamped around her. A knife flashed, its cold blade pressed against her throat.

"Go!" she shouted at Gregory.

He looked at her, at the men approaching, then at the knife at her throat.

"Get your hands off of her," he said to Vega quietly.

"Give me the money!" the Mexican shouted.

"Don't, Gregory!" Violet said. "He'll kill me anyway. Run!"

His eyes met hers, and she saw panic and confusion, but worst of all she saw hesitation.

"Go!" she shouted again. "You can't do anything for me!"

His jaw clenched, and he stared at a spot behind her, which she could only assume was Victor's ugly face.

"Let her go," he said again. "Let her go first, and I'll give you the money."

Instead of answering, Vega shouted down the street, "Hurry! I am being robbed!" The man with the tin star and his compatriots were almost there.

"Gregory!" Violet shouted. "Go!"

His eyes met hers; then he wheeled his horse around and did exactly what she'd told him to do, exactly what she'd have expected of the Gregory she'd met outside of St. Louis. He ran.

Chapter Thirteen

Gregory cursed his conscience. Again he was reminded why he'd never bothered to have one before: the damn thing was dangerous. He should be long gone from here by now, but instead he'd stuck around. He'd found an abandoned mine shaft a ways from town and hid out. He couldn't leave Violet at the mercy of the Mexican, hadn't wanted to in the first place. If they'd both been captured, however, neither of them had a chance.

There were men searching for him. He'd heard them on occasion as he hid in the brush. He'd overheard one say the gringo bitch was locked up in jail, so he was thankful Violet was still alive. The sack she'd tossed him in the streets of Independence held a considerable amount of money—more, he suspected, than she'd get from any bank. Why had she gone back to that horrible place? How had she known the Mexican would have so much stashed at his whorehouse? What the hell was going on?

His gaze strayed to the sack. He could set himself up for a lifetime with that amount of money. He could become anyone he wanted to become, buy anything he wanted to buy. He wouldn't have to answer to Miles; he wouldn't have to marry well; all he had to do was take it and walk away.

But that would mean leaving Violet behind. It would mean breaking his word to Miles and doing exactly what everyone expected of him, even Violet. A shuffling noise broke into his thoughts. He drew his gun. Sunlight filtered in from the front of the shaft. Several shapes scurried toward him.

"Hold it right there," he called.

Someone gasped. "Don't shoot us, mister."

"Come closer." Squinting in the dim light, he recognized a couple of them. They were the young women from the Mexican's place, only they had a young man with them. "What are you doing here?"

The young man stepped forward and raised a gun. "I'm the protector of these girls. What are *you* doing here is what I want to know? Is he one of Vega's men?" he asked the girls.

Gregory recognized the bold girl he'd met outside the saloon. She spoke up: "No. I've seen him before. He was with *her*."

"Her?" Gregory asked. "Are you talking about Violet?"

"She said her name was Vengeance," the girl answered. "And I imagine she's just about the finest woman put on this earth. She set us free."

That sounded like something Violet would do: risk her life to save someone else. People who really weren't worth saving . . . like himself.

"Come in," he said. "Before someone spots one of you. And you," he regarded the young man. "Put that gun away before it goes off and gives our location away."

The young man eyed him a moment longer, then slid his gun back into his holster.

"Have anything to eat, mister?" the bold girl asked. "We've been dodging Vega and a couple of his men for two days and ain't had a bite."

He nodded toward his packs. "Help yourself."

The small group converged on his supplies like buzzards on a dead cow. He noticed what one girl had slung over his shoulder and tensed.

"Where did you get those saddlebags?"

She clutched them to her chest. "*She* gave them to us. Made us a map and told us where she'd hidden the money. Don't be thinking you're going to steal it from us. She said the money was ours."

The young man drew his pistol again, and fast enough that Gregory didn't think the girls had anything to worry about with him as protection.

Gregory shook his head. Violet hadn't been able to rob a bank yet and not end up losing the money. "Cool your heels, young man. I won't try to take your money."

"Is she here with you?" a girl who stood close to the young man asked. "I'd sure like to thank her for what she did for us."

"No. She's not here." His voice had a hollow sound to it, and he knew it had nothing to do with the rock walls surrounding him.

"But she got away, right?" the bold one asked. "Even if she didn't kill Vega like she said she would. If she didn't get away, we'll have to go back for her. It's the least we can do, considering what she did for us."

A lie had always come easily to his lips if the circumstances dictated. He felt that in this case, they did. He'd told Violet these girls were none of their concern. She'd shown him otherwise. He couldn't send them back to that hellish place, for that foul man to abuse.

"Yeah, she got away," he said.

"I knew you were special when you gave me that money and didn't even want nothing for it," the bold girl said. "You and her, Violet, you go together. You're both special."

They were both crazy; he'd admit that much to himself. He'd been having suicidal thoughts. Thoughts of storming into Independence and rescuing Violet. But that would be insane. It would be something she would do for him.

"I'm riding out," he told the girls. "I'll leave most of the supplies for you. Stay here until I've led Vega and his men away from the area." His gaze met the young man's. "You are man enough to see that these girls are taken care of properly?"

Stretching to his full height, the youngster stared him bravely in the eye. "I would have killed Vega already, but I had to think of them and getting them

177

to safety. My family has a nice farm fifty miles from here. The girls will be safe there until they decide what they want to do, or where they'd like to go."

Gregory figured the boy could get the girls to safety and watch out for them. He nodded, and began gathering his gear.

"I hope I find a man like you someday," a thin blond girl said. "A good one who doesn't just want to throw me on my back for an hour or beat me because he's mad at the world."

What these girls had endured at such a young age sickened Gregory. "I'm sure you will," he said. Men like him were a dime a dozen. He planned to ride out, and yes, to hopefully draw any men combing the area away from the mine, but he couldn't say in which direction he would ride—down the road with Vega's money, or back to Independence.

The jail cell reminded Violet of Vega's dirty back rooms. She sat on a thin cot, her legs drawn up to her chest. She'd been given a short reprieve. Vega and a couple of the sheriff's men had gone to search for the girls and for Gregory. She prayed they would be unsuccessful.

Two days had passed since Vega had ridden out. She hoped the fact that he hadn't returned was a good sign. The sheriff gave her bread and water to eat. He'd also done his fair share of staring at her, as if trying to decide what size rope he'd need to fit around her neck, or maybe what he could get away with before the hanging.

"Were you one of Vega's girls?"

She glanced at him through the bars. He sat behind his desk, unmoving. Violet had nothing to say to him. He wasn't the same sheriff she remembered who'd accepted bribes from Vega to look the other way, but she imagined he was the same type; otherwise Vega would have been run out of town.

"You're a brave woman, risking Vega's wrath," he said. "If he doesn't find his girls and his money, you're in for a hard time."

Hard times were nothing new to her. They just seemed harder now because she'd lived a more than decent life beneath Miles Traften's roof. He'd spoiled her for finer things—at least for the company of finer people. People who cared about her, made her feel loved and important. She'd repaid Miles and Lilla by becoming exactly like her kin—robbing banks, trying to kill people. Now she was in jail, with no possible hope of escape or rescue.

She couldn't count on Gregory. He had more sense than to try something so foolish. A coward would run, and keep going, and she was glad of that. She wouldn't have Gregory's death on her conscience along with everything else. And she prayed that the girls had found the young man who was supposed to watch over them.

"Don't cotton to what he does, myself," the sheriff said. "But he pays me good to tolerate him and his taste for young girls." His gaze ran over her. "Me, I prefer my women to be women. Like you."

"And I prefer my men to be strong enough to stand up against what shouldn't be tolerated," she snapped. "A man a dollar can't buy."

He laughed. "Hell, there ain't too many men—or women—a dollar can't buy. I bet even you have your price if it would get you out of that cell."

Did she have a price? Yes. The safety of her brothers and her sister. They had loved each other in a house where there was little love to be found. She would do anything to go back and have the sense to think of them before her own greed for revenge.

The sound of horses scattered her thoughts and announced the end of her reprieve. Only the sight of Vega's red, angry face when he barged into the jail brought Violet any measure of comfort. He had returned empty handed.

"Out!" he shouted at the sheriff.

The man with the badge smiled casually at her, rose, and sauntered toward the door. "Don't kill her," he warned Vega, then winked. "At least not yet."

Vega glanced at Violet and sneered. "Yes. You can have her when I am finished. Bring your friends. All of them."

Violet found herself in another nightmare—one in which she would not wake safely in Gregory's tender embrace. Vega plucked the keys from the sheriff's desk and approached her cell. She stood but kept her back straight, her head high. Inside she might be terrified, but she would never let him see it, not even when she drew her last breath.

"You were always a stubborn girl. But you were my favorite." He stuck the key into the lock and opened the door. "I would have given your father much more than a case of whiskey for you."

He meant to slash into those tender wounds, those scars that would not heal. Why couldn't her father have been Miles Traften? Why couldn't she have at least been loved and valued, even if she was poor? How could Violet put herself at this man's mercy again?

That answer, unlike the others, was simple: her thirst for vengeance had brought her back to this place. She must live—or die—by her decision.

"If you intend to touch me, then kill me instead. I would rather be dead than suffer your filthy hands on me again."

He closed the door. "Oh, you will suffer; make no mistake about that."

Violet refused to back away or cower in fear when he approached. Fear gave him pleasure, made him feel powerful, and she would not give him that. He grabbed the back of her neck and ground his mouth against hers. She brought her knee up between his legs. It was a tactic Lilla's husband, Grady, had once shown her in order to defend herself. It worked. Howling with pain, Vega doubled over. Violet made a break for the cell door.

As he'd done at his saloon, he grabbed her hair and pulled her back. She propelled herself against him, hoping to knock the breath from his body by forcing him against the back wall. She didn't have enough weight to do much damage, but he did bang his head on the bars of her cell window. He roared like an angry bull and started after her. Suddenly he had a thin rope around his neck. Attached to the other end of that rope was a pair of strong hands.

181

"Run, Violet!"

"Gregory?" she whispered. Her heart leaped with joy.

"Hurry, Violet! I have your horse. Let's go!"

Vega's face started to turn blue. He choked and sputtered. Violet rushed from the cell, dug through the sheriff's desk and found her gun. There was another gun beside hers. Violet picked it up. She had a feeling it was loaded.

"Violet!" Gregory yelled again. "Come on before the sheriff returns!"

She could tell Vega was close to passing out. She ran to the cell. Violet wanted him to know who it was who killed him. Her hand shook, but she raised the weapon and pointed it at him.

"Violet?" She saw Gregory through the cell window, staring at her. "What are you doing?" Then . . .

"Do it," she heard Victor rasp. "I want to see if you have the guts."

Her hand shook harder.

"Violet," Gregory yelled again. "Put that gun down and come on. I know he deserves it for what he's done to those girls, but you don't have the heart of a killer. I know you."

Did he know her? No, he didn't know her at all. Violet swallowed the sudden lump in her throat and tried to squeeze the trigger. She couldn't. After all Vega had done to her, to others, she still couldn't find the courage to kill him. Or maybe it wasn't a lack of courage that stopped her. Maybe Gregory did know her better than she knew herself. She lowered the gun.

Vega grinned at her before his eyes rolled back into his head and he passed out. Violet slipped the gun into her holster and ran outside. Gregory was winding his rope around his saddle horn. He looked at her strangely for a moment, then smiled.

"You coming or not?"

She couldn't help but smile back at him. "You're crazy. You know that?"

"Yeah, I know. I should be halfway across Kansas with that money you stole from the Mexican, but here I am, breaking you out of jail. But we'll talk about that later. We'll talk about a lot of things."

She stopped smiling, and so did he.

Chapter Fourteen

They rode hard for three days. Violet had never been so tired in her life. Gregory pushed her and the horses relentlessly, but knowing that they had a dangerous man with the law in his pocket chasing them was a strong motivation. And she knew that when they slowed down he'd have questions—questions she'd find hard to answer. But she would answer them, and answer them truthfully.

Gregory had risked his life to save her again. Obviously her plans were becoming too dangerous. Violet didn't want to see him get hurt or killed on account of her, so she shouldn't involve him with her any more. The best way to get rid of him was to tell him the truth. Then she wouldn't bother to hide the saddlebags of Vega's stolen money. After he heard what she had to say, Gregory would take the money and go. Or at least she thought he would. At one time, she would have been more certain.

There were other banks to rob before she reached Coffeyville. She would face those and her father alone, just as she felt certain she would end up facing Vega alone again. He more than likely knew where she was headed. If he didn't, it wouldn't take him long to figure it out.

"We should stop for the night," Gregory said. "We can both use some rest."

Violet nodded in weary agreement. "And a bath. Let's find a spot close to water."

He glanced up at the dark clouds gathered overhead. "Doesn't look like water will be a problem. We're in for a storm. The only good thing about that is, whoever might be trailing us will have to stop and take cover, too."

A low rumble of thunder verified his suspicions. Violet smelled rain. She also felt the weight of the coming confrontation. It might be easy to convince him that she felt moved to help the girls at Victor's place. That she had gotten lucky about discovering the money. That she was an angel who went around rescuing poor souls in need—but those explanations would all be lies. Gregory deserved better.

He'd proven himself to her. He could have easily taken the money she'd stolen from Vega and moved on. It had been a considerable amount, certainly enough to set him up nicely somewhere.

Instead he'd come back for her. He'd told her how he'd met Vega's escaped girls in the mine—he'd even traded some more money to them so that she could have her saddlebags back. And then from the sound of it—although he hadn't said so—he'd risked being caught to see that those girls and the young man escorting them escaped. He was no longer the man she thought he was; he'd earned her respect, and maybe more than that. But *she* hadn't changed, and she'd never been who he thought she was. She had to right the wrongs she'd committed against him so that he could move on.

They found a spot where the trees would give them a measure of cover from the rain. Gregory strung blankets together with the same rope he'd used to strangle Vega. It wouldn't be much protection when the sky opened up, but it was better than nothing. He unsaddled the horses and brought their saddles and blankets beneath the small tent.

Having given Vega's girls most of the supplies, Gregory and Violet had both had very little to eat during the past three days. She was starving.

"Looks like jerky or beans," he said, digging into their packs. "I'd hunt, but we can't risk shooting off a weapon. I'm going to rig up a snare, see if I can't catch us a rabbit."

"I'd better round up some wood before the rain starts." Violet rose and started gathering sticks. She gave Gregory a few branches she thought would work for a snare. While she worked, she watched him. He took a knife and thinned pieces of his rope to tie the snare together.

"Is that 'something you learned in Wyoming that you didn't want to?' " she called.

He nodded. "Came in handy a couple of times

186

along the trail. What I wouldn't give right now for a big steer to slaughter."

Violet closed her eyes for a moment and sighed. *A bubble bath and a steak.* She remembered days in her childhood, days at Vega's whorehouse, when she was dirty and hungry. She'd thought she'd come a long way since then, but here she was again, hungry and dirty. Now, she had to come clean with Gregory.

She got the fire started while Gregory went to set his snare. Violet opened a can of beans, curling up her lip. If she never ate beans and jerky again, it would be too soon. And all too soon Gregory was back, settling next to her while she dished them both a plate of food.

"You were meant for finer things than this, Violet," he said, indicating their skimpy meal and the tent they sat beneath. "You should be home, safe under Miles's roof. You shouldn't be out robbing banks to ransom a man undeserving of you, or risking life and limb to rescue pitiful young creatures—"

"They are not pitiful," she interrupted sharply. "And they are not *creatures.* They are human beings and deserved better!"

He sighed. "The plight of those girls sickened me, but it wasn't our business, Violet. If you go around trying to right all the wrongs in the world, you'll always be getting into trouble. You have to turn a blind eye once in a while. Walk away, even if you don't want to."

"I couldn't walk away," Violet said quietly. "I consider Vega my business. Do you think that the girls escaped? Did their young man seem capable of taking care of them? We should have found a way to bring them with us."

After removing his hat and setting it beside him, Gregory said, "The girls are fine, I'm sure. That youngster seemed very capable—and as for bringing them with us, well, young girls are as much trouble as babies. And I don't care for babies."

Hoping to avoid the questions she knew would come from him, she asked, "You don't like babies?"

He wrinkled his nose. "No. They smell; they're messy and loud. I like to avoid them if at all possible." His gaze met hers and he sobered. "Violet, what were you thinking inside of the jail when you aimed that gun at Vega? I know that animal doesn't deserve to live, but it wasn't your responsibility to kill him for those girls' sake. Do you want the law chasing us for murder, too?"

Guilt came close to consuming her. "I never meant to put your life in danger." Violet tilted her head to the side and stared at him. "Why did you come back for me? Why didn't you take the money and run?"

Gregory studied his supper, then shrugged. "I don't know. Maybe because that's what you expected me to do. Maybe because that's what I expected of myself. I guess I wanted to surprise us both."

"And that's the only reason?"

He smiled. "Well, there's still the partnership."

She lowered her gaze. "Yes, there's still the partnership."

Suddenly, he reached out and lifted her chin so she would have to look at him. "I knew you wouldn't leave me behind if the situation were reversed. I guess I'm aspiring to be more like you. Brave. Unselfish. Those girls consider you an angel. You can't buy that kind of respect."

Instead of feeling a rush of pleasure from his compliment, she felt miserable. "I'm not brave and unselfish. I'm not who you think I am."

Gregory released her chin and shoved another spoonful of beans into his mouth. "Well, no, you're not an ordinary young miss used to a life of luxury. But your heart is in the right place, which is more than I can say for most people. More than I've ever been able to say about myself. You—"

Unable to bear any more praise, Violet placed her fingers against his lips. His delusions about her only made telling him the truth more difficult.

"My heart is *not* in the right place, Gregory. I don't have a heart. Not one that isn't full of hate. I meant to kill Victor Vega when I went to his whorehouse. I would have, had I remembered to load my gun again after you cleaned it. Then, inside the jail . . . I wanted to kill him. I wanted to kill him so much it hurt."

Gregory's brow furrowed. "I can't say that he isn't a man the world wouldn't be better off without, but I know you, Violet. You're not a killer. The girls had some misconception that you meant to kill him, but—"

"They were right. I had every intention of killing him. But not for them, for me."

Confusion still clouding his eyes, Gregory asked,

"Why would you want to kill him if not for the sake of those girls?"

A streak of lightning split the sky. A large clap of thunder followed. It seemed a fitting prelude to what she was about to tell him.

"Because I was once one of Vega's girls."

The jerky he'd been in the process of bringing to his mouth halted midway. "What?"

She knew he'd heard her clearly. His mind couldn't accept what she'd told him. "My father, my real father, sold me to Vega for a case of whiskey when I was fourteen."

Gregory dropped the jerky in the dirt. "That can't be true."

Violet glanced away from the surprise, the repulsion that crossed his handsome face. "I wish it were a lie, one I had fabricated for the purpose of fooling you. But I've been fooling you since the day we met, fooling Miles's proper friends and all of St. Louis for the past three years. Lilla isn't my cousin; she's my savior. She was the kind soul who rescued me from a saloon in Texas and gave me a new life."

Now he was the one who had trouble meeting her gaze. It was as if by looking into her eyes he'd be forced to acknowledge what she'd told him was the truth. "The saloon where Lilla taught charm lessons to those . . . women? You were one of them?"

"Yes," she answered. "I didn't entertain men in the back rooms. I cleaned up the place, cooked for the girls. Because of Vega and my abusive father, and what they'd both done to me, I was terrified of men. Lilla took me away from that life. Miles tried to give me another one. But the nightmares wouldn't let me rest. I want my revenge. I want to rescue my sister and brothers from the bastard who sired us."

Gregory rose and walked away. He stood with his back to her. "So what you're telling me is that you've been lying to me all along? There was never an outlaw named Tip you had to ransom from his gang. Never a doting father in Boston you defied when you wouldn't marry the man of his choice. Never—"

There was silence for a moment, as if he were digesting all she'd told him; then he asked, "And Vega? He made you work for him in that horrible place?"

Violet wanted to lie again, to tell him she'd escaped Vega before he could do anything to her, but she had to tell him the truth—all of it. "Vega didn't share me with other men. He kept me for his own private sport. He beat me, he raped me, and one day I ran away. That's when I met up with Sally and her girls headed for Texas. Sally took me in. She bought me old dresses and let me do all the work around the saloon. In exchange, I didn't have to entertain men in her back rooms."

"Then you met Lilla and she changed your life?"

"She gave me a better one," Violet admitted. "But in the end, it really didn't change anything, did it?"

He turned to her then, and she wished he hadn't. The hurt, the anguish in his eyes felt worse than any beating she'd suffered in the past. "Why couldn't you have just stayed put, Violet? Gone on deceiving everyone? No one had to know. You could have kept your secret and found a decent life with some unsuspecting fool."

Her heart twisted. "So you believe only a fool would marry a woman like me?"

He ran a hand through his hair and turned away again. "I don't know what I think, Violet. All I know at this moment is that I should have killed that bastard before we left Independence."

The heavens opened up and rain poured down. Gregory walked away. Violet called his name, but he kept walking.

She had known he would shun her when she told him, but she hadn't known how much it would hurt. Not until this moment. Somewhere deep inside, Violet had hoped her past wouldn't matter. She had hoped Gregory could accept her unconditionally.

She let the rain put out the campfire, just as the truth had put out the fire she knew once burned for her inside of Gregory. Rising, she walked out into the rain, letting it soak her to the bone, wishing it could wash away her sins, the hate in her heart. She wanted to be all Gregory had thought she was: good, pure, worthy of a man's love. But, as she'd once told Lilla, wishing didn't make it so.

From the corner of her eye, she saw Gregory return. He glanced at her, his clothes soaked; then he crawled beneath their shelter. He didn't come to her. He didn't take her in his arms and tell her the past didn't matter to him. Tomorrow he would be gone. She knew it as surely as she knew Vega would come after her. It was just as well, she told herself. It was what she'd intended—what she'd wanted—to put him out of harm's way. A long, jagged streak of lightning flashed. Thunder rolled.

"Violet!" Gregory shouted. "Get in here before you get yourself killed!"

At least he still cared whether she lived or died. A thought occurred to her: Gregory would likely be gone come morning, and he no longer believed she was a virgin to be protected. She'd told Vega she'd been with another man—that he no longer held exclusive knowledge of her body. She might die at Vega's hands; she might be caught during the next robbery and hanged. She wouldn't go to her grave with the stench of the demon still clinging to her, without ever knowing how it should be between a man and a woman.

Before she lost her nerve, she started to strip off her wet clothing.

Gregory shrugged out of his wet shirt. He'd give Violet a minute more to take cover; then, if she didn't show up, he'd go out after her. Thoughts whirled through his head; emotions became jumbled inside of him. He felt anger with her for deceiving him, rage on her behalf, disappointment that she wasn't all that he thought her to be. He also felt like a fool. He'd been so sure she was a lady; she must have been laughing at him every mile they'd crossed together.

If she'd worked in such places as Sally's Saloon, if Victor Vega had made her his whore, she wasn't at all the innocent he had once believed her to be. Hell, she probably knew things, had done things, that would make him blush. She proved him right a moment later. The lightning flashed. She stood outside the tent. And she was stark naked. He sucked in his breath at the sight. She was all womanly curves, dripping wet, the kind of woman all men dreamed about bedding . . . but not the kind they married.

"What are you doing, Violet?"

"I—I want you."

His heart softened at the fact that she was naked and cold, enough to cause her to stammer her words; but then he caught the look in her eyes.

"No, you don't. You're still afraid of me."

She ducked inside of the tent. "I am afraid," she admitted. "I'm afraid because Vega abused me. He hurt me, raped me. He beat me because I wouldn't do the things he wanted, because I would never willingly submit to him."

Her words cut through him. He didn't want to imagine her at the foul man's mercy. And he hated the thoughts running through his mind, as if she were somehow to blame.

"I'm sorry," he said, and he was. He just didn't know if he was sorrier for her, or for himself because she wasn't all that he had wanted her to be.

"I was just a little girl," she whispered. "I didn't know what he had planned for me when my father sold me to him. I thought maybe I would cook for him, or clean, or fetch—"

"Don't." Gregory didn't want to hear about her suffering. It made him suffer, too. It made him feel helpless, and the rage—God, it churned such murdering rage inside of him!

"I *want* you to know. I want to tell you," she persisted. "Vega is the reason I scream in my sleep. He's the reason why, when you first touched me, I was afraid. He's the reason I never thought I could want a man . . . not the way I want you."

He'd once considered making Violet his mistress. The thought of her having been with another man hadn't bothered him then, but he hadn't felt the things he felt for her now.

"How could your father sell you?" he demanded. "What kind of a person does something like that?" The harshness of his voice made her move away from him. Gregory tried to calm his raging emotions. "I'm having a difficult time dealing with this."

She glanced up at him. "*You're* having a difficult time? How do you think I feel?"

What he thought was *her* shame had now become his own. She'd known he was an insensitive ass from the start. And he was. So what was she doing sitting before him, exposing her body, exposing her soul? "What do you want from me?" he asked.

Her voice shook. "I just want tonight. I want to be with you. I want you to show me that being together doesn't have to be humiliating or disgusting. I want you to erase what he did to me."

This experience was a first for Gregory. He'd never felt pain for another person, or confusion over his own feelings. He'd always known what he wanted in life, had always gone after it, and in whatever way it took. No one had counted on him, had expected more than deceit, greed, or lies from him. He had to be honest with Violet.

"I don't think I can do that. You're never going to forget what he did to you."

In a voice tinged with accusation, she whispered, "And neither will you. You don't want me now."

Her eyes burned into him, daring him to admit otherwise. He had trouble ignoring her nudity, only shown to him in flashes of lightning. She was perfect . . . the most beautiful woman he'd ever seen. A single tear caught a flash of light as it rolled down her cheek. He couldn't keep his distance from her any longer. Gregory pulled her into his arms. He felt the chill of her skin against his and grabbed a saddle blanket, wrapping it around them.

In spite of the warring emotions inside of him, he kissed away her tears. His lips traveled to hers of their own accord; his body reacted to her despite the turmoil that raged in his mind.

"Love me," she whispered. "Just for tonight, forget who I really am."

Could he forget? More important, he supposed, could he make her forget? The feel of her firm, round breasts pressed against his chest, the sweetness of her kisses, tempted him to give her what she wanted, to take what he wanted in return. She understood it was just for tonight—hadn't asked for anything else, didn't demand he be more of a man than he was.

"Are you sure, Violet?" he asked.

The lightning flashed again. Resolve shone in her tear-filled eyes. "Yes. I'm sure."

Chapter Fifteen

And Violet *was* sure as Gregory eased her down onto the ground. Seeing Vega again had made her all the more certain. Gregory might be right: perhaps nothing would erase what had happened to her in the past, but being with a man she cared about, one she knew would risk his life for her, even if he couldn't love her, was as good as she might get. With the possibility of death hanging over her, Violet wanted to experience all life could offer. At least what Gregory would give her.

He kissed her again, pressed his warm skin against hers to chase the chill from her bones. He still wore his pants, which were soaked from the rain. A moment later he struggled out of what little clothing he wore. When he stretched out beside her, she fought panic from returning. Lightning exploded outside the ragged covering of their small tent. He stared down at her.

"Don't be afraid of me, Violet. Nothing I do is going to hurt you. Everything I do, I do only to give you pleasure."

Since she could trust him with her life, she had to trust him with her body, as well. "I trust you."

Her words seemed to cause him pain, maybe a moment of fear. He was thinking about tomorrow, when he would leave her. She feared he'd pull back again, tell her that he couldn't be with her. She might lose him, but she refused to lose this opportunity.

"Touch me," she encouraged softly. "I like the feel of your hands on me, your mouth—"

He stopped her with his lips. This kiss felt different. Committed. At least for the night. Gregory was bolder than he'd been in the past, maybe because her innocence was no longer an issue with him, maybe because there was no doubt in his mind about what she wanted. His tongue teased hers, demanding a response from her. She slanted her mouth against his and sucked him inside. He groaned; then his hands slid down her body. His fingers brushed her nipples. His mouth followed, bestowing the exquisite torture she had already experienced with him once before.

She threaded her fingers through his thick, damp hair. He continued the torture until she couldn't take his teasing; then she forced him back up to her waiting lips. His kisses grew deeper, more demanding, and fueled her own sense of urgency. His fingers slid down her flesh, past her waist, which caused her a

The Best in Historical Romance!
Get Four Books Totally FREE*!

A $23.96 Value! FREE!

moment of alarm, but he didn't grope her in a crude manner, or hurt her in any way. Instead he gently stroked her—found a place within her she hadn't known existed. A place that sent a tingling sensation pulsing through her.

Even the proof of his arousal couldn't bring fear to the surface, not while he continued to love her with his mouth and his skilled fingers. He broke from her lips to kiss her neck, to nuzzle her ear, and she was grateful for a chance to catch her breath. Only she couldn't catch a normal breath, and she couldn't stop the soft moans of pleasure that escaped her. She felt as if something was building inside of her, something that wanted out.

The pressure increased. She arched against him, struggling to grasp the unknown. Her stomach muscles tensed. A feeling of intense pleasure washed over her; then the world as she knew it ceased to be. She exploded, her nails digging into Gregory's shoulders, her body convulsing until she cried out. He kissed her again, whispering her name while she clung to him, dazed by what she'd just experienced.

He moved atop of her and nudged her knees apart. Visions of past terrors suddenly clouded her mind. A man, looming over her, forcing her legs open. She knew what happened next. Painful penetration. Humiliation. Helplessness. Bile rose in her throat. She almost smelled the stench of Vega's body, the foulness of his breath. In her mind, she heard his vulgar taunts, his promises that she liked what he did to her, that her body wanted the degrading joining of his flesh and hers. *"You are mine,"* she heard him whisper. *"You will always be mine."*

"No!" Violet screamed. She struggled and tried to scratch his face. Her hands were captured and forced above her head.

She squeezed her eyes closed. "Not again! You will not do this to me again!"

"Violet? Violet, look at me!"

It wasn't Vega's voice, but she was afraid to open her eyes. Afraid that the lightning would flash and she would see the devil again, drawing back his hand to strike her for fighting him.

"Don't hit me," she pleaded.

The strong hands holding her wrists suddenly released her. The weight pressing her down lifted.

"Violet, open your eyes. I'm not him. I'm not going to hurt you."

She trembled. As she'd done after each time Vega raped her, she curled herself into a ball. She felt the gentle touch of a hand upon her hair.

"I'm sorry, Violet. I'm so sorry for what he did to you. Goddamn that bastard to hell!"

Violet stuck a fist into her mouth to keep from sobbing. Vega would *never* allow another man to erase what he'd done to her. She'd been fooling herself to think she was ready to be with Gregory. Tonight had proven Vega still controlled her. She hated him, and hated herself for giving him the power.

"I'm so ashamed," she whispered, then turned to look at Gregory. "We can try again. I—"

"No," he said, his voice still laced with huskiness. "You're not ready. I told you—I can't undo what he did to you. It has to be your decision, Violet. It can't be because you want to chase him from your nightmares. It can't be because you think it's what I expect. It has to be because something inside of you tells you that it's time to let him go, to let go of the past."

He was right. As long as vengeance burned in her heart, there was no room for anything else. "I can't let it go. I've carried the hate around with me for too long. It's become my reason for living."

"And is it worth dying for?"

She couldn't answer, and he didn't act as if he expected one. Instead he rose and moved out into the rain. She watched the storm silhouette his magnificent body. He was too beautiful for her to look at, too good for her, even if he had made his own past mistakes. He gave her pleasure, and he was decent enough to control himself when her fear overtook her passion. He hadn't gotten angry and tried to force her in order to find his own pleasure.

The only other man she'd met in her life who could give without demanding something in return was Miles. Tonight Gregory had proven he was that type of man as well. He would likely be gone tomorrow, and she would still be on her quest for vengeance, never knowing what might have been between them. She pulled a saddle blanket over her and turned away from the sight of him.

Later, she felt him settle beside her. When he did, she fell asleep. Dreams did not terrorize her. She slept like the dead, and awoke to the inevitable: Gregory no longer slept beside her.

Violet's gaze strayed to where his horse should have stood tethered beside hers. The animal was gone. The money, too, she had no doubt. Gregory would have reviewed his options and realized that stealing the money was the smartest. She'd been fooling herself to believe he could give without taking.

The fact that Gregory hadn't roused her before he left was upsetting. It was past dawn, and Vega might have caught her. Hadn't Gregory considered that possibility? She hurried into her clothes. There was no going back. She'd come too far. She'd crossed the line the minute she robbed the first bank in St. Louis. All the lies, the stealing, the attempted murder—it all had to be for something . . . and maybe for something other than revenge.

Violet wanted her sister to have a choice in life. She wanted Rose to someday find a man who made her feel the things Gregory made Violet feel. She wanted her to see the side of life Miles and Lilla had introduced—that there were compassionate, decent people in the world. Rose was still young; maybe her heart wasn't as hardened as Violet's had become. Maybe there was hope for her. And her brothers. Violet wanted to make sure they didn't end up robbing banks for a living, treating women disrespectfully, beating them because they knew no other way.

Her resolve strengthened, Violet lifted her saddle from beneath the soggy tent. She froze. Her saddlebags lay beneath.

Violet dropped her saddle and grabbed up the bags. Her hands trembled when she opened them.

They were still stuffed with money from the last robbery. "What in the world?" she whispered. Why hadn't Gregory taken the money? He knew she hadn't hidden the bags. Was he crazy? He wouldn't be taking her back to Miles to collect his partnership position in the company. Unless he wanted to end up doing some type of menial labor, which she knew good and well he considered beneath him, what could he have been thinking?

When a possible answer drifted through her mind, her blood ran cold. Surely he wasn't so foolish. She left the tent and approached her horse. Because of the rain, Gregory's tracks were easy to follow. As quickly as she could, Violet ran to saddle her horse. She threw her saddlebags over the horse's rump and mounted up. The muddy trail Kline's horse had left led her up to the main road. He didn't ride ahead; he didn't go to the other side in what she would think an effort to skirt Vega if he were following them. He rode straight down the road, back toward Independence.

"Fool," she said in a snarl; then she kicked her horse into a run and raced after him.

Gregory knew the taste of greed, a thirst for power, the desire for earthly possessions. He'd never hungered for justice. Not until he'd watched Violet change from a warm and willing woman into a terrified little girl before his eyes. If he'd known what he knew about Victor Vega the day he rescued Violet from the jail in Independence, he wouldn't have stopped choking the man; he would have castrated the bastard and watched him slowly bleed to death. He'd been wrong to stop Violet from killing Vega: the man deserved to die for what he'd done to her.

He had mixed emotions about Violet. She'd looked so sweet as he watched her sleep this morning. So innocent despite the abuse she had suffered. But he'd still left her. A better man would be stronger, would know how to love her despite her past. A better man wouldn't have been chasing her around with thoughts of what she might get him in regards to material possessions or prestige. She had no earthly wealth, certainly no pedigree.

Violet deserved a man who could accept her unconditionally. Gregory wasn't that man. He didn't know how to be—he hadn't been taught. He could do only two things for her: leave her the money so she could follow through to see her sorry father behind bars, and make certain the man trailing her never laid a finger on her again. He would kill Victor Vega. The man wasn't a human being. He was an animal.

Since he didn't know if Vega would come alone or bring men with him, Gregory guided his horse off the main road. He doubted if he and Violet had gotten much of a head start. A day, probably, at the most. He'd try to get the drop on the bastard, make sure he was alone when he dealt with him.

It occurred to him that he might not beat Vega. That he might be killed instead. But there didn't seem to be a choice. He couldn't let Vega live, knowing the man might find Violet farther down the road, knowing what he would do to her if he caught up.

Visions of Violet at the horrible Mexican's mercy made his blood lust grow. Memories of Violet's screams last night, of the way she'd curled herself into a ball as if she might disappear, strengthened his determination. No woman should suffer that type of degradation.

Around midday he spotted smoke from a camp-fire. Gregory rode as close as he could without being spotted. He tied his horse to a tree and proceeded on foot. There were two men seated around the fire, eating. One of them was the sheriff from Independence. The other was Vega. Gregory figured he could hit the bastard with a bullet from here, but that wasn't good enough. He wanted the man to see who killed him, and to know for what reason. He would bide his time, wait until Vega left to attend personal business.

The longer Gregory watched him—eating, laughing, and pretending to be a human being—the more his rage grew. He shook with it before Vega finally rose, unbuckled his gun belt and laid it on the ground, said something that received a laugh from the sheriff, and sauntered off into the trees. Gregory crept toward the place he'd seen the Mexican disappear.

He had to get the bastard farther away from his companion. Otherwise, as soon as he fired his gun, he'd have to deal with the sheriff, as well. He didn't hold with murdering a man he had no reason to kill—in fact, he had never killed a man in his life. But then, he'd never met one who deserved to die more than Vega.

The saloon owner had just finished buttoning his pants when Gregory came up behind him and shoved his gun into the back of his head. "Don't make a sound or I'll shoot you." He cocked his gun to assure Vega he meant his words. The man started to turn, but Gregory dug his gun barrel deeper into his neck. "If you call out, you're a dead man."

The Mexican nodded. Gregory made certain he stayed behind him, his gun cocked and ready. If Vega tried to call for help, he'd kill him without batting a lash, and suffer the consequences, whatever they might be. He wasn't man enough to accept and love Violet for everything she was, or had been; but he could do this for her.

When they reached Gregory's mount, Gregory moved around to face Vega, his gun pointed at the man's ugly face.

"Who are you?" the Mexican asked in a growl.

"Justice," he answered quietly. "Justice for all the young girls you've raped and beaten."

The saloonkeeper squinted at him. "I know you," he said. "You came into my place and refused my girls; then I saw you with *her!* You have my money!"

"You won't need it in hell." Gregory kept his gun steady on the man, then untied his horse. "Walk," he ordered, motioning with his gun.

"Is she with you?" Vega asked, but moved as he'd been instructed.

"No. She's long gone."

He glanced over his shoulder insolently. "A pity. I would like to get between her legs again."

Gregory came close to shooting him. Instead he

cuffed Vega on the back of the head. "Shut up! Say another word about her, and I'll blow your head off without giving you a chance to defend yourself."

"Ahh, you are the one she mentioned," the Mexican said with a sneer. "Her man."

"Just keep moving," Gregory ordered.

"You can shoot me, but it will not change things. I still had her first, and she was sweet. So young, so full of spirit—at least, until I beat it out of her."

The man deserved to be shot. Gregory's finger tightened on the trigger. "She got the drop on you, didn't she? She ran away from you. She set your girls free. She stole your money. You didn't beat a damn thing out of her."

"I underestimated her," Vega admitted. "I will not do so the next time."

"There won't be a next time," Gregory assured him.

They walked a considerable distance before Gregory told Vega to halt. He tied his horse up again, then ordered his prisoner to turn around. The sight of the man alone was enough to make Gregory pull the trigger. Vega was scum, worse than scum.

But even after all that Gregory had done in his past—the blackmailing, trying to ruin Wade Langtry because he didn't believe the man had the right to mix with decent society, his greed for the finer things in life and desire to get them with the least amount of effort, Gregory realized he didn't have it in him to gun a man down in cold blood. He was a lot things, most of them bad, but he knew if he didn't at least give Vega a fighting chance before he killed him, he could never live with himself. Fighting fair was a cowboy code of honor. Gregory guessed more than manure had rubbed off on him during his three-year stay in Wyoming. He tossed his gun in the dirt a short distance away.

"Go for it," he said softly.

The Mexican glanced at the gun, back at him, then smiled. "You are a fool."

Vega threw himself forward onto the dirt. Gregory was on him in an instant. The Mexican turned and struck out at him, hitting Gregory squarely on the jaw, but he didn't feel the pain; all he felt was the desire to kill. He balled up his fist and hit Vega in the face, making the man's head bang against the hard ground. He rose, kicked his gun into the brush, and allowed his opponent to gain his feet.

"Do not let a man up once you have him down," the Mexican taunted. "I hope that whore is worth dying for, because I am going to kill you."

Gregory punched him again. The man stumbled back, roared, and charged. His bulk slammed Gregory up against the trunk of a tree and knocked the breath from his lungs. Momentarily stunned, Gregory felt his opponent begin to choke him. Gasping for breath, he knocked his head against Vega's and threw the man off balance. He brought his fist up and hit the man hard enough to knock him off of his feet.

"Get up, you sorry bastard," Gregory rasped. "I want to beat you some more before I kill you."

Vega rolled and gained his feet, but in the process,

he'd come up with something he hadn't held before—a long knife.

"I will cut you up before I finish you," Vega panted in response. "You will not be so pretty to look at anymore."

Braving a quick glance toward where he'd kicked his gun, Gregory saw no sign of the weapon. Vega lunged forward and cut his shirtsleeve. He felt a stinging in his shoulder. It didn't hurt enough to distract him from his intention, though: Vega wouldn't leave the clearing alive.

They circled one another. Vega smiled smugly.

"I like the thought of killing her man. Maybe I will cut off your privates and give them to her as a gift when I catch up with her. I have another gift I will give her, too." His grin stretched. "Can you guess what it is?"

Too much rage made a man blind to danger. Gregory tried to ignore Vega's taunts and stay focused on the knife. It flashed again, and he managed to avoid it. He kicked out and swept Vega's feet. The Mexican stumbled but didn't fall. The man's face turned red.

"Did she tell you my special name for her?" Vega asked. "Did she tell you I called her my little *puta*? Did she tell you she liked what I did to her?"

Ignoring Vega's foul remarks became harder. Gregory had to shut him up. He didn't want to hear the man speak Violet's name, let alone hear his vulgar taunts. Rushing forward, he grabbed Vega's wrist. The man tried to cut him, but anger like he had never experienced gave Gregory the strength to keep Vega from succeeding. The knife quivered and came dangerously close to his neck. Gregory shoved Vega back, but he couldn't make him release the knife. The Mexican raised the blade and started forward.

"Stop right there, Vega!"

Lucky for Gregory, Vega had been as startled by the interruption as he was, or he might have a knife protruding from his chest. Violet had arrived, and she held a gun trained on the Mexican.

"Gregory, back away from him."

"Violet," he said in a growl. "Get the hell out of here and down the road like you should be!"

"This wasn't your fight, Gregory," she said, never taking her eyes off of Vega. "This was between him and me."

"I'm making it my fight," he argued. "You should be nearing the Kansas border by now."

"Going home to see your father?" Vega spoke up. "That is what I thought. Do you plan to kill him, too? I do not think you will, *puta*. I do not think you have the courage to kill either of us."

Gregory had once thought the same about Violet. He'd since learned she could be unpredictable. He feared Vega had made the mistake of underestimating her again.

Chapter Sixteen

Violet wanted Gregory out of the way, but he refused to give up his ground. She thanked God she'd arrived in time to save his life. If Vega had killed him, she wouldn't be able to live with herself.

"Pull the trigger, *puta*. Prove me wrong," Victor taunted.

"Don't talk to me," she ordered. "I can't stand the sound of your voice. I can smell you even from over here. Gregory, please leave."

"A woman shouldn't have to handle scum like him," Gregory insisted.

"A woman shouldn't have to handle a lot of things," she countered, and her gaze went to him. He'd told her he wasn't brave, but he'd proven himself to be honorable. She realized in that instant that both words meant the same thing. "I don't want to see you hurt."

Their gazes locked for a moment. It was a moment that proved deadly. Vega grabbed Gregory from behind and quickly brought his knife up.

"Drop the gun, or I will slice his throat from ear to ear," the Mexican shouted.

Gregory tried to twist away, but Vega held tight. Violet saw a stream of blood run down his neck.

"Don't fight him," she said. "He'll kill you."

"Good," Gregory huffed. "Then you won't have any reason not to put a bullet between his eyes."

Violet lowered her gun. "Let him go, Vega. We'll send him on his way, and then it will be just the two of us."

Vega grinned. "Like old times, eh?"

"Yes," she whispered. "Like old times."

"Like hell it will." Gregory smashed his elbow into Vega's gut and managed to struggle away.

Vega raised his knife. Violet raised her gun. Her bullet traveled faster than his blade. The force knocked Vega back. He stared at her for a moment, glanced down at the red stain spreading across the front of his shirt, then looked back up. "I underestimated you again," he said, then crumpled to the ground.

She stared at his motionless form, her gun still aimed and ready. Gregory walked over, kicked the knife from Vega's grasp, and bent down. He placed a hand against the man's throat.

"He's dead."

The gun in her hand shook. "You're sure?"

"Yeah," he answered. Then he rose, searched the brush, and appeared with his own gun, which he placed in his holster.

Violet lowered her weapon. She didn't feel like she'd thought she would. She didn't feel suddenly cleansed. She didn't feel as if some long, choking thirst had been quenched. She'd killed a man. A man who deserved to die—not only for what he'd done to her, but what he'd done to many young, innocent girls—but some part of her was repelled by what she'd just done. She felt bile rising in her throat. A moment later she stumbled to the brush and retched.

"You had no choice, Violet." Gregory knelt beside her. "If you hadn't killed him, he would have killed both of us—I can assure you of that."

"I know," she agreed, her voice shaky. "It just doesn't feel like I thought it would . . . killing him. I took a life."

Gregory lifted her chin and forced her to look at him. "He took yours a long time ago. It seems fair to me."

But she still lived and breathed, regardless of what Vega had done to her. She could have chosen another path rather than the one she had taken. Miles and Lilla had given her that chance, and she'd thrown it away to come and do . . . this?

"We have to get out of here," Gregory said. "Vega wasn't alone. The sheriff from Independence—"

"Is right behind you with a gun aimed at the back of your heads. Don't make a move, either of you."

Fear clutched at Violet's insides, making her feel ill again. Now she had gotten Gregory further trapped into her problems. She would be the death of him yet.

"I shot Vega," Gregory called out. "She didn't have anything to do with it. Let her go."

The sheriff laughed. "She's wanted for robbery, and now you're both going to jail for murder. Both of you, get up slowly, put your hands behind your heads, then face me."

Violet did as instructed, but her mind worked frantically. "I shot Vega and I robbed him," she said, turning to face the sheriff. "This man has nothing to do with any of it."

"I figure he's the one who broke you out of jail," the sheriff countered. "He's also the one who took Vega's money and ran. He's already confessed to killing—"

"That's a lie," she interrupted. "I killed Vega. And you know why."

"Be quiet, Violet," Gregory whispered beside her. "Let me handle this."

"You can sort out your stories in jail," the sheriff said. "I have your horses gathered up with mine. We're going back to Independence; then the both of you are going to swing."

Violet and Gregory moved forward, their hands behind their heads. The sheriff kept his gun trained on them.

"Vega deserved to die," Gregory said. "You know that."

"He was one sick bastard," the sheriff agreed. "But he paid well, and now the both of you are going to pay."

They reached their horses, and Gregory did something that confused Violet: he went to her horse as if it were his mount.

"What about the money?" he asked the sheriff. "Wouldn't that ease your conscience over Vega's death?"

"Have you got it?" the sheriff asked, his eyes suddenly bright with greed.

Gregory slapped Violet's horse on the rump and yelled, "Yaw." The animal took off.

"Yeah," he answered. "And there it goes."

The man steadied his gun on Gregory; then his gaze darted toward the retreating horse.

"No telling how far that horse can run in the time it takes you to get us mounted up and on our way," Gregory drawled. "Or who might come across her before you do."

"You swear the money is on that horse?" the sheriff demanded.

"In the saddlebags," Gregory answered. "No one is going to care what happened to Victor Vega. He went after his runaway girls; he didn't come back. End of story."

Their captor rubbed a hand over his jaw. "Folks have been on me for some time to shut him down, run him out of town," he admitted. "I don't particularly take to his brand of entertainment. Still . . . he paid me well to look the other way."

"All we're doing is the same," Gregory pointed out. "The way I see it, we just did you a favor. Now you can return it and have Vega's stash in the bargain."

The man pursed his lips for a moment, stared down the road, then placed his gun in his holster. "Get the hell out of my jurisdiction. I never want to see either of you again."

Stunned, Violet watched the sheriff mount his horse and take off down the road. She glanced at Gregory. "How did you know he'd take the money over taking us in?"

He shrugged. "I know men like him. Greed is what drives them. Money comes first. He preferred it over saving Vega's girls, stopping the wrongs done to them, so I figured he'd prefer it over us."

Violet remembered that the sheriff had told her both men and women would do anything for a dollar, and he'd just proven himself right. She wanted to curse Gregory for even coming after Vega, but time was an issue. "You should get going."

He glanced at the one horse remaining. *"We* should get going. Knowing our luck, your horse stopped a few feet down the road and was on her way back. The sheriff can still get the money and take us in."

"Right," she agreed. "We'll ride together for a while before we part ways."

"We'll have to pick up an extra horse somewhere," he added, but that was all.

She noticed the cuts and bruises on him. "First, I need to look you over. Clean you up. We'll find a place to stop farther down the road."

"I'm all right, Violet," he argued. He swung up onto his horse, then looked back to where they'd been.

216

The urge to turn and glance at Vega's body was strong. Violet's head started to turn.

"Don't look back, Violet."

Gregory held a hand out to her, and it reminded her of the night in Sally's Saloon when Grady Finch had held his hand out as well; and of Lilla telling her in the buggy on the way to the WC Ranch not to look back. Violet had a problem with not looking back. Even though Violet had said the same thing to Vega's girls, she herself was incapable of not looking back. The fact that Victor Vega lay dead a few feet away was more than enough proof of that. But Gregory was right regarding this circumstance. Vega wasn't worth the trouble, or the guilt she felt over killing him.

Her hand slid into Gregory's strong one, and he helped her into the saddle. It was a tight fit, but she was happy to have him with her . . . for the time being. He couldn't stay with her. She had banks to rob and another man to punish. She had her siblings to save. And she had a feeling he would try to talk her out of following through with the rest of her plans.

They rode in silence and as fast as they dared on a horse carrying two riders, so they had made it only to the place they'd camped the night before when darkness began to settle over the land. Violet hadn't bothered to break camp as she'd been in such a hurry, and their tent remained intact.

"Ever get the feeling you're walking backward?" Gregory commented dryly. He helped her off the horse.

Violet moved to the makeshift tent. Their blankets had dried during the day. "I'm going to check your snare," she called to Gregory as she set off. "Maybe we'll have rabbit for dinner."

"If you have one, I'll skin it," he called back.

She cocked a brow at him. "Do you know how to skin a rabbit?"

"I'm not helpless," he said. "I did learn a thing or two about survival in Wyoming."

"Yes, you did," she conceded. "Y-you held your own with V-Vega." Her mind shied away from what had happened earlier, from the sight of Vega's face, from his look of surprise when she'd shot him.

"I would have killed him," Gregory assured her. "You should have ridden on, as I expected you to do."

"And you shouldn't have gone after him in the first place," she shot back. "You're smarter than that. What were you thinking?"

He looked at her, stared into her eyes. "I was thinking about last night, and how I'd make sure he never touched you again."

Embarrassment over her failed attempt at love-making mixed with her guilt and confusion over her reaction to killing Vega. She felt on the verge of breaking down.

"I don't know who I am anymore. I guess I've never known. I don't belong in the world I left behind, and I don't belong in Miles's world. I have no place."

He sighed, then walked over to her. "At least you haven't stepped on everyone in your way while trying to find it. Why don't you rest? I'll check the trap."

"I'm exhausted," she said simply. "Who knew killing would be such tiresome work?" Then she burst into tears. Gregory's arms went around her. She clung to him. "Why didn't killing him feel good, like I thought it would? Why do I feel remorse? How could I, after what he did to me?"

His hand slid over her hair. "Because you're human, Violet. But you did what you had to do. You feared for my life, and you knew that if you let him live, he'd come after you. He would have killed you, too. And he would have raped and beaten you again first."

"I know," she admitted, taking a deep breath. "I'm not sorry he's dead. But I guess I'm sorry that I'm the one who killed him."

"That's why you should have let me do it."

She glanced up at him, still crying. "I never wanted you along to do my killing for me. I never even wanted you to know the truth about my past." She paused. "I think you should leave."

He shook his head. "I can't—there's only one horse, and I'm not leaving you afoot. Besides, I thought I might talk you into going home now. Home to Miles."

She broke free of his embrace. "You know I won't go back. Not until I've done all I intend to do."

Gregory took her shoulders between his hands. "Let it go, Violet. Can't you see what's happening? This quest for vengeance is tearing you apart, making you become someone you don't want to be."

"I am who I am," she retorted. "You know that."

She knocked his hands from her shoulders and moved away again. "No man would want me knowing the truth, and I can't find myself one of those 'fools' you talked about to deceive. I can't live under Miles's roof for the rest of my life, allowing him to care for me. So what are my options, Gregory?"

She waited for him to answer. He didn't. Violet walked over to the tent and squatted beneath it. She lay on the hard ground and closed her eyes. She was tired and confused. And all she wanted was to sleep—to forget.

Gregory roused her a short time later.

"Wake up and eat something."

It surprised her to see that he'd skinned and roasted a rabbit. "My skinning knife was in the packs on my horse," she said. "What did you use?"

"My hands," he answered dryly. "Not as entertaining as a game of billiards at a gentlemen's club, or a good round of poker, but one must make sacrifices."

She felt bad for him. Of course, it wasn't her fault that he'd followed her into a life of crime and hiding out, but that of his own greed. Heaven knew he'd earned that partnership Miles had offered him. And at least he fit in somewhere, could have something like a business. Violet had no idea what she intended to do once she rescued her siblings. She'd have to care for them in some way. And there were four of them. Her brothers were old enough to work, but she'd wanted to make certain all had the opportunity to receive schooling.

Reaching for a plate of roast rabbit he'd prepared

for her, Violet asked, "Before you knew about the truth, what were your intentions toward me?"

He glanced up. "I told you my intentions were honorable. I believe I have proved that they were."

"No. I mean the first time you met me outside of St. Louis. You wanted me to look you up. For what purpose?"

For all that had happened to her, Violet was naive at times. Her question proved it. "I think you know what for." Gregory went back to his dinner.

"Did you believe I was a whore who worked in a saloon or a brothel?"

Her question startled him. The idea had never occurred to him. "No," he answered. "I thought you were a kept woman."

Her brow furrowed. "What's the difference?"

He wondered why she was asking. Maybe she wanted a distraction so she wouldn't have to think about Vega, or the fact that she'd killed him. He himself certainly wouldn't judge her concerning that. The man needed killing, and if Violet hadn't done it, he himself would have.

"The difference is that a kept woman attends solely to one man's needs and is therefore considered the more respectable of the two professions."

"Hmmmm," she responded, then went back to eating.

His curiosity got the best of him. "Why are you asking?"

"I'm considering what I'll do once I've rescued my sister and brothers and must care for them."

Gregory almost choked on his food. "Think of something else."

"What do you suggest?"

Work for men was sometimes hard enough to find. For women . . . well, Violet wouldn't have many choices. Women helped their husbands in businesses. Women sometimes cooked for patrons in a boardinghouse or hotel, but he didn't imagine the wages were good. Nothing he could think of would provide her with the funds to care for herself, much less four younger siblings.

He said instead, "Everything considered, Violet, I don't think you'd make a good mistress."

She lowered her gaze. "I suppose not. Not unless I can overcome my fear of . . . of, well, that."

He didn't like the idea of Violet with nowhere to go and no one to look after her. "I hope this helps you to see the sense of giving up your quest and returning to Miles. Maybe he can do something about your brothers and sister."

Her head snapped up. "I told you before, I don't want Miles involved in my dirty business. Besides, I can't go back now. Even though I acted in self-defense, I went back there to kill Vega and that's what happened. I'm not worthy to live beneath Miles's roof. I never was."

So they were back to what she'd been avoiding to begin with. "You don't have to tell everyone everything about yourself, Violet. Not even Miles. Don't tell them that—"

She shook her head. "I'm not like you. I can't fool people into believing something that isn't true. I couldn't bring myself to mislead Miles about all that's happened. Or trick some gentleman into believing I'm a lady, and an innocent one. I think my best option would be to become a man's mistress. One who has money and can support me and my family." She looked at him with a steady glint in her eye.

His anger rose. What was she thinking? She who couldn't even make love to him, with some other man? "And you plan to do this where?"

"Not in St. Louis, of course," she assured him. "But it should be a large city where there are several well-to-do gentlemen in need of a mistress."

"And what the hell do you mean, you're not like me?"

Calmly, she explained, "I meant I can't pull the wool over people's eyes and make them believe I'm a gentleman, all the while lying in wait to stab them in the back or marry their daughters for a dollar. Did you love Lilla Traften?"

Her words were cutting him to the quick. "No."

"But you wanted to marry her."

"Yes."

"Because you saw her as a means to an end. You never saw her as a person."

"That's not true," he defended. "Lilla is very beautiful. Of course I noticed that."

"How fortunate for her," she snapped. "I don't imagine it would have mattered had she not been beautiful, would it?"

He didn't need reminding of his past mistakes. "What in the hell do you want from me, Violet?"

223

"I want you to leave!"

Oh. He understood now. But she wouldn't run him off. Not until he was good and ready to go. Besides, he still held out hope that he could talk her into returning to St. Louis. He would take his partnership, and Violet . . . he didn't know about Violet. He did know that with all he had on her, he could blackmail Miles from here to eternity if the notion struck him. He hated that the thought had even crossed his mind.

"I'm not leaving," he said.

"Then you will make yourself useful," she demanded.

He rolled his eyes. "I think I've come in pretty handy a couple of times already."

Her eyes met his. Her chin lifted, which told him she was about to say something shocking. "I want you to help me overcome my fear of . . . of that."

Chapter Seventeen

Gregory was glad he didn't still have food in his mouth, or he would have choked again. "Why? So you can become another man's mistress?"

"If I have no choice," she answered. "I'll look for suitable work first, but I think I should be prepared—in case becoming a kept woman is my only option."

"How can you even consider it after what's happened to you?"

"That's why I need you," she persisted. "I think that you could help me. I think you might be the only man who can—"

"Now hold on," he interrupted. "I'm not going to help you become a whore."

"I already am one," she said. "I'm just not good at it."

Her response made him furious. He threw his plate aside. "You are not a whore! You were raped. That isn't the same thing."

"It is in most men's opinions," she said. "I'm ruined, Gregory. You know it and I know it. Your thinking changed about me the minute I told you the truth. I should get used to it."

He ran a hand through his hair. The truth was hard to swallow. He didn't like the way he viewed what had happened to Violet, but he was trained to think and respond a certain way. And he realized most other men were, too. A woman's highest asset, other than if she brought money to a marriage, was her virtue. Wasn't it?

"Besides the obvious, what do you expect me to do?" he asked.

She seemed to ponder the question. "I must have control or I panic. I want you to allow me to do anything I wish to you, and for you to promise not to do anything to me unless I ask."

He laughed. "Are you serious?"

"Yes."

Her big blue eyes stared at him truthfully and trustfully. Again Gregory felt moved that anyone would trust him like this. Especially this woman, who had been so misused. He wouldn't agree to her proposal for the sake of her becoming someone else's mistress, though. If he could get Violet over her initial fear of physical intimacy, she might be able to look toward a future with a man who was a husband, rather than simply a provider. Gregory felt certain such a man existed. One who would love her despite everything she'd done, or all that had been done to her. He admired Violet; he respected her. It would just take someone stronger than himself to marry her.

Of course, this could be a trick. "What if I refuse?" he asked.

"I don't need you. I'll give you the slip and go on my merry way, and you can go back to Miles empty-handed."

"Back to Miles?" he asked. "Why would I bother going back to him?"

She looked him over. "As a trade, after I've rescued my family, if you do this for me I will return with you to St. Louis. But only to thank Miles for his kindness to me before I set out on my own. And only to make certain you receive your partnership."

"So you'll think of this as purely a business deal?"

"If you'd like."

"Only, I'm the . . ."

"Yes, you're the whore," she finished.

It wouldn't be the first time he'd whored himself to make a deal. It really was a shame, a beautiful woman like Violet, frightened of expressing passion, of receiving a man's desire. He could count it as a good deed, couldn't he? He'd stopped himself before, but here she was threatening him if he didn't. . . .

"I guess if it would help you out," he said.

"Good," she responded. "Take off your shirt."

He blinked. "You want to start now?"

She rolled her gaze. "No. I want to check your cuts

and bruises. Do you still have the whiskey you bought at . . . in Independence?"

"Yeah. I'll get it and unsaddle the horse."

The chore gave him time to find a moment of conscience. Miles wouldn't approve of the bargain that had just been struck. He had to assume Miles didn't know everything there was to know about Violet, though. It wasn't as if he were taking advantage of a virgin, or deflowering a young, well-to-do miss for the purpose of forcing a marriage between them. The bargain was only about physical indulgence. Violet was even the one who'd instigated the agreement. Hell, he was doing her a favor, helping her to get past an obstacle so she could move on with her life.

He unsaddled his horse, grabbed the whiskey, and returned to the tent. Settling beside Violet, he removed his shirt. She took the whiskey, dabbed a little on a cloth, and administered to his cuts. He had a good nick on his arm, and one on his neck.

"It's not too bad," she said of the scrape. "A couple of minor cuts, and your jaw is bruised."

"I said I was all right."

"You could be dead." Her voice sounded funny.

He glanced at her. She stared at him in the oddest way—as if she saw something different from what anyone else saw when they looked at him. "But I'm not, and neither are you," he retorted. "Vega has tortured you enough in this lifetime. Let him go, Violet. He's gone forever now."

She nodded, then lowered her gaze and continued to search his body for cuts. When she brushed across his nipple with the damp cloth, it hardened. Her fingers brushed it in the next instant. "If I put my mouth here, do you feel the same things I do when you put your mouth against mine?"

"I . . ." He cleared his throat because his voice sounded high. "I don't know. I don't know what you feel."

A moment later she leaned forward and ran her tongue over his nipple. He sucked in his breath. She took his nipple into her mouth. His hands strayed to her long hair. He twisted his fingers into the silky strands, pulling her face up to his.

"I didn't ask you to kiss me," she said.

Gregory groaned and released her. She returned to cleaning his cuts as if nothing had happened between them. When her hand moved down his stomach, his muscles tightened, and that wasn't all that hardened.

"Last night, what you did to me. A-are there ways a woman can give a man pleasure without . . . without consummating the act?"

Snatching the bottle from her, he took a long swig. "Yes."

"What are they?"

"My God, Violet, you worked in a saloon in Texas, where there were women who pleasured men. Didn't the girls talk amongst themselves? Didn't—"

"I didn't pay them any mind when they talked about that," she interrupted. "And in Independence, Vega sometimes said he wanted me to do things, but I didn't understand them, and I wouldn't do anything willingly, so he'd just get angry and beat me."

Gregory ran a hand through his hair and took another drink. "I swear, Violet. I don't know how a woman who's been forced into your situations manages to stay as innocent as you are."

"I wasn't a woman," she reminded him. "I was a girl. And I wasn't the least bit curious about something that had been only degrading and painful to me."

She was a woman now—a very desirable one as she sat staring at him, her hair down around her shoulders and her tempting lips slightly parted.

"A woman can please a man with her hands or with her mouth," he said.

Her blue eyes widened a fraction. "Her mouth?"

The heat from the fire suddenly felt too hot. He'd never had a conversation like this before. The only women he'd been with knew all about pleasing men, and about being pleasured by them.

"Just like I can please you with either."

"You can?"

Gregory slapped a hand across the back of his neck and rubbed. "Yes."

She sat for a moment, as if weighing what he'd just told her. "Show me."

"What?" He cleared his throat again. "Uh, which . . . what . . . You or me?"

"Me," she answered. "Show me what you can do with your mouth."

He laughed, although he realized it was a nervous one. "It's not that simple. You'd have to allow other things to happen between us. Let me kiss you, undress you, touch you. You'd have to trust me, Violet, and give me rein to do what I must."

"*Can* I trust you, Gregory?"

Good question. He wasn't sure. To go so far with her, then back off . . . Of course, that was what he had agreed to do. And he had done it before. He remembered her terror yesterday. It had been easy to walk away when she'd been afraid. He had cared enough to do so. He had simply to remember that her problems with intimacy couldn't be overcome in one night—no matter how well he showed her pleasure.

"Yes, you can trust me," he said.

She drew a shaky breath. "Then . . . I give you permission to do what you feel is necessary, but I don't give you permission to go any farther than giving me pleasure."

Being given instructions dampened a little of his ardor. He wasn't sure tonight was a good night to show her anything. "Maybe we should wait."

But when she glanced up at him, he saw desperation in her eyes. "I don't want to think about what happened earlier. About what I did. What I have left to do. Tonight I don't want to feel remorse, or regret, or shame. I just want to feel pleasure, your lips against mine, your hands on my skin, your—"

Gregory leaned forward and kissed her. He couldn't blame her. He didn't want to think about what had happened earlier either. Where they had been, or where they were headed. He just wanted to concentrate on Violet, and giving her pleasure. He waited until she kissed him back before his hands strayed to the buttons on her shirt. Slowly he unfastened each one, breaking from her lips to kiss each strip of soft, smooth skin he exposed.

His mouth felt indescribable. Against her skin, it was warm, moist, seeking. . . . Violet tried to relax. She'd promised to trust Gregory, and he'd proven to her before that she could. He pushed her shirt off her shoulders and tugged her shift from where she'd tucked it into her pants. He didn't rush, but teased her nipples through the thin fabric. She moaned and struggled to remove her clothing. He stilled her motions, easing her shirt off, gently pulling her shift over her head before his mouth returned to her breasts.

He tortured her hardened nipples until she squirmed beneath the tender onslaught of his tongue. Caught up in the pleasure, she hardly noticed when he unfastened her pants and slid them down over her hips. He left her gasping, breasts aching, then kissed her stomach, her hipbone. He pulled away, removing what clothing remained on her body as he went. His hands slid up her bare legs. His fingers stroked the insides of her thighs. She felt them tremble, but she felt no fear of him.

She already knew the magic his fingers worked, so when he touched her there—the place that made her tingle and pulse—she almost sighed with relief. He gently stroked her, brought her breathing to a labored pace, made her hot and moist. She moved against him, increasing the pressure, her body already educated about where her efforts would lead. But he removed his hand. The tide she'd been riding sank before it could crest. She moaned in frustration.

A moment later she felt his mouth against her, the pressure of his tongue taking up where his fingers had left off. Had she not been so desperate to find the exquisite release he'd given her before, she might have protested the intimacy, the indecency; but her bones turned to liquid, her blood turned to fire, and all her inhibitions trickled away.

The tide lifted her again, churned by the white-hot flame of his tongue. Violet trembled, caught up in a whirlpool of emotion, drowning, gasping, moving against him until she crashed to shore. She arched upward, shattered, the experience even more excruciatingly pleasurable than the last time he'd brought her to this unknown world.

Her body shuddered, she moaned his name, and a moment later he was there, kissing her, holding her while she grappled to return to earth. The feel of his rigid member pressing against her leg through his clothing brought her back quicker than she would have liked.

She knew he wanted her. But she wasn't ready—she feared she would react the way she'd reacted the last time he'd settled between her legs. He must have sensed her withdrawal; maybe the sudden tensing of her body had told him what she hadn't, because he groaned and rolled away from her.

Gregory felt as if he were about to pop. He was pleased he'd pleased Violet, but he wasn't too pleased about the rest of their agreement. Following through with it might kill him. He scrambled out of the tent, one intention on his mind, and he didn't care if he had to take care of it himself. As he walked, he unfastened his pants. He breathed a sigh of relief just to be free from the garment's tight restrictions.

"Gregory?"

He stopped, his breathing labored.

"Are you all right?"

"No," he said. "Go back inside the tent."

"W-what are you doing?"

"I have to get rid of a problem. If I don't, I'm not sure I can leave you alone for the rest of the night."

"C-can I do something for you?"

His body pulsed at the possibility. He was glad he wasn't facing Violet. "What did you have in mind?"

"What were you going to do?"

He wasn't sure he wanted her to know, but if he didn't tell her, she'd probably just follow him. He sighed. "I'm resorting to what a man doesn't like to have to do."

"Would it help if I did it for you?"

Biting back another groan, he answered, "I'm not sure you're ready yet."

The heat of her hand against his back startled him. "I could try."

Slowly he turned to face her. Even in the darkness, he saw that she wore her shirt, but nothing else. His problem grew worse. "You'll have to touch me, Violet. Are you ready to do that?"

"I think so," she whispered.

He took her hand and brought it to his sex. She nearly snatched her fingers away; then she seemed to gain control of her fear. She wrapped her hand around him, which was enough to almost send him off. He held his breath. Slowly her hand moved down his length.

"You're big. And hard . . . but you're smooth, almost like velvet, and hot." She explored him until he wanted to clamp his hand over hers and make her get the torture over with. Finally she asked, "What do I do?"

He showed her. She caught on quickly, and quickly had him gasping, moving against her hand. He reached inside her open shirt, touched her breasts, teased her nipples until they hardened. He kissed her neck, nipped at her flesh, then groaned as the pressure built. He imagined being inside of her, feeling her moist heat wrapped around him; then he exploded.

The force of his release nearly sent him to his knees. He pulled away from Violet, slammed up against the side of a tree, and grappled with the fading shudders that pumped his seed from him. It took him a while to recover. Violet brought him back to earth.

"Did I hurt you?" she asked.

Taking a deep breath, he fastened up his pants and turned to face her. "No, Violet. You gave me the same kind of pleasure I gave you earlier." He pulled her into his arms and kissed her.

"I'm glad," she said against his lips. "I like pleasing you, being pleased by you."

If she kept up that kind of talk, he'd be ready for her again in a matter of minutes. Gregory turned her toward the tent.

They settled down together, Violet snuggling up to him, and he thought she fell asleep the moment her head hit the ground. Gregory stared at her, the darkness allowing him only shadows and shapes. Violet sighed, the contented sound a man liked to hear from a woman.

Gregory's arms went around her. He didn't think he'd have much trouble falling asleep either. He would have trouble, however, dealing with how right Violet felt in his arms. She felt as if she belonged there, had always and would forever belong here beside him.

He didn't like those thoughts. They scared him. No matter what she made him feel, how much he desired her, Violet was just another deal, another opportunity, another woman. He had to remember that . . . or become enough of a man to deserve her.

Chapter Eighteen

Things weren't as cozy the next morning. Gregory tried to talk sense into Violet, but she wasn't of a mind to listen. And he wasn't just trying to talk her into being reasonable for his own good, but for her own, as well.

"This scheme of yours is never going to work. You're lucky you haven't been caught before now, or killed!"

"It hasn't gone exactly as I expected," she admitted, bending to roll their blankets into bedrolls. "I could just ride to Kansas with the intention of getting my brothers and sister away from the bastard, but I want him to pay for what he's done."

"I thought you had already come to realize that the taste of vengeance isn't as sweet as you thought."

Her gaze skirted him. "So what do you think I

should do, just forgive him? He sold me to a man like I was property! He beat my mother, probably to death. He beat the rest of us, too, when he'd had too much to drink, which was all the time."

"What he did was wrong. It was more than wrong," Gregory agreed. "But revenge has you placing your life on the line to get even with him. If you get caught, or killed, how are you going to help your brothers and sister? Besides, men like your father will usually see to their own sorry end. And whether you like it or not, he's your flesh and blood."

"Don't remind me," she snarled. Violet stared up at him. "I've never told you my real name, have I?"

"It isn't Mallory?"

Of course, he had an idea Mallory wasn't her last name. He knew Miles had a sister in Boston whose married name was Mallory, and Violet had admitted—

"Dalton."

"As in . . . the Doolins and Daltons?"

"The same."

He ran a hand through his hair and whistled. "And here I thought you had no pedigree."

She rose, walked over to him, and shoved the bedrolls into his arms. "You may be good with your hands and with your mouth, but you're still an ass, Gregory Kline." She started to walk away.

Not about to let her off so easily, he said, "You didn't answer my question. How is getting killed or caught and sentenced to hang going to help your family?"

"For one thing, if my father is in prison, I don't

have to worry about him coming after us. Or sending his no-good, thieving relatives looking for us. He sent me to prison. He committed me to a living hell, and I intend for him to suffer the way he's made me suffer. The way he made all of us suffer." She walked over and retrieved the horse he'd saddled.

"It would still be smarter to return home and get Miles to use his money and his influence—"

"This is my family!" Violet shook her head and stared at him. "I waited for two and a half years for the detective I hired with my allowance from Miles to find my brothers and sister again. They had already left the old place when I first sent him to check on the situation there, probably running because the law figured out my father allowed gang members to hide out there in exchange for liquor. I'm not going to put off helping them again. I'm not going back, not without them. Not until my father is behind bars where he belongs!"

Detective? That must have been the unsavory sort Violet had been seen meeting with in St. Louis, Gregory realized. "Or until you get killed during one of these robberies, or caught by a posse. Is all this really worth the risk?"

"Don't you understand even a little? I'm doing this for my family. Wouldn't you do the same? Wouldn't you do anything you had to do to rescue your brothers?"

Gregory took a moment to consider her question. He didn't like the answer. "No. We were never close. Every man for himself. That was the way we were raised."

"Then I pity you."

He moved close to her. "You pity me? My parents were very wealthy. We had standing in the community. We had fine clothes and fine carriages to impress everyone. We had—"

"Material things," she cut him off. "But no love to go along with them. We might have been poor, might have had to scramble for every meal put on the table, might have had to put up with beatings from my father, but my sister, my brothers, and I, we loved each other."

The passion flashing in her eyes told him how much she loved her siblings. Gregory envied her in that moment. He envied her commitment, her love, even though she said her heart was full of hate.

"I'm happy there has been something good about your life," he said. "I wish my family had been closer. I wish my parents hadn't been so busy trying to make a cent that they'd given one about us. But what you're doing is still crazy, Violet. It's dangerous and it's gone on too long!"

"Well, it, may not be smart, but at least I'm doing it for love," she snapped, staring into his eyes. "Not because there is some materialistic reward attached to it or because I've found a way to get my hands on a lot of money that doesn't belong to me. You have your reasons for doing what you do, and I have mine. And I think mine are better."

She turned away, then, having slashed open his gut with her words. What was he doing here? Following her? Allowing her to get him mixed up with her crazy plans? He should have deserted her long ago.

And returned to what? *Nothing.* He had nothing without Violet.

"Are you coming, or staying?" she asked after mounting the horse. "I have to get moving. I need to rob another bank."

The words were spoken as casually as if she might have said she had dishes to wash or clothes to hang. Gregory shook his head and mounted up behind her. He would continue to try to talk reason with Violet. In the meantime, he just hoped she didn't get the both of them killed.

She clucked and sent the horse toward Kansas. Farther down the road, there was no option but to go into a small town for supplies and another horse. The town wasn't much, but it did have a hotel—and a bank.

"Don't even think about it," he said as they rode past the building. "I'm too tired to run."

"I'm tired, too," she admitted. "And I'd love a long bath and a real bed to sleep in."

"I think we've played this out before."

She turned in the saddle to look at him. "I'm serious this time. I'm dirty and exhausted."

They were both dirty and exhausted. He thought he could trust her this time. "All right. But just in case, let's get a horse and supplies first. If you pull something in the morning, I want to be prepared."

Violet soaked in a tub of bubbles. Gregory sat upon the bed, waiting for his turn and looking as if he wished a strong gust of wind would come along. They'd purchased a horse and supplies, and he'd sent their dusty clothes out to be laundered. Violet longed to wear a dress again. To feel pretty and feminine.

"Do you think our clothes will be back in time for us to dress and have dinner downstairs?"

He didn't answer. He kept staring at the bubbles.

"Gregory?"

His gaze snapped up. "What?"

"Our clothes? Do you think they'll be laundered and back in time for us to dress and have dinner downstairs?"

"I imagine."

She laughed at his intent expression. "Do you think you can stare the bubbles away?"

He gave her a burning look. "I'd like to climb in with you."

"There isn't much room."

"I know."

She'd done worse than take a bath with him, and . . . "You can't do anything to me unless I give you permission," she warned him. "But if you abide by the rules, you may join me."

He frowned. "Maybe I'll just save myself the torture."

His response disappointed her. She'd like to see him strip down. It wouldn't bother her in the least to run her hands over his soap-slicked skin, or to have him rub his over hers. She'd also been thinking about last night.

"Gregory, why couldn't a woman and man just

please each other with their hands and mouths? Why do the other at all?"

He glanced up. She thought he looked more uncomfortable than he had a moment before. "For one thing, if a man and woman want children, they have to do the other."

"But suppose they don't want children? Could a man be content—"

"No," he assured her.

"Why not?"

Unbuttoning the collar of his shirt, he answered, "Because a man wants to do the other more than he wants to do anything else."

She didn't understand. "But why? If he can receive pleasure just as easily—"

"Violet," he warned. "This is not a decent conversation."

The urge to laugh overtook her. Beneath the bubbles she was naked, and he sat in the same room, watching her bathe. They'd already done things together she had never thought she would do with any man, at least willingly, and things that all of society would censure them for.

"You're prudish," she said with a smile.

His face darkened a shade. "I am not."

Her smile stretched. "Yes, you are. You want to do these things with me, but you don't want to discuss them."

"Discussing them only makes me want to do them more," he explained.

It was her turn to frown. "And you still want to do the other more than anything else?"

"When or if you're ever ready," he answered, loosening another button on his shirt. "Until then, I suppose I will settle for the other."

"You're very obliging," she retorted.

"Under certain circumstances."

It occurred to her to wonder how many similar circumstances he'd been in. He'd told her before that he'd been with more than one woman, more than two. Why did he think that was all right for him, but not all right for her?

"You're also a hypocrite," she decided.

His brow lifted. "A hypocrite?"

She nodded and soaped her arms. "It's all right for you to be less than pure, but it isn't all right for me."

"It has been that way for years, Violet. Understood and accepted among society."

"Well, I don't accept it!" she said, suddenly furious. "My situation was not one of my own making. I didn't willingly give up my virtue. Yet here I am, forced to consider whoring for a living—"

"You have other options." He walked over, then bent down behind her. "Let me wash your back?"

She gave him the soap. "While you're at it, explain my other options."

"You can always take your siblings and start fresh somewhere. Say you are a young widow. I don't know why I didn't think of that before. You're very beautiful, Violet. I'm sure you could attract any number of wealthy men, and marry one rather than become his mistress."

His hands felt heavenly against her skin. "But that would be lying to him. As I've said before, I wouldn't want to fool a man into thinking something about me that wasn't true."

"You didn't mind fooling me."

"But I had no intention of marrying you," she pointed out. "And I did tell you the truth, even when I could have gotten away with lying to you further."

"Yes, you did."

By the flat way he said it, she figured he wished she hadn't told him. At times—like now, when he became silent—she almost wished she hadn't told him, either. He wouldn't have gone after Vega. He wouldn't have forced her into a confrontation where she'd ended up killing the bastard. And though she was glad Vega was dead, she wished she hadn't learned she was capable of killing a man. For now she had to kill her father.

"I'd like to get out now," she said. "Would you leave while I dry off?"

"I could help you."

If Gregory was nothing else, he was a distraction when guilt and dark thoughts plagued her. He'd also saved her life and fought for her honor. And he was honest—more honest with her than she'd been with him.

"It's broad daylight," she said, and suddenly felt uncomfortable, even after all they'd done together. He rinsed her back, then rose and snatched a towel. He held it as if waiting for her to rise.

"You have nothing to be ashamed of, Violet. Your body is beautiful, perfect to me."

She blushed with pleasure at the compliment, which was a change. When she'd worked at Sally's

Saloon, she'd tried to hide both her beauty and her figure. She'd considered them curses. Vega had always leered at her body, made her feel dirty and ashamed, but she liked the way Gregory looked at her, as if she were an exquisite painting. She rose and stepped out of the tub. He wrapped the towel around her and steered her toward the bed.

After many nights of sleeping on the hard ground, Violet thought the plump feather mattress felt heavenly. She sat on the edge, waiting to see what Gregory would do next. He took the towel from around her shoulders and began to pat her skin dry. He started at her neck and gently kissed each patch of skin he dried.

The towel's rough texture made her nipples harden. When he noticed that, Gregory's mouth found them. Violet gasped softly and twisted her fingers in his hair. He moved lower, drying her stomach. She felt her breath lodge in her throat when the towel touched the sensitive place between her legs. His mouth was there a moment later. She moaned and closed her eyes.

Her body understood the sensations he offered now, how to relax and let him bring them to her. He pushed her trembling legs farther apart, his fingers lingering over her thighs, then moving up around to her hips to press her more firmly against his mouth. His tongue teased her, pleasured her until she felt the building inside of her, the tightening of her stomach muscles, the desperation to find release from this mixture of torture and ecstasy.

She moved against him, gasping, moaning, writhing until the whirlwind caught her up and carried her away. He moved back up, gently easing her onto the bed while her body still convulsed and trembled. He kissed her, a deep, passionate kiss that nearly melted her bones.

"You can't know how much I want you, Violet—want to be inside of you. Feel you wrapped around me."

He almost made her want the same—he'd given her pleasure and she wanted to give it to him as well—but she couldn't bring herself to give him permission to invade her body, to stab so painfully at her.

"Part of me wants that, too, Gregory. But I'm afraid. Afraid that I'll remember again, confuse you with Vega. You can't understand how much he hurt me. How he ripped and tore and left me bleeding. I'm not sure those wounds, the ones inside of me, will ever heal."

Gregory trailed a fingertip along the side of her face. "I think they will someday, Violet. I think they're beginning to heal already." He rolled away from her, rose and started getting undressed.

"Do you want me to—"

"I'm taking a bath," he said in explanation for undressing.

"The water is cold by now."

"Good," he grumbled. "Take a nap. After I bathe, I'll get our clothing and we can go downstairs for dinner."

She threw a portion of the quilt on the bed over her and closed her eyes, but not fully. Beneath the

247

cover of her lashes, she watched him undress. She grew hot and tingly, even when her gaze lowered to the part of him standing proudly at attention.

Perhaps her mind *had* begun to let go of her past. Gregory had already shown her that there was another side to what she'd experienced with Vega. Oh, how she wanted to experience that.

Violet heard him settle into the tub, and closed her eyes. She would give the matter more thought. She would not again rush into something she might be unable to carry through. She felt certain that even Gregory, as much as he'd kept his word to her so far, had limits to his tolerance.

Chapter Nineteen

Gregory wondered when he would snap, Violet looked so ravishing. For dinner, they were posing as husband and wife, and although Violet's dusty men's clothing had earned her a curious inspection from the proprietor of the establishment when they'd first entered, now she looked elegant, a combination of innocence and sensuality. So much so that all Gregory could think of was getting her out of her feminine trappings and pulling the pins from her upswept hair, and tumbling her into the bed so he could prove to her she had nothing to fear from him.

He was slightly annoyed that he couldn't be more patient, that although she'd certainly offered him alternatives in finding his pleasure, he wanted most what she withheld from him. It was like being presented with a feast, then told that only the appetizers were to be sampled.

To add to his irritability, the dining chamber of the hotel was small. He and Violet were forced to join a young couple at their table. The couple had a baby with them who cried, which added to his nasty mood.

Polite introductions were made. It felt odd to introduce Violet as his wife, but she hardly noticed him stumble over the word, so enthralled was she with the child. Its parents kept ogling and crooning over it.

"May I hold him?" Violet surprised Gregory by asking.

The woman—what was her name? Martha something—gladly handed the child over.

"He's beautiful," Violet said softly, then laughed as the toothless creature gave her a wide smile. "Isn't he sweet?" she turned to ask.

Gregory eyed the child a moment. A stream of drool streamed from the baby's mouth. "Lovely," he said, then turned his attention to the food being offered.

"How old is he?" Violet asked.

"Six months," the mother proclaimed proudly. "And the joy of our lives. Do you and Mr. Kline have children?"

"No," Gregory quickly answered.

"Well, you should," the woman fussed. "They add so much to a marriage."

"We've only been married for a short time and don't wish for so much to be added," he countered.

250

Glancing at the woman's husband, he asked, "What is your business, Mr. . . . ?"

"Burton," the man supplied. "I manage the bank."

Gregory's gaze went to Violet. She'd stopped playing with the child. "Is that so?"

The man nodded. "Not that there is much to manage in a town this size," he said with a laugh. "But I do handle the payroll for a section of the Rock Island Railroad. A lot of responsibility there."

"And I wish he didn't," the wife sounded off. "I wouldn't worry nearly as much about him all alone in the bank if he didn't."

"Oh, Martha, you know nothing ever happens here. It's one of the reasons we like it," he explained. "A fine place to raise our son."

"And his brothers and sisters to follow," Martha said, smiling sweetly at her husband.

Gregory was glad he hadn't eaten yet or he might have lost his supper over the loving glances the pair kept exchanging. He also suspected Violet had begun to have more on her mind than children. The banker had dangled bait that he doubted she could resist.

"A large payroll," she said. "That is a responsibility."

"But my Seth can handle it," Martha said. "So what are you doing so far from your home in St. Louis?"

Gregory waited to see what Violet would come up with as an excuse. Looking over, he saw that the creature in her lap seemed to be squirming in his direction.

"Gregory is in the cattle market. We're looking for ranches to acquire."

"So you're a rancher?" Mr. Burton eyed his neatly cleaned and pressed suit as if that wasn't what he expected in a rancher.

Gregory gave a warm smile. "No, I don't run the ranches; I simply acquire them for the cattle company of which I am a partner."

"Oh, a partner?" The man beamed at him, as if he'd just bragged of running the country. "Never could see the appeal of herding around a bunch of smelly, bawling cattle. Sounds like dirty work."

"It is," Gregory assured him.

"I think the little one wants you to hold him," Violet spoke up. And suddenly she thrust the slobbering thing at him. Gregory didn't know what to do with it. He held the baby beneath its flailing arms. It grinned and more drool ran from its mouth, down its clothes, and onto Gregory's suit pant leg. The baby's face turned red, and a moment later Gregory's nose twitched.

"Here." He tried to hand the smelly baby back to Violet.

"He likes you," she said, and he saw the mischief sparkle in her eyes.

"He's such a sweet baby," its mother said. "He simply loves everyone."

The child grabbed Gregory's nose with drool-covered little fingers. Gregory was not amused, though the rest of the table broke into laughter.

"He, ah, smells funny," he explained to the mother. His voice came out nasal-sounding because the child had refused to release his nose.

"He needs changing," the woman agreed. She rose and took the creature away.

Gregory used his napkin to wipe up all the drool left on his face.

"Babies are somewhat messy," the father apologized jovially.

Gregory did not comment. He was starving, and would much rather have Violet to himself than deal with this family. The woman returned and the husband rose to get her chair. Their baby seemed less good-natured than before. It fussed and carried on to the point that Gregory had a headache.

A person appeared to take their orders, and Gregory breathed a sigh of relief when the food was finally brought around. Strangely, though, Seth Burton's wife took one look at the meal, turned pale, and clamped a hand over her mouth. She quickly rose, thrust her child into her husband's arms, and hurried outside. Her husband, looking alarmed, also rose. He shoved the baby at Gregory and hurried out after his wife.

"You again," Gregory growled at the child. It promptly spit up all over his suit. He cussed and handed the baby to Violet. As he cleaned himself with a napkin, he heard her laughing.

"It's not funny," he snapped. "It's disgusting. I told you that I don't care for babies. There's always something foul coming out of one place or another from them."

"Well, I love babies. I think they are as sweet as angels."

He glanced at her, and for a moment was struck dumb by the beauty of her face and the sight of the child snuggled up near it. The picture caused a very strange reaction in him. He felt suddenly weak in the knees. Perhaps he was about to throw up, he decided a moment later.

The woman and her husband returned. She smiled weakly and reclaimed her child. "I hadn't told Seth yet, but I think we are already expecting again. I thought one couldn't conceive while breast-feeding," she finished, suddenly looking less than enthusiastic about motherhood. The man also seemed more subdued. The baby in Martha's lap settled to sleep and the rest of the meal passed in relative silence.

"I think children should be born with only a short amount of time between them," Violet proposed as they neared finishing their food. "They are closer that way."

"Do you believe so?" Martha asked hopefully.

"I certainly do," Violet said. "My sister and I were six years apart, and I wish we'd been closer in age. We would have had more in common."

At her last remark, Gregory noticed Violet pale. She probably realized that it wouldn't have been good at all. Her father might have sold them as a pair. As Gregory contemplated that, he considered that maybe Violet was right, and the man did deserve to be terribly punished.

"What do you think, Mr. Kline?" Mrs. Burton asked.

He wasn't in the mood for conversation anymore. His suit jacket reeked of baby vomit, Violet wouldn't let him make love to her, and he'd had enough. "I believe if two people are of a mind to consort with one another, they should be willing to suffer the consequences. After three or four of those little monsters, maybe the two of you will realize what's causing the problem."

Shocked silence followed his remark. He glanced up from his meal. Violet cast him a dirty look, rose, and ran off.

"Excuse me," Gregory said, throwing his napkin in his plate before he stood. Then he threw down money to cover the bill and left.

"With pleasure," the bank manager growled after him.

Violet was waiting for him in the room, her hands planted upon her hips. "You may have been raised with manners, and I may have acquired them only in the past three years, but even I know how rude that was!"

He shrugged angrily. "I just stated the obvious."

"You're a fine one to cast stones. I believe a while earlier, had I given you an opportunity, you would have gladly rutted with me in this room—consequences be damned!"

"That's not true," he argued. "I would have taken precautions."

Her eyebrows lifted. She was obviously taken aback by the thought. "What sort of precautions?"

He tugged at his collar. Here they went again. "Since you'll bother me until I tell you, I wouldn't have spilled myself inside you."

"Oh," she said, and her cheeks turned pink. Then

she sat on the bed and said, "Well, it wouldn't have mattered anyway. I-I'm barren."

He felt a wave of sadness go through him. "Are you certain?"

"I can only assume so. Because of Vega," she added softly. "I mean, surely at some point over those two years . . ." She turned away and began plucking the pins from her hair.

For some reason, Violet's inability to have children bothered him. It seemed unfair. She'd looked so beautiful holding the child downstairs, so natural. If or when she put this nasty business of her father behind her, it would be a crime for her not to have a husband and children.

"Maybe I'll go back down and apologize to the Burtons," he suggested.

"I believe you should," she agreed. "I'm going to bed to get a good night's sleep. Undisturbed," she added meaningfully.

He took it he'd be sleeping on the floor again. He also wondered if she wanted a good night's sleep so that she could pay Mr. Burton a visit first thing in the morning. Since Violet seemed dead-set on arriving in Coffeyville with a trail of robberies to implicate her father, Gregory would either have to thwart her plans before she placed herself in danger, or throw in his lot with her.

Gregory still didn't hold with bank robbing. *As if blackmail and stealing from those I know is so much more honest*, the snide thought crossed his mind. But dammit, Violet's sorry father did deserve to pay for what he'd done. If there was a payroll inside of Mr.

Burton's bank, and a large one, maybe that would be good enough for Violet's scheme. Maybe then she could get on with her plans and get this business behind her . . . and maybe he could resist stealing it from her and proving that he hadn't changed at all.

A persistent knocking awoke Violet. For a moment she couldn't remember where she was, or why. She hoped Elizabeth, Miles's housekeeper, would sweep into the room carrying a tray of breakfast. Then she remembered she wasn't beneath Miles's roof anymore. She struggled up, glancing toward the floor where she'd heard Gregory settle for the night. He wasn't there.

The blankets he'd used were folded and neatly stacked on the end of the bed. She rose, grabbed her robe, and struggled into it before answering the door. The hotel proprietor stood outside.

"Your husband has asked me to relay a message to you."

Her mind still groggy, she almost informed the man that she did not have a husband. "Gregory?"

He nodded. "He says you are to meet him downstairs. He said that he has gone to fetch the present you wanted for your father, and that you should be ready to leave with all due haste."

"A present? For her father? Leave in all due haste?" She felt her gaze widen. That bad feeling settled over her again. When the proprietor kept staring at her, she asked, "Mr. Kline did settle our bill, didn't he?"

"Oh, yes," he assured her. "A very nice man, your husband."

"Yes," she agreed dryly. "Very nice." She closed the door. How could Gregory dare rob Mr. Burton? Sure, she'd shown an interest when the man told them that he managed the bank, and yes, she had considered robbing the bank when they'd first ridden into town. But that was before she'd met Seth and his wife—had eaten dinner with them and held their firstborn in her arms. Now it would be rude to rob them. Mr. Burton could lose his position. He could be hurt! They had a baby, and another on the way. What was Gregory thinking?

Violet hurried to get dressed. She only hoped she could stop Gregory before it was too late.

Chapter Twenty

Violet entered the bank just as Gregory pulled his gun on Mr. Burton. He had a bandanna tied around his face, which concealed his features nicely. The gun swung in her direction, which angered her almost as much as the sight of Mr. Burton with his hands in the air, looking as if he might faint. Violet stormed to Gregory's side.

"Don't point that thing at me. How dare you pull a stunt like this with Mr. Burton! He's a decent man, and he has a new baby and one on the way! You are compromising his position!"

"Mrs. Kline," Seth Burton squeaked. "Please don't rile this man. You'll get yourself shot."

"Oh, nonsense." She reached out and snatched the gun from Gregory's hand. "Get out before I shoot you!"

Gregory had the sense to do as he was told. That was when she noticed something odd: the gun she held didn't look like Gregory's gun. A moment later Gregory rushed into the bank, his face flushed, and he was out of breath.

"Don't, Violet!" he shouted.

"Oh, my God," Seth Burton said under his breath. "Your wife has just stopped a robbery!"

Gregory's gaze went to the gun in her hand. "What are doing with that?" he asked.

Violet's knees went weak. "You weren't just here?" she whispered.

"No," he whispered back. "What's going on?"

"Mrs. Kline." Seth Burton placed a hand against his heart and came around from behind the teller's cage. "You are the bravest woman I have ever met."

She nearly fainted.

Gregory steadied her. "What happened?" he demanded.

"I'll tell you what happened," Mr. Burton crowed. "I was in the process of being robbed when your wife came in, marched right up to the outlaw, and snatched the gun from his hand. She gave him a good tongue-lashing, too!"

"You did?" Gregory asked, his face turning pale.

She nodded. "I thought . . ." Her gaze strayed to Mr. Burton. "I thought it was very rude of him to try to rob a nice man like Mr. Burton."

"You could have gotten killed," the bank manager fussed. "And over so little. The railroad payroll went out on a stage before dawn, headed toward Topeka. I had little in the way of money here in the vault."

"The payroll is on a stage?" Violet asked, recovering herself. "Well, that is nice to know." If she and Gregory robbed the stage, surely Mr. Burton couldn't be held accountable or be hurt. "I had only come in to tell you good-bye and to say what a pleasure it was to meet you and Mrs. Burton last evening."

"You're leaving? But you must stay. I will introduce you to the sheriff and throw a party in honor of your bravery."

"The sheriff?" both she and Gregory asked in unison.

"Actually, it was nothing," she said to the bank manager. "Mr. Kline and I must be on our way. We have other business to attend to."

"My wife is always doing things like this," Gregory assured the wide-eyed Mr. Burton. "She'll make an old man of me before my time."

"Well, yes," Mr. Burton agreed. "You really must take more care, Mrs. Kline. Too much courage isn't always an admirable trait in a woman."

"I will try to suppress it," she answered. "Do give my best to your wife."

The man smiled. "I can hardly wait to see her, so I can tell her. In fact, tell the whole town."

"In her condition, I wouldn't advise telling her that your life was in danger this morning," Violet suggested.

He frowned. "Perhaps you're right. But I must tell the sheriff what happened. He's grown lazy. As I said last evening, nothing much goes on in a town this size, and—"

"Yes, you should tell him," Violet agreed, her mind working. "In case something happens farther down the road."

Gregory glanced at her and frowned.

"The robber knew about the payroll," Seth Burton confided. "I told him that I didn't have much, and he said he knew otherwise. Then I told him that the stage had already taken the payroll. He may go after it."

"Yes, he might," Violet agreed.

"Maybe he won't," Gregory countered.

She cut her gaze at him. "I'm nearly positive that he will."

Gregory sighed. "Good day then, Mr. Burton. And I guess good-bye."

"I hope you'll stop and visit us again on your way back to St. Louis."

"If we're alive—ah—able, we will," Gregory said; then he took Violet's arm and ushered her from the bank.

They'd barely made it outside when he started in on her. "Good God, Violet, you could have been killed!"

She wanted to punch him. "Yes, and it would have been your fault! What was the message about going to fetch a present for my father if you weren't intending to rob Mr. Burton?"

His face flushed. "Actually, I did intend to rob him, but when I came outside I ran into his wife coming from the mercantile. She had to chat about this and that and then she asked me to hold the damn child while she dug a handkerchief out of her bag to wipe the baby's snotty little nose, and then, well, I realized I couldn't rob a man whom I had just insulted the previous evening. And then there was the . . ."

"The baby?" she asked, raising her eyebrow. "You didn't want to put his father in danger, did you?"

"No," he agreed, as if he'd just admitted to a much worse crime. "Take away the slobber and the stench, and the child was very nice."

"I believe you really are developing a conscience," Violet mused.

"And it seems yours has finally decided to make an appearance, too."

Violet felt a warm feeling in the pit of her stomach when he smiled at her. She shook off the feeling. "Well, it's time to put conscience aside. We have a stage to catch."

"I know there's no sense in asking, but I'm assuming you don't mean a stage traveling home to St. Louis?"

He didn't deserve an answer. She rolled her gaze and hurried toward the hotel, intending to change from her dress into her outlaw clothes.

They argued again just before they rode out of town.

"I insist on doing this alone," Gregory said.

"I said you could come along with me to Kansas. I didn't say that you could participate in my dangerous schemes, and I certainly didn't say you could do them alone!"

"Well," he argued. "If you won't give up your plans, I have to become a party to them. It's too dangerous for you. The stage might be heavily guarded. Besides, if you mistook the man who intended to rob Burton for me, then I'm closer to his size. This way, after the heist, the driver will give a description that matches the man Burton will say tried to rob him."

Violet hated to admit it, but Gregory was right. And, if she did it this way, she could pin the earlier attempted robbery on her father too. Of course, she hadn't pulled a robbery to date that had gone according to her plans. She wanted this to work, and it would work best if it was a lone man, certainly not one whom anyone would even consider to be a woman.

"First we have to catch it," she said. "We'll see what kind of guard there is and decide from there."

Gregory nodded and they kicked their horses out.

It took most of the day at a hard pace before they saw the dust of a coach spiraling ahead, but from all indications, they'd caught the stage. Gregory couldn't say he was happy to see their quarry, but then again, he also couldn't say the sudden leap his heart gave wasn't anticipation, which his newly found conscience tried to veil as worry. He and Violet left the road and raced through the trees. There were four armed guards, and from what Gregory could see, no travelers inside the coach.

Violet pulled up to slow her horse, forcing him to do the same.

"There are too many," she said. "It's too risky."

"I can handle four," he assured her.

"Well, I'm not going to let you," she argued. "I

wouldn't want something to happen to you. I mean, I wouldn't want that on my conscience, as well."

"Well, you're sure as hell not going to rob the stage," he said. "I wouldn't want anything to happen to you, either."

"Too bad the reward Miles offered you wasn't for dead or alive," she snapped.

He couldn't have an honest emotion as far as she was concerned. "Yeah, too bad," he agreed.

"I guess that's it then," she said with a sigh. "We'll just have to find another bank along the way to rob. It's too bad. I imagine a railroad payroll is pretty big. The law would be relentless in pursuit of anyone brave enough to take that money."

Gregory imagined the payroll was bigger than even Vega's stash. A lot of money. Enough to buy a man a new identity . . . or to buy a woman one. "Let's trail them for a while. They can't make it all the way to Topeka without stopping somewhere. Maybe we'll come up with something."

A little before dusk, the stage finally pulled into a swing station. It was an adobe structure with a water trough and a corral full of horses. Two men and the driver dismounted from the coach. The other two handed down what appeared to be a strongbox to the guards waiting below. The driver and a man who'd come out of the station looked to be arguing. The stationmaster shrugged, and the driver stomped away and began unhitching the coach.

"What's going on?" Violet asked.

"I imagine he's just changing the horses."

After the driver unhitched the horses and led them

into the corral, he walked to the road and squinted into the distance. He glanced up, shook his head, and walked back.

Gregory glanced up, too. Dark clouds had gathered overhead. They were in for another rainstorm.

"Why was he starting down the road, as if he expected to see someone?" Violet asked.

After thinking about it for a moment, Gregory answered, "His replacement, the guard's replacements. They were supposed to be here, maybe."

"So now they have to wait."

He nodded. "And a storm's blowing in. If we're going to take that strongbox, we need to do it now."

"There are four guards, the driver, and the stationmaster watching over that payroll! Even if we both go in—"

"We won't go in together," he interrupted. Gregory knew Violet could be a damn good actress if measures called for it. "We'll go in separately, you as a woman and me as a man. Change back into your dress."

"My dress?"

He nodded. "I'll explain while you get ready."

Gregory had a good plan. Violet wasn't certain she could pull it off, though. He studied her, messed up her hair, and then reached down and tore the sleeve of her dress from her shoulder.

"This is my best dress," she huffed. "And now you've ruined it!"

"You need to appear as if you've been running for your life," he reminded her. "Besides"—his gaze drifted over her body—"showing off some of that pretty skin of yours will distract the men."

It seemed to be distracting him. He kept staring at the exposed flesh of her shoulder. Violet waved a hand in front of his face. "What are you thinking?"

His answer wasn't flattering. "I'm thinking about all that money." He reached out and touched her bare shoulder. "You know, with a haul like that one, we could go anywhere we want to go, buy anything, become anyone we choose."

She swatted his hand away. "That money doesn't belong to us. I intend to make sure the good people who worked hard for it receive it . . . just at a later time."

"There's that conscience again."

She glared up at him. "Where's yours?"

Gregory shrugged and walked away. "Just thinking out loud."

Violet couldn't help but feel pleased that he'd said "we" when referring to them, as if they had a future together. But she wouldn't build her life the way her kin had, stealing from others. She would make sure this money would be returned when her father was caught. And the fact that Gregory wanted to purchase her a new identity told her that he still couldn't accept her for who she was. He might have won pieces of her heart since that first morning they met outside of St. Louis, but for them to be happy, he'd have to love her despite her past. She knew that.

"Go over the plan again," she said.

He did, and quickly, because darkness would soon be upon them. Since she wore a dress, Gregory helped her mount. He took the seam at the hem of her garment and ripped it to display a good portion of her leg. She gasped in displeasure.

"It was ruined anyway, right?"

"Am I to play the part of the distraught wife set upon by an outlaw, or a brazen whore looking to help them pass the time?"

He frowned over the amount of leg he'd displayed and tried to bunch the material together again. She clucked her horse forward and forced him to move back.

"Violet," he called.

She glanced over her shoulder.

"Be careful."

"You're the outlaw this time—you be careful."

Their gazes held for a moment. She thought he would say more, and suddenly she wanted to say more, but he walked toward his horse and began preparing for his role in the robbery.

"Ready?" he asked.

"I'm ready," she whispered; and she wished she'd made love with him completely, because she wasn't certain whether either of them would live through the dangerous stunt they were about to pull.

"Go," he said, and she kicked her horse into a full gallop.

She made the main road and raced toward the station. When she got within shouting distance, she started screaming. The men stumbled out of the adobe house like drunks from a saloon at closing time.

"Help me!" Violet shouted. "Please help me!"

One man snatched her horse's bridle. Another tried to soothe the excited animal.

"What happened, ma'am?" the man she recognized as the stage driver asked.

She placed a hand against her pounding heart. "My husband and I were set upon by an outlaw. He shot Gregory. Oh, my God, I think he killed him!"

The stationmaster stepped forward. "An outlaw? Were you robbed by this feller?"

A sensible conversation outside was not in the plan, so Violet swayed. She tumbled from her horse, hoping that one of the men would catch her. One did.

"Let's get her inside and out of the heat," he said, and he carried Violet toward the structure. That was when she realized she still didn't like to be touched by a man . . . any but one.

The others followed. The man who carried Violet set her upon a crude wooden chair. All of the others pressed forward, looking at her expectantly. For a moment panic almost overwhelmed her.

"Can you tell us what happened?" the driver asked.

She drew a shaky breath. "This morning I intruded upon a robbery in progress at the bank in Harvest Grove. Luckily the man was frightened away, and dear Mr. Burton wasn't harmed. My husband, Gregory . . ." She paused to allow tears to rush to her eyes. "We had business elsewhere and took to the road right after the robbery. This man must have spotted us and recognized me as the woman who'd stopped his earlier plans. He shot my husband."

Again she paused, as if she couldn't go on.

"Tom, get her a glass of water, for Christ's sake," one of the guards ordered.

"Did the man harm you?" the stationmaster asked, glancing at Violet's torn clothing, and a bit too long at her exposed parts, she noted.

She accepted the glass of water, greedily drank from it, and handed the glass back.

"When Gregory fell from his horse, he told me to keep riding. He told me to save myself. I've been running for a long time, afraid to even glance back to see if the outlaw still pursued me. I veered off the main road, hoping he would pass me, but I didn't see him. The trees and brush tore my clothing."

One man glanced toward the door, as if he meant to check and make sure the outlaw hadn't followed her to the station. Violet grabbed his shirtsleeve.

"I fear my husband may be dead," she cried, then rose and threw herself into his arms. "Oh, dear Lord, what will I do? How can I go on without him?"

The man awkwardly patted her on the back. Violet jerked away. "I can't breathe." She walked to the open doorway and turned back. When the group of men all took a step toward her, she held up a hand to ward them off.

"Please, a moment to catch my breath."

"We were at the bank this morning, too," the stage driver said. "I bet that robber was after the railroad payroll."

Violet wondered where Gregory was. She couldn't keep the men at a distance for long, or inside of the swing station.

"Mr. Burton expressed the same concern," she agreed. "He said he'd told the robber the payroll was already—"

Suddenly she felt the cold barrel of a gun pressed to the back of her neck. An arm went around her throat.

"Nobody move or I'll kill the lady."

"Oh, Lord," Violet whispered. "It's him. The man who shot my husband!"

One of the stagecoach guards' hands slid toward his holster.

"Don't!" Gregory shouted. "I'll kill her. I swear I will."

"Please don't let him do this," Violet pleaded. She summoned more tears. "If you care nothing for me, think of my unborn child."

The guard's hand moved away from his gun.

"All of you, remove your gun belts and throw them on the floor," Gregory ordered—quite impressively, Violet thought.

She made a choking sound even though Gregory didn't hold her tightly. The men hurried to obey his instructions.

"The payroll," Gregory barked. "Open that strong-box."

"We ain't got the key," one of the guards said. "It's in the bank at Topeka."

"Bring the box over here."

When no one made a move, Violet made more choking sounds. One of the guards hefted the strong-box and brought it over.

"Back off," he ordered the guard, and after the

man rejoined the others, Gregory shot the lock on the strongbox. Then he kicked it open with his boot. Violet had trouble not gasping. The chest was loaded with more money than she'd ever seen gathered in one place. She heard Gregory's slight intake of breath close to her ear.

"Stationmaster," Gregory said. "Whichever of you is him, get me a couple of flour sacks and put the money inside. Put all the gun belts in one, too."

The stationmaster, glaring at Gregory, did as he was told. "There's your money, and you have our guns," he said in a growl when he'd finished. "Now let the lady go."

Gregory laughed. "Not until me and the money are away from here. And none of you had better come after me or she'll get a bullet between the eyes, baby or no baby." He pulled her backward.

Violet whimpered as he dragged her from the station, loaded down with sacks of money and heavy gun belts. The men gathered at the door, watching, waiting for him to slip up.

He forced her to the water trough, where he pitched the sack of gun belts. He told her to open the corral gate and held the gun trained on her the whole time. Acting terrified, Violet opened the gate. Gregory made her mount his horse, then climbed on behind. Grabbing the reins to the horse she'd ridden into the station, he wrapped them around his saddle horn. Then he fired shots in the air, scaring all the other horses out of the corral. Now the stagecoach guards were not only without weapons, they were without horses, too.

"Better cast them one more pathetic glance for good measure," he whispered in Violet's ear.

She remembered the day she'd sat in Vega's wagon as it rolled away from her family's pitiful shack, staring back at her mother in helpless appeal. She tried to summon that same expression. Like her mother, the men did not come after her.

They had almost made it out of sight of the swing station when the sky opened up and Gregory drew his horse to a stop. She slid from his horse, planning to mount her own. Violet heard Gregory curse and thought it had to do with the rain—until she noticed him staring behind them. A group of mounted riders approached the swing station.

"Who is it?" she asked. "The guards' replacements?"

He nodded. "Yeah, dammit. Now they've got double the men to come after us."

She cursed too, but under her breath. *Of all the rotten luck!*

"Hurry and mount up," Gregory said. "This rain will buy us a little time."

They rode hard. Rain poured from the sky. Lightning crackled around them and made their horses nervous.

"We're leaving tracks," Gregory called. "We'd better find somewhere and hole up."

Riding in a dress had started to rub the sensitive skin of Violet's thighs raw. She nodded and followed him off the road. They picked their way through the woods. The cover was good. She hardly felt the rain, canopied overhead by tall leafy trees.

Ronda Thompson

Gregory helped her dismount. "We did it, Violet," he said, his eyes awash with excitement. "We pulled it off."

She couldn't and wouldn't share his excitement. "Not yet, we haven't. Those guards will be combing every inch of this territory in search of us for taking that payroll." She didn't want to be caught before she avenged herself or her father.

"Have you ever seen so much money in your life?" Gregory asked, his spirits obviously undaunted.

The last thing she'd ever intended was to instill in Gregory a love of such crimes. The things she'd done were not things she felt proud of—they were simply necessary evils to further her plans. But now that he saw how easily such riches could be obtained . . .

"Gregory," she warned. "I think I've corrupted you."

He pushed her up against the side of her horse, pressing against her, his lips only inches from hers. "I want to be corrupted." His gaze lowered to her soaked, torn, clinging dress. "And I've never seen a woman who looked more beautiful wet."

Violet was certain the rush of warmth that spread through her had nothing to do with excitement over the robbery. The danger of their situation was much too real. But that also meant this moment in time could be all they had left. Staring into Gregory's eyes, she realized there was no one she'd rather be with if the end did come.

She wasn't going to waste any more of the time they had together, not a moment of it. Violet leaned forward and kissed him. The fire in her grew. Their mouths moved against one another, demanding, wild, uninhibited. For the first time in her life, Violet wanted a man. Wanted *all* of him. Gregory.

"I want you," she whispered. "I want all of you."

Chapter Twenty-one

Gregory pulled back and stared into her eyes. "Are you sure this time, Violet? Because—"

She placed her fingers against his lips. "I'm sure."

Reaching behind her, he snatched their blankets from the backs of their saddles, grabbed the thin rope he used to string them together during rain, and proceeded to prepare them a shelter. Violet walked to a tree and leaned against it. She didn't think she'd ever seen him move so quickly. He kept glancing at her, the fire in his eyes scorching. There was also some doubt there, as if he expected her to change her mind at any second.

As a show of her commitment, she removed her shoes, then reached up beneath her torn gown and slid her expensive silk drawers down her legs, stepping out of them. Gregory had barely gotten blankets spread on the ground but abandoned his task. He walked over to her and, without saying a word, reached out and grabbed the back of her neck, bringing her lips to his. His hand slid over her exposed shoulder, and with a yank did away with what was left of her sleeve. He broke from the kiss, his lips moving down her neck, across the rise of her breasts. Violet tugged her dress lower.

His tongue teased her nipples through her shift; then his hand slid up her thigh. The tear in her dress gave him easy access to the place he sought. He stroked her there, made her hot and wet and achy for him. She unbuttoned his shirt and shoved it from his shoulders. He stopped long enough to shuck the damp garment. Their lips met again, his fingers found her, and hers went to the fastening of his pants.

Bravely she freed him from his confines and wrapped her hand around the hot, hard length of him. He groaned against her lips, gathered her up, and carried her beneath their makeshift tent. Their clothing quickly disappeared. Again his fingers found her, and hers found him. He made love to her with his kisses, with his fingers, until they moved against one another, until she began to tremble beneath him.

She groaned when his fingers ceased their steady strokes, but he showed her how to create the same torturous friction by rubbing his engorged member against the pulsing place between her legs. And her pleasure was increased, for she was controlling him, moving him against her. The pressure built as she continued. She heard his labored breathing next to her ear; then his hand replaced hers. He continued to rub himself against her, but he also did more.

He slipped inside of her, only enough to make her gasp in surprise. He gasped, too, but she didn't think it was in surprise. Before her mind even fully registered what he'd done, he was out again, applying pressure where these wonderful sensations were centered. He continued until she felt ready to burst; then again he penetrated her.

There was no pain. Instead, it felt as if he filled her completely. But she knew he hadn't. There was more of him.

"Gregory," she whispered, suddenly unsure of her decision.

"I'm not going to hurt you," he promised, but his voice was husky, laced with a passion she knew he couldn't rein in this time. She'd allowed him to go too far. She had no choice but to trust him.

As if he sensed her sudden distress, he withdrew and again stroked her until she forgot what he intended, forgot everything but the quest to reach release. She felt her passion building again, waiting to explode . . . then he switched tactics. He entered her again, gently and not as far as she knew he would reach. Magically he moved, in a way that he could be both inside of her and stimulate her at the same time. It was tremendous.

Violet's soft moans of pleasure made controlling his passion next to impossible, but for her, Gregory battled his own desires. For her, he'd go slowly, make certain he didn't frighten or hurt her in any way. Despite her toughness, her courage, she was still a delicate flower. A tender bud who had yet to bloom. He wanted her to open for him, to find the sunlight, to let go of her darkness.

The first arch of her hips against him pushed him deeper and nearly shattered his control. She felt so warm and tight, he could easily give in to his pleasure and forget about hers. But he couldn't be selfish, not with a woman as giving as Violet. Not with a woman who trusted him, of all men, above all others.

He captured her sweet lips. She trembled beneath him. When she sucked his tongue into her mouth, he slid himself deeper. She gasped softly; then he grasped her hips and showed her how to move against him, how to stimulate herself.

She caught the rhythm quickly, and he gave her control. How much of him she would take into her body would depend on how hard she arched against him. Her tentative movements proved grueling. Gregory waited as patiently as the circumstances would allow as Violet struggled against him, searching for her own release. He continued to give her more each time she moved and, at last, after what seemed an eternity, he was fully imbedded within her.

It was heaven. He might explode just from the sheer bliss of feeling her wrapped around him. He stilled the motion of her hips or she would set him off without her. Now he must take control.

* * *

Gregory filled her completely, and yet Violet felt no pain, only a hunger: a desperate need for what only he could give her. She wanted to arch against him again, to feed her need for release, but he had stopped her movements. He pressed his forehead against hers, breathing heavily; then he began to move slowly, steadily, in and out until she couldn't keep still. She moved with him, against him, creating friction, that wonderful heat where their bodies joined.

Their kisses further inflamed her. They were breathless brushes of lips merged with her soft sounds of pleasure and his masculine groans. She'd never known it could be like this with a man, and realized in her heart that it couldn't—not with any man, only with him. She felt no fear, no pain, no degradation, just pleasure and the certainty that, as with Vega, she would never be the same. But, unlike with Vega, this memory would be one she cherished.

Gregory's rhythm increased, and she matched him, took all he had to give, until they could no longer kiss, only gasp and stare into each other's eyes. The pressure inside of her built, clawed to get out, and she broke, splintered apart. She wrapped her legs around him and clung to him, moaning his name. He thrust harder, deeper, then she felt him tense, heard his groan of surrender. He kissed her face, whispered her name, convulsed inside of her.

"I'm sorry, Violet," he whispered. "I should have pulled away before . . . I couldn't, you feel too good."

She wasn't certain what he was talking about. Violet couldn't imagine why he was apologizing to her. He'd just changed her life. He rolled to his side, still holding her in his embrace. She buried her face against the warmth of his neck. His breath stirred the damp tendrils of hair framing her face. Then she cried. She cried because he wasn't the first, wasn't the one who had led her gently down the path to womanhood. She cried because Vega had made something so beautiful, so ugly.

"Did I hurt you, Violet?" Gregory asked.

She shook her head. "No. I'm crying because I wish you were the first."

He kissed the tears from her cheeks. "I am the first. The first to give you pleasure. This . . . us—it was different for me, too."

She lifted her head to look at him. "In what way?"

He stared into her eyes. "In a way I can't explain."

And he didn't bother to try. Instead he kissed her again. It was a long, deep, wet kiss that heated her blood, and she supposed his, because she felt him growing hard inside of her again. She wasn't even aware that a man could perform the act more than once in one night. Vega had quickly found his pleasure with her when he'd raped her, then rolled away and began snoring. But Gregory was nothing like Vega. What he made her feel was nothing like she'd ever felt before. And he would make her feel that way again—and still later, again.

The sound of gunshots woke her. Violet bolted up and turned to wake Gregory, only to find him gone. She clutched a blanket around her and crawled outside of the makeshift tent. The sight that greeted her was confusing. Gregory sat mounted and had the reins to her horse tied around his saddle horn. He pointed his gun skyward and fired a couple more shots.

"Gregory!" she shouted. "What are you doing?"

His gaze snapped to her. For just a second she saw something in his eyes she'd seen last night when he made love to her. A softness—something very close to love?—before his gaze hardened.

"I'm doing what's best for you, Violet."

"Best for me?" Her confusion grew. "If you keep firing that gun, you'll bring those guards from the swing station right to us!"

His jaw clenched. "I know. I don't want you to get hurt. Get dressed and be ready for them when they come."

A horrible suspicion made her stomach churn. "Gregory, don't do this to me. Don't—"

"Play your part, and you'll be fine," he interrupted. "You were never cut out for this life, Violet. You deserve better."

Anger raced through her, as strong as the passion she had felt for him the previous night. "You're damn right I deserve better! I trusted you! You can't leave me here!"

He stared at her, as if memorizing everything about her; then he glanced away. "Trusting me was your first mistake. Once a wolf, always a wolf."

Adding to her panic, he turned his horse away. "Gregory!" she shouted, then ran after him. He kicked his horse, dropped her valise, and left her standing in the dust. "You sorry son of a bitch!" she yelled, but her voice broke. Tears streamed down her face. She collapsed on the ground. Ten minutes later, that was how the posse found her.

Ten men surrounded her. One of them moved forward. Violet recognized him as one of the guards from the swing station. "This is the woman he took as a hostage. Are you all right, ma'am?"

Violet sat in the dirt, wearing only a blanket, tears streaking her face. She knew what they were all thinking. She shook her head. "No. I am not all right."

The man dismounted and walked to where she sat. "Do you have some clothes to put on?"

Her gaze darted toward her valise. "He at least left me that much dignity."

"Which way did he go?"

Gregory was smart. He would head in the opposite direction from Topeka, thinking those pursuing him would be searching ahead rather than behind them. Violet nodded to the north. "He took off that way."

"We heard gunshots," one man in the group said.

Numbness spread over her. She knew she should be feeling something—anger, hurt, something—but it was as if to do so would take more energy than she could muster.

"I managed to wrestle his gun from him," she maintained enough sense to explain. "I tried to shoot him but I missed. He took the gun from me and ran. I realize now the only reason he didn't shoot me was because he knew the gunfire would draw you men."

"We'll catch him," the guard promised. "He'll pay

for what he's done." He spun the cylinder of his revolver.

Once, those words might have soothed Violet. Her life had become about revenge. Yet regardless that Gregory had tricked and abandoned her, she didn't want to see him captured. She certainly didn't want to see him shot from the saddle as he tried to escape. Her numbness began to fade. Emotion rushed to the surface, and the truth found her: she loved him. God help her, but she did.

And for a moment last night, when she'd looked deep into his eyes, she'd thought he loved her, too. She'd thought nothing mattered but the two of them, and being together. She'd believed that somehow, some way, she had managed to make him love her despite her past. Through eyes threatening to water, she watched the guard walk to her valise and pick it up. He brought it to her.

"You need to get dressed. We'll see you safely back to the swing station."

A handful of men stayed, but the rest rode off in search of their quarry. Violet thanked God they believed her and rode in the opposite direction Gregory had gone. She felt eyes boring into her, speculation churning in the minds of the remaining men.

"Could I have some privacy?" she muttered, keeping her head bowed.

"Oh, sure. Let's give her a few minutes," the head guard said to the others.

Violet needed more than a few minutes to deal with what Gregory had done. It might take a lifetime. He'd said he didn't want her to get hurt. Was that really the truth? Or had the temptation of the money finally proven too much for him? A discreet cough reminded Violet that now was not the time to sort through her feelings, or to let anger get the best of her. She rose, moved into her makeshift tent, and dressed. She chose another dress, a plain one, but wore a pair of men's pants beneath.

Her gaze strayed to the blankets, and memories flashed through her mind—of Gregory making love to her. She quickly glanced away, grabbed her valise, and crawled outside. She walked to where the men sat mounted, their backs to her.

"I don't have a horse," she said.

"You can ride with me," the same guard who'd approached her earlier said. "You can wait at the swing station until we catch the son of a bitch."

The idea of riding double with the man didn't appeal to Violet. The idea of them catching the "son of a bitch" appealed less. Still, Violet let the guard help her onto his horse. She kept her valise, which luckily didn't hold much, between her front and his back.

The journey to reach the swing station seemed to take an eternity. For one thing, a woman didn't make love to a man all night and ride a horse comfortably the next day.

Once the guard helped her dismount, he said, "I'll stay here with you, ma'am. The rest of you, ride the road behind us and make sure that outlaw didn't change directions."

Violet hoped her face didn't show her distress over his order, but then again, maybe she should respond. "What about my husband? Did anyone find him?"

The guard's face reddened. "Well, we ain't exactly looked, ma'am. Your health and the outlaw being our major concerns."

She grabbed the man's sleeve. "I have to know if he's dead or alive. He may be lying hurt, bleeding . . . or if he's dead, I need to know."

The guard glanced at the others, then back at her. "How far back would you say it was that he fell from his horse?"

"I-I'm not certain," she stammered. "Five miles?" At his frown, she added. "Maybe less. I was fleeing for my life and can't be sure."

With a sigh, the guard turned back to the mounted men. "Have a look-see. Make it quick, and hurry back if you find anything. If you don't, keep riding. If you haven't caught the outlaw by dark, report back here."

"Thank you," Violet whispered.

The guard nodded and indicated that she should go inside. The stationmaster was there. He glanced at her, then quickly glanced away.

"Can I get you something, ma'am?" he asked. "Some food? Water?"

"No," she answered. If she could find a way to sneak out, she could steal a horse and be on her way.

"You should," he insisted. "For the baby and all."

"The baby?" Oh, she'd forgotten the drama she'd added to her abduction. "I suppose you're right."

"At least you know . . . I mean, that it's your husband's child and all."

She wanted to roll her gaze, but she refrained. Of course a man would automatically assume that if an outlaw had abducted a young woman and kept her overnight, he would have raped her. She supposed if it really had been an outlaw with her, she no doubt would have been assaulted.

"Yes," she agreed. "At least I know that."

"Sit," the guard suggested. "I'm keeping a close watch. He won't get his hands on you again. I'm sure the sheriff in Topeka will want to have a long conversation with you in case we don't catch the varmint."

"The sheriff?"

He nodded. "For a description and all. You, ah, did get a good look at him, right?"

She lowered her gaze, and the blush she felt spreading over her cheeks wasn't simply good acting. "Yes. I got a very good look at him."

"I figured as much," the guard said. He pulled out a chair for her.

Violet had become a prisoner. Even if the man suspected she had nothing to do with the payroll robbery, he wouldn't let a witness out of his sight—unless Gregory was caught, and she didn't even want to think about that.

The meal the stationmaster prepared stuck in her throat. He wasn't a good cook. The structure was one large room, but the only places to rest were the stationmaster's dirty cot or the floor. Violet chose the floor. She rested for a while. Exhaustion from a night of very little sleep caused her to drift off.

The sound of men returning roused her. She scrambled up, fear that Gregory would be with them making her heart pound wildly inside her chest. After the men shuffled in, and her gaze had roamed every face, she breathed a small sigh of relief.

"He just vanished," she heard one guard complain to the stationmaster. "Gone, like a wisp of smoke." The same man glanced at her. "Sorry, ma'am. We didn't find your husband, either."

Her legs almost buckled with relief. Violet moved to a chair and sat. She buried her face in her hands and wept. Of course, the men didn't know she cried from happiness rather than sorrow or frustration. Gregory had gotten away . . . at least for now.

A hand touched her shoulder. She jerked free. The guard who'd watched her during the day said, "The driver is going on to Topeka tomorrow. You can ride in the coach. A handful of us will accompany you; the rest will keep searching."

She supposed she could arrive in Topeka under worse circumstances. The guards could be taking her in as a prisoner, rather than as a witness against the man who'd robbed the payroll. But then, that was what Gregory had intended when he'd left her. But was that all he intended? Would he meet up with her later? Or would he take the money and run?

Those questions plagued Violet throughout the journey to Topeka the next day. The bouncing coach constantly reminded her of her and Gregory's night together. She was sore, and in a place that kept making hard contact against the seats every time the stage hit a rut in the road. How could Gregory do this to her—make love to her, stare into her eyes with what she believed were feelings that went deeper than passion, and then abandon her?

He'd made love to her because that was what she had asked him to do, a small voice inside her head reminded her. He'd also talked about how she and he could take the money and go anywhere they wanted, become anyone they chose. But now . . . every man for himself, that was how he'd been raised.

Violet ached in more places than one by the time the coach pulled into Topeka. She hated the way she stared out the windows, looked at every face she saw walking the streets in the hope that one would be Gregory's. But his face was not to be found among any. The coach pulled up in front of the sheriff's office. The guards climbed down. One opened the door and helped her out. All escorted her inside.

The sheriff was an older man, one who ironically reminded her of Sheriff Johnson in St. Louis. He glanced up from his paperwork. "What's going on?"

One of the guards quickly explained the circumstances, admitting rather shamefacedly that they hadn't apprehended the robber.

"And you were taken as a hostage by this man?" the sheriff asked.

Violet nodded. "H-he also shot my husband, but Gregory hasn't been found, either."

"I'll take over from here," the sheriff said to the guards. "Mrs. . . . ?"

"Kline," she supplied.

"Would you have a seat? I need to ask you a few questions."

As the others left the jail, Violet seated herself across from the sheriff.

"Now, tell me everything that happened," he said.

She calmly told him that she and her husband had been traveling from their home in St. Louis across Missouri to Kansas to look at ranch property. She told him about meeting the Burtons in Harvest Grove, and about walking into the bank to bid Mr. Burton good-bye when she'd found herself caught up in the middle of a robbery. Violet made sure to mention that Mr. Burton had worried over telling the robber that the payroll had already been taken by the coach. She told him that Mr. Burton expressed his concern that the robber might pursue the coach in hopes of stealing the money.

"And you and your husband were ambushed by this man on the road?"

"Yes, he shot Gregory and I ran from him, but then he found me at the swing station and took me as a hostage so he could steal the money."

The sheriff scratched his chin. "That was convenient for him, you being there and all. You and the payroll."

A prickle of unease lifted the fine hairs on the back of her neck. "I would rather think it was more convenient that the stage had stopped there for a change of horses. The swing station was my only hope of protection from the man. I was relieved when it came into view."

"Of course," he agreed. "And your husband hasn't been found?"

She tried to summon tears, but she guessed she'd already cried herself dry. "No."

He sighed, then glanced down at his desk. "Another robbery. I've been getting some strange wires from towns ranging from St. Louis all across Missouri. Confusing messages about robberies being pulled." His gaze drifted over her. "While the reports have varied, I wonder if it's not the same guy carrying out the robberies. Or, perhaps the same gang. Some reports have even gone so far as to suggest a *woman* was involved."

Violet's heart lurched. This was what she'd wanted—sort of. She'd wanted all the robberies to be blamed on one man: her father. But not her. She tried to keep her face blank. "That is strange," she agreed. "But I don't see where it has anything to do with me."

His eyes roamed her again, and in a speculative manner. "I hope you understand that it is my duty to make certain of that before allowing you to leave."

If she gave him time to fit too many pieces of the puzzle together, she feared he might arrive at the correct conclusion. "I'm not sure what you're saying, Sheriff."

"First things first," he commented. "Can you describe this man you say took you as a hostage?"

"Yes." This was what she'd wanted all along. She described her father—to best of her ability, since she hadn't seen him in six years. "And he bragged to me about his name," she added, hoping to throw suspicion off of herself.

The sheriff's brows lifted. "He told you his name?"

She lowered her gaze. "I would rather not go into the circumstances regarding it, but he said his name was Dalton."

"Dalton? Hmmm. That is an interesting coincidence. The man, or woman—the clerk wasn't certain later—that robbed a bank in St. Louis claimed the name of Dalton. In fact, many of the robbers mentioned that name."

Violet tried not to squirm. "Well, it was obviously the same man, then."

"Didn't you just tell me that *you* were from St. Louis?"

Her gaze snapped up. "Yes, I am. What of it?"

He shrugged. "Just seems like another coincidence. Have you got anyone there who might give you a character reference? You *and* your husband?"

By placing her in this circumstance, Gregory had forced Violet to do what she'd never intended—bring Miles into her plans. But she had no choice. "Miles Traften is my uncle. He's a very prestigious man in St. Louis. Maybe you have heard of him?"

The sheriff looked as if his dessert had just been snatched from him. "Yes, I have heard of him. Very well-to-do, I understand."

"I have been provided for quite nicely," she said, and infused enough snootiness to her tone to make him blush. "I have no reason to steal money. And neither does my husband, who is a partner in one my uncle's lucrative businesses."

"I guess not," the sheriff agreed. But when he

looked at her, she saw suspicion still clouding his eyes. "You don't mind if I send for him? Just to make certain you are who you say you are?"

Violet didn't have to pretend she was outraged. She rose. "Are you calling me a liar?"

"I'm just doing my job, ma'am, and hope you won't take offense."

"Well, I am offended," she shot back. "I have been taken hostage by a bank robber, a man who shot and probably killed my husband, a man wh-who took advantage of me, and you are insinuating that I have something to do with a string of robberies that have taken place across the territory?"

"Why were you and your husband traveling by horseback, Mrs. Kline?" he asked. "With your means, surely you could have traveled in comfort across Missouri to Kansas."

"We like to ride," she huffed. "We enjoy seeing the countryside."

"Where exactly is your destination?"

She said the first thing that came to mind. "Coffeyville."

"Coffeyville?" His bushy brows rose again. "A town rumored to be a Dalton hangout? I believe one of them even lives there on the outskirts of town, although the law has never been able to catch him at anything other than being drunk."

Her stomach knotted up. She shouldn't have said Coffeyville. Not in the same conversation as the name Dalton. She'd backed herself into a corner.

"Another coincidence, Mrs. Kline?" he asked when she didn't speak.

Although it sickened her, she had no choice but to say, "I think you had better send for my uncle."

"Oh, I will," he assured her. "And I think you should stay here in Topeka until he arrives. I will, of course, provide you with an escort."

A guard. Not one to protect her, but one to make sure that she couldn't leave. Well, Violet had eluded Gregory more than once—though she'd used unscrupulous methods. Certainly she wouldn't kiss some strange man or try to get him into bed with her in order to escape. Gregory . . . well, Gregory had been different . . . or so she'd thought.

"Am I to be kept in jail until my uncle arrives?" she asked, lifting her chin.

"Of course not," the man answered. "I will secure a room for you at one of our fine establishments."

"I have no money. My h-husband carried our funds."

"Well, since they didn't find his body, maybe he is still alive. Maybe he'll show up in Topeka and the two of you will be reunited."

"I pray that is the case," she said, praying the opposite given the sheriff's suspicion.

If Gregory did something foolish, as he had in Independence, and tried to rescue her, they would both be labeled as outlaws. The pieces of the sheriff's puzzle would snap firmly into place. Even if Gregory reappeared as her wounded husband, the sheriff might find it suspect unless Miles arrived and backed up their story.

"If your uncle is Miles Traften, I'm sure he'll be happy to settle your bills once he arrives, Mrs.

Kline." The sheriff rose. "Now I figure you'd like to clean up and rest."

"Yes," she said, and allowed the lawman to escort her from his office.

The room he secured for her was nice—the best money could buy—but it didn't change that it was a jail cell. Her own personal hell. She wondered how long she would be detained in Topeka. She still had plans to complete. With or without Gregory, she had to rescue her sister and brothers. And with or without her plan to frame him, she had to confront her father.

Chapter Twenty-two

A whole month! Violet paced the confines of her room. Where was Miles? Each day that passed made the sheriff more suspicious of her, and each day reminded her that she had unfinished business in Coffeyville. Gregory had indeed abandoned her. Violet had trouble coming to grips with his betrayal. She suffered a variety of emotions: anger at him one moment, hope the next.

Hope that he would rescue her. Dreams that he would come with her to Coffeyville. Fantasies that he would ask her to marry him—would agree to take her family in as his own. But her wishes were like the stories Violet's mother had once whispered to her in the dark: they were only fairy tales.

She had to be strong now, more than ever. No one would make her feel discarded or dirty again. She wasn't trash, and her siblings weren't trash, either. She'd already fought one demon from the past, and won. There was only one left, and she would face him, too. She didn't know how she would do it, though.

A guard or the sheriff accompanied her everywhere she went now. People stared, whispered about her. Miles's refusal to answer the sheriff's wire, they said, was an indication that he might have no idea who Violet Kline was, and had therefore ignored the summons.

Of course, she couldn't have told the sheriff she was Violet Mallory—and Miles was smart enough to make the appropriate inferences. So Violet was worried. And her confinement drove her crazy. She felt tied into knots. If Miles didn't make an appearance soon and clear her of suspicion, she'd have to take matters into her own hands.

A soft rap on the door made her jump. She wondered for a moment if simply willing Miles to appear had worked, and rushed to the door. Miles did not stand on the other side. The sheriff had come to call, and brought a man with him. One she'd never seen before.

"Mrs. Kline," the sheriff drawled sarcastically. "One of your escorts mentioned that you haven't been eating well. He did so in the company of a man who happened to be on the payroll stage that was robbed. The man commented that you pleaded with them to spare the child you carried, if not yourself, and he worried that you should take care to eat. I thought it best to have Dr. Mosley have a look at you."

Violet felt her mouth drop open. She quickly closed it, her mind working frantically. "I—I fear, everything considered, all that's happened, well, I fear I might have lost the child."

The sheriff didn't appear a bit surprised. The doctor, on the other hand, frowned.

"Then I should check you over for certain, Mrs. Kline. Sometimes such a loss can cause infection. Our good sheriff has need to worry."

The good sheriff was trying to trip her up. Uncover another lie. The sheriff smiled at her, and Dr. Mosley stepped inside of the room and closed the door.

"Remove your gown, please," he ordered.

Violet's hand flew to the lace of her collar. The man was old, but he was a man all the same. "I assure you, I am fine. An examination is unnecessary."

He cast her a stern glance. "I am the doctor, not you, Mrs. Kline. If you are fine, I should be the one to assure you, not the other way around."

She decided that maybe being honest for a change might help her situation. "I am uncomfortable with men touching me," she admitted.

The man sighed. "I have heard the rumors, Mrs. Kline. That outlaw, he had you overnight, and, considering how you were found, it is an easy assumption to make that the foul man took liberties with you."

Well, the foul man had. And he'd done a good job of it, too. Violet didn't dream about Victor Vega anymore. She dreamed about Gregory, about his hands on her, his mouth. In the mornings she awoke, throbbing for the feel of him inside of her, her breasts aching for his touch.

"Yes," she answered simply.

The doctor shook his graying head. "I'm sorry for you, but now an examination is even more necessary. The man could have—"

"I told you, I don't feel comfortable with this," she interrupted.

"I will be gentle," he assured her. "And as quick as possible." His gaze hardened. "The sheriff will count your refusal to see to your own good health as suspicious."

The sheriff was already suspicious of her. The man she claimed as her uncle had not arrived to verify her story. The husband she claimed had been shot had been found neither dead, nor alive. She had no choice but to allow the doctor to examine her. With trembling fingers, Violet unbuttoned her gown.

The examination was embarrassing. Violet didn't care if the man was old or not; having his fingers probing and poking her was almost more than she could stand. She was thankful he was true to his word and didn't take long.

"You may dress, and—"

A knock sounded at the door. The sheriff and his impatience to uncover another lie, no doubt.

"Finish dressing and I'll be back to you in a moment," the doctor said.

As he moved toward the door, Violet hurried to do his bidding. She'd barely gotten her dress buttoned up when a man stepped into the room. Her knees nearly buckled.

"Miles," she whispered, tears rushing to her eyes.

"Violet, thank God you're all right." He held out his arms and she rushed into them. She glanced over his shoulder and saw the sheriff frown. She smiled at him.

"Then this woman truly is your niece?" he asked.

"Of course she's my niece," Miles snapped. "And I demand to know what in heaven's name is going on here?"

"It's a long story, Uncle Miles," she said, then looked at the sheriff. "Perhaps these good men will allow me time to tell it to you."

Miles glanced around the room. "Where is Gregory?" he asked in a snarl.

Violet felt a lump form in her throat.

"Her husband?" the sheriff asked.

"Her—"

"Husband," Violet interrupted, staring into Miles's wide eyes. She felt tears gather. "I'm afraid he might be dead."

At least Miles appeared upset by the news. "Dead? But how, what, and why—"

"Shot by an outlaw chasing us," she explained. "Please," she beseeched the sheriff and the doctor. "Allow me time to break this horrible news to my uncle."

She thought the sheriff would argue, but the doctor stepped forward and took the lawman's arm. "She should be allowed her privacy, Ben." He smiled sadly at Violet. "It's early yet, and you're not far along, but I'm fairly sure you didn't lose the child. You are still pregnant."

The sheriff looked less than pleased again, she noted as a dark cloud descended upon her. Miles's mouth fell open. The men left the room. The door closed. Violet saw spots dancing before her eyes. Then she saw nothing.

"Violet! Violet!"

She felt her wrists being rubbed. A voice floated to her from faraway. Miles's voice. Was she at home, then? No wait, she wasn't in St. Louis. She was in Topeka, suspected of robbing a stage, or of at least being in cahoots with the robber. She *had* been in cahoots with him. She had done more than pull off a few bank heists and the stage robbery with him. She was pregnant.

Suddenly she bolted up, gasping for breath. Miles's bleary face came into focus. He looked pale and shaken.

"Violet? Are you all right?"

No, she wasn't all right. She was on the brink of hysterics and couldn't seem to control her emotions. Violet burst into tears. Miles's arms went around her.

"Oh, Miles," she said softly, clinging to his solid strength. "I've done some horrible things."

He patted her gently on the back. "Violet, tell me what's going on. And . . . why this farce of your being married to Gregory Kline?" He suddenly pulled back from her. "Oh, Lord, you're not really married to him, are you?"

301

"No," she quickly assured him.

After breathing a soft sigh of relief, he tensed. "Then whose child are you carrying?"

Tears welled up in her eyes again. "His," she answered weakly.

"That sorry bastard," Miles thundered. "Is he really dead?"

She shook her head. "No. He took the money we robbed from the stage and—"

"And he left you to answer for the crime," Miles said in a growl. "I'm glad he's not dead, because I am going to kill him!" He rose and started pacing beside the bed. "I asked myself why I entrusted you to him once he'd left. I was desperate, but even so, I knew he'd do something underhanded. After a week passed and he didn't return, I called myself a fool and set out in search myself."

Violet was confused. "Then, you didn't get the wire the sheriff sent to you?"

"No," he answered. "I've been traveling what I assumed would be your route to Coffeyville. Upon my arrival in Topeka, I did what I've done during my journey at every town: I stopped by the local sheriff's office and asked after you. Once I'd entered and introduced myself, the man jumped up and said he had been waiting for my arrival. You could have knocked me over with a feather. He said he had you safely secured in a hotel here. Then he started to ramble on about robberies and you being taken hostage and, well . . . I shut him up and demanded to see you."

Thank goodness Miles had shut the man up before too much conversation passed between them. "I'm glad you demanded to see me right away," she said. "Because I've lied to him." Her voice broke. "I've lied to you; I lied to Gregory. My whole life since I left Texas has been a lie."

Miles walked to the bed and sat beside her. "I know about your past, Violet. At least most of it. Lilla told me. Only because she wanted me to understand you, understand the screaming at night, your fear of men. I knew your father had sold you to a man at fourteen. Lilla allowed me to fill in the rest. That's why when you disappeared, I feared you had gone to seek revenge."

She felt miserable, sick, and just plain scared. "You were right. I did. I have. I killed a man in Independence. The same man who beat and raped me." Then she burst into tears.

Miles reached over and took her hand in his. "Had you told me his name and where to find him, I would have done the job for you long ago."

Shock still overwhelmed her, and Miles's reaction added to it. "You're not repulsed by me? You're not—"

"I'm not judging you, Violet," Miles interrupted. "It isn't my place." He squeezed her hand gently. "You have been like a daughter to me these past three years. I have grown to love you, and to love you without condition. Regardless of who you were or what you've done, I see inside of you. I see the goodness there."

A compliment had never made her feel so low. Miles didn't see the same thing she saw when she looked in the mirror. "All I see is the hate, the anger,

303

and the bitterness over the fact that my whole life couldn't have been what it's been like with you for the last three years. My father is a drunkard who beats those he should love the most. My mother was a coward who couldn't stand up to him." Her head bowed with the shame she felt. "I'm not good. I can't forgive the way you have forgiven me."

The man who'd treated her so kindly during the past three years tilted her chin up, forcing her to look at him. "Not until you learn to forgive yourself, Violet. Deep inside, you still think what happened is your fault—that you could have changed things, done something other than what you did. You're not like your father, Violet. You're not like your mother, who stood by and watched, too afraid to stand up for her own children. If you can't love who you were, love who you've become: a strong, courageous young woman."

What she'd become was a thief, a killer, and a woman carrying a child out of wedlock. She felt overwhelmed. "What am I going to do?"

"We'll think of something," Miles assured her. He straightened, released her hand, and the softness faded from his eyes. "I'm assuming Kline seduced you. He talked you into this wild payroll robbery. Hell, for all I know, he was the one who robbed the bank in St. Louis. The incident took place on the very day he arrived back from Wyoming."

"And the very day I disappeared," she reminded him. "I robbed that bank and you know it, Miles." She drew a shaky breath. "In fact, I've robbed two since, and I stole money from Victor Vega before I killed him. Gregory did not seduce me; I—I wanted to be with him."

Miles shook his head as if he couldn't accept the truth. He rose from the bed. "I don't understand, Violet."

She assumed he meant why had she had robbed banks. "I had this plan to set my father up. I want to make sure he goes to prison for what he's done to me."

"So the payroll? You pretended to be a hostage so Gregory could rob it—that was your idea?"

"No," she admitted. "That was Gregory's idea. And it worked, but then . . . well, he took the money. He fired shots in the air to make certain those looking for us found me."

With pinched lips, Miles said, "Well, at least he's done one smart thing in his life. Better that you were caught and believed to be the hostage rather than hunted down and shot for taking that payroll."

"I'm not sure those were his motives," she admitted. "I thought he might come for me, but he hasn't."

"And he never will," Miles assured her. "Gregory can be very charming. He's a wolf in sheep's clothing. Always has been and always will be. I'm sure he misled you."

Violet straightened upon the bed. As angry as she felt with Gregory, she also felt moved to defend him. "He never lied to me. He never tried to make me believe he was anything other than what he was— an admitted coward. A man who placed his own wants and desires above everyone else. Yet he proved otherwise on several occasions. He risked his life for me, for a group of girls who had also been abused by Victor Vega. He even went to confront Vega when I told him the truth about my past. He went to kill him, only I ended up doing the honors."

Miles snorted in disdain. "Gregory Kline? That *is* who we're talking about, isn't it?"

Passion renewing her strength, Violet rose from the bed. She felt dizzy for a moment but steadied herself. "You may be forgiving of me, Miles, but you never were where Gregory was concerned. Even when he worked hard for you in Wyoming, you wouldn't give him the respect he deserved. You marked him off your list of worthy men long ago, and you never intended to let him back on it."

Miles glanced around. "Where is your hero now, Violet? The fact that he isn't here, has left you with child and probably headed for parts unknown with enough money to set himself up nicely, is testament enough to his character."

It was an observation with which she couldn't argue. One she didn't want to deal with at the moment. Violet suddenly felt exhausted, and so much raced through her mind. Good Lord, she was going to have a baby. She needed time to absorb all that had happened in the past hour.

"I'm happy to see you, Miles, but I'm tired. I'd like to rest for a while."

"Of course," he said. "I will secure a room and we'll talk more later. I will get you out of this mess and back home where you belong."

She watched him walk to the door and open it. A guard stood outside. Miles bristled.

"What are you doing, young man?"

"I—I . . . well, I'm watching—that is, protecting Mrs. Kline."

"I will assume that duty now."

The guard's face turned red. "But the sheriff—"

"And I will speak with the sheriff," Miles interrupted. "You may leave and find something else to do."

Miles was a gentle soul with Violet and his daughter, Lilla, but he was a raging bull with any man who dared lock horns with him. The guard backed down and hurried off.

"We will dine together in an hour."

"Yes," she said, then watched him close the door. A second later Violet realized Miles trusted too much those he shouldn't, and those he should, not enough. She'd been freed from her prison. And she had a mission to complete.

Chapter Twenty-three

Gregory watched from the shadows. Something had gone wrong. Miles Traften crept along the darkened streets, glancing over his shoulder as if he felt eyes following him. What was he up to? And where the hell was Violet? Gregory had spent a good two weeks trying to trip up those stage guards, making false trails then doubling back. Then he'd come to Topeka. He'd been waiting, watching, knowing if Violet got into trouble, she'd send for Miles. And Miles had arrived two days ago. If everything had gone smoothly, Traften and Violet would have already left for St. Louis. They hadn't.

Obviously everything had not gone smoothly. Gregory cursed under his breath and left the shadows. He should be halfway across Kansas by now. He should be planning where he'd go, and what identity he'd choose to give himself, but instead he'd hung around. He couldn't leave Violet, not until he knew she'd be all right.

Miles stopped at the livery. He opened the doors and slipped inside. A moment later another man—one Gregory could only assume was the owner—stepped out, stuffing a wad of bills into his pocket. Miles might not believe money could buy happiness, but he obviously knew it could buy anything else—including the opportunity to make someone look the other way.

Gregory crept to the livery and went inside. Miles was in the process of saddling a horse. Not two, he noted, only one.

"Going somewhere, Miles?" he asked.

The man spun around. He squinted in the dim light from a lantern. His eyes widened. "You," he said in a growl. "What are you doing here, Kline? I figured you'd be halfway across the state by now."

He wasn't in the mood to mince words. "Where's Violet?"

"Violet is none of your business!" the older man said in a hiss. "You stay away from her. You've already caused her enough trouble."

Gregory approached him. "I figured you'd get her out of whatever trouble she might get into. But something's happened, hasn't it? Does the sheriff still think she was in on that robbery? Is he too honest for you to buy off? What's going on, Miles?"

The man punched him. Gregory stumbled back a step. He wiped the blood from the corner of his mouth.

"Don't think I won't hit you back, old man," he warned. "My days of courting you are over."

"If you don't get out of my sight, and stay away from Violet, your days are numbered, Kline!"

Traften didn't intimidate Gregory, though. Not anymore. Not with Violet's future on the line. "I'm not leaving until you tell me what's going on."

Miles glared at him. "I don't have time for this, Kline. I have to catch up . . ." His voice trailed off.

Gregory's gut twisted. "With Violet. She gave you the slip, didn't she?"

Miles turned away. He slapped a saddle on the back of his horse. "What she did or did not do is no longer your concern. I will take care of Violet. Take your precious money and get the hell out of here."

"She's headed for Coffeyville," Gregory said.

"I know that," Miles barked.

Gregory was curious about what else Miles knew. "Do you know why?"

The man cast him a dark glance. "Yes. I know all about Violet's past. So don't think you're going to shock me with the details."

"You could have told me what I was getting mixed up in."

Miles pulled the cinch on the saddle tight. "I wasn't sure about everything. Lilla only told me a little."

He'd thought he knew Miles. Knew his type. At one time he thought they were both the same type. "You were aware of Violet's past, and you took her into your home? Doted upon her? Treated her—"

"I love that girl," Miles interrupted angrily. "Do

310

you have any idea what kind of person she is? How strong she is to have overcome all that's happened to her without letting it destroy her? Yes, she sought vengeance for the wrongs committed against her, is still seeking it, but can I blame her? No. Even after what you've done to her, she still defends you to me. She believes you are brave and honorable. But you and I know better, don't we, Gregory?"

An awful feeling washed over him. One he'd never felt before. Or not for a long time. He felt shame—deep, soul-shaking shame that Violet still saw in him what no one else could see. Shame that she still might believe in him when he'd given her no reason.

Miles brushed past him, leading his horse. "Take the money and run, Gregory. Prove her wrong." He paused. "And you lied to me. You said you'd behave like a gentleman with her. I know you have not."

It surprised him that Violet would tell Miles they had been intimate. He couldn't imagine why she would. "I didn't seduce her," he said. "And you knew she wasn't innocent when you asked me to make that promise."

Miles face looked red by the flimsy lantern light. "I also knew she wasn't with child at the time!"

Gregory felt as if he'd just been gut-kicked by a mule. A moment later, relief spread through him. "You don't understand, Miles. Violet must have failed to tell you that she only pretended to be with child when I took her hostage during the robbery. It was just a ploy to win the men's sympathy."

Miles glared at him. "Tell that to the doctor who examined her two days ago because the sheriff

311

wanted her story verified." He sighed, disgust evident on his weary features. "But never fear, Gregory. I'll take of Violet and the child. You and I know they will both be better off without you."

The truth wasn't any easier on him the second time around. He was going to be a father. Gregory couldn't even fathom that type of responsibility. And Violet—what had she thought when she'd learned the news? He shouldn't have just assumed she was right when she'd said she was barren. He should have taken precautions in spite of her beliefs, as he'd claimed he would. But he hadn't, because he was selfish. He'd been thinking only of his pleasure, not her safety or her future.

Miles was right: he was no shining example for a child. He was no decent man who could love and protect Violet—love her because of her goodness, instead of resenting her for a past over which she'd had no control. Violet and his child both deserved better than a man like him—a man who spent a night making love to a woman—a woman who stirred emotions inside of him he'd never felt, a woman he was in love with—only to leave her come morning.

And yes, he'd done what he thought was best for her . . . but he'd also done what everyone expected from him: he'd taken the money and run. He'd wanted to buy himself a new life. One he could be proud of. He wanted the respect and prestige that he could never earn from those who already knew him, but that he might easily purchase from unsuspecting fools.

At that moment, Gregory hated himself more than

he imagined either Miles or Violet could or ever would. What he hated the most, as he watched Miles shake his head and walk away, was knowing that even now he didn't have the courage to be more than either of them expected.

"Sorry, Violet," he said softly. "Every man for himself."

Horse thievery: another crime Violet had added to her long list of hanging offenses when she'd escaped four days ago. She'd had no choice. It wasn't as if she'd been able to run around Topeka purchasing what she needed, even if she'd had the funds to do so. She'd donned her man's disguise, slipped from the hotel, and had taken her pick of horses tied to a hitching post outside one of the local saloons.

In the saddle packs, she'd found hardtack. She still didn't have a gun, though. Nor did she have any evidence to set up her father for her crimes. She had nothing. Nothing but the courage to face Harold Dalton again, and her determination to see her siblings rescued from the drunken bastard.

But Violet realized all that she had been given in that moment. If her journey since the morning she'd robbed the bank in St. Louis had led her down the wrong path, it had also shown her the way. Violet had learned things about herself she didn't know. She'd found courage even while staring her worst nightmare in the face. She felt compassion for others, like the poor mistreated girls she'd freed from Vega's whorehouse.

She knew that although outlaw blood ran in her

veins, a life of crime was not for her. Neither could she ever give a man her body, without first giving him her heart. She was worthy of a man's love, and worthy of loving him in return. It no longer mattered to her that her father didn't love her, that he'd mistreated her. Life had sent her people who did love her, who had treated her kindly.

The most important lesson that Violet had learned was that no matter how far a person sunk into the mud of life's injustices, he or she could pull themselves out. Yes, she'd been dealt a cruel hand, but she had been given a chance to draw new cards.

Who a person became was up to them. She would face her father again, but not as a beaten, frightened child. She'd face him with pride over who she'd become, not with her head bowed in shame over who she once was. And her child, the one she carried inside of her, would not grow up feeling shame, either.

Her hand strayed to her still flat stomach. She'd been too tied into knots during her stay in Topeka to notice her lack of a monthly flow. It had never occurred to her that Vega might be the one who couldn't reproduce, which was obviously the case. Now she understood why Gregory had apologized to her after they had made love. He'd planted his seed inside of her. One that had taken root.

She couldn't think about her current situation now—not the possible responsibility of raising a baby on her own, or how she would support the child, and her siblings. Violet only knew that she would find a way. And deep down, she didn't believe she'd have to have to find her way alone.

Even if Gregory hadn't shown up to rescue her in Topeka. Even if he'd abandoned her after a night spent making love, she still believed in him. Maybe she was a fool, a fool in love, but some small part of her held out hope he'd change his mind, change directions, change everything he'd been taught to believe . . . for her.

Miles would come after her, too; she knew that with certainty. She'd only thrown him off for a day. After penning him a note begging off dinner because she didn't feel well, she'd deceived him once again. But she'd had good cause. She'd slipped away, afraid to involve him further in her troubles. She wasn't certain her blood father wouldn't kill her given half a chance, and Violet knew he wouldn't hesitate to kill a stranger. Miles had done too much for her. She couldn't ask him to risk his life, as well. Though she still feared he would follow her, she hoped he would arrive too late to be in any danger—or of any help.

Weary from the grueling pace she'd set for herself, Violet found her bedroll and settled on the hard ground. She'd been riding for the past four days. She had to reach Coffeyville before anyone caught up with her . . . and the pregnancy caused her to tire easily. She worried about pushing herself when doing so might cause her to lose the child. She wanted the baby. She loved Gregory.

She almost smiled while imagining his expression were he to learn the news. He wouldn't be able to see himself in the role of father. She could, though. Gregory's problem was that no one had ever believed in him. No one had ever counted on him. No one had ever trusted their life to him, or the life of another. He didn't know himself. Not the way she knew he could be.

As she settled down for the night, she stared up at the stars overhead. She ached for Gregory. Burned for him. She'd been waiting for him all of her life; she just hadn't known it. She closed her eyes and willed him to come to her—begged him to love her, and sometime during the night, he did.

His mouth found hers in the darkness; his hands cupped her swollen breasts. She inhaled his scent, reveled in his body heat warming her chilled skin. His mouth moved lower, his tongue teasing her nipples. His long, slender fingers moved down her skin, found the core of her, where she pulsed with need for him. He stroked her until she writhed, until she begged for more. Then she felt the thickness of him, the hard, hot length of him sliding inside of her. She moaned his name, dug her nails into his broad shoulders.

"I love you, Violet," he whispered. "I love everything about you."

His words poured fuel over the fire raging inside of her. Violet arched against him, gasped for breath. "I love you, too," she said in a moan. "I'll always love you."

He drove harder, deeper, faster, and she rode the wave of pleasure only he had shown her. She clung to him, striving, reaching, matching his movements in order to find release. It was almost upon her when she felt him slipping away. She tried to grab him, to pull him back to her, but he left her. Violet sat up, trying to grasp thin air. Sweat coated her body. Dawn streaked the sky. "Gregory," she whispered. But he did not answer. He was not there—had never been there except in her dream.

Violet tried to slow her breathing, the pounding of her heart. She'd wanted to take Vega's power over her and give it to another. Gregory had it now. The ability to slip into her dreams. To be so real she thought she still smelled him on her, felt his warmth, the lingering taste of him upon her lips.

Where was he? Why couldn't she command him in life as easily as she had commanded him in her dream? His voice still echoed in her ears. *"I love you."* Violet shook her head, trying to get the sound, smell, and feel of him from her. She rose, her legs aching from too many hours in the saddle, and prepared for what she must do. Today she would reach Coffeyville.

Chapter Twenty-four

The run-down cabin where she'd grown up came into view. Violet nearly retched at the sight of it. There was no flood of fond memories, recollections of a childhood spent laughing, running carefree through meadows of wildflowers. There were only thoughts of beatings, and crying. There were stories whispered to her in the dark by her mother—maybe the only hope she'd been able to give. Stories with happy endings. Considering, Violet didn't think hers would be one of them.

The place seemed quiet. Deserted. She hoped it wasn't. To come all this way, to do all she'd done, only to find her family gone again—that would be the cruelest injustice. She nudged her horse forward. A figure stepped out onto the porch. Violet jerked her mount to a halt, her heart pounding; she didn't want to be seen.

"Get your skinny ass back in here and fix me something to eat!"

Violet's blood ran cold. She knew that voice, and the tone of it hadn't changed in six years. The figure on the porch, a young girl, ran a hand through wild hair. Shoulders slumped, she stared back at the open doorway.

"Rose!" the voice shouted again. "If I have to tell you again, I'll beat you black and blue."

"Rose," Violet whispered. Tears sprung to her eyes. Her sister had been a child when Violet had been sold. Now a young woman stood before her, hints of maturity apparent through her thin shift. Violet could have been staring at herself, all those years ago.

"I'm coming," the girl shouted, then went back inside.

A quick glance around the area didn't turn up her brothers, but Violet did spot a small cross sticking up out of the ground. Two sticks tied together, as if crafted by a child. Her mother's grave. Violet nudged her horse toward the cabin.

Once she reached the shack, Violet dismounted. The porch steps still creaked beneath her feet, as they had always done. She walked through the open door. Her sister stood at the table, dishing beans onto a plate. She glanced up, her blue eyes fusing with Violet's.

"Hey, hold it right there!"

Ronda Thompson

She heard the sound of a rifle being cocked. Violet turned to face a dirty, unshaven man who stood with a weapon aimed at her. She removed her hat and let her hair fall down around her shoulders.

"It's good to see you again, too, Father," she drawled.

Harold Dalton's mouth dropped open. She'd taken him by surprise. But only for a moment. His next words didn't surprise her at all.

"What the hell are you doing back here, girl?"

Her stomach churned at the mere sight of him. Violet felt no love stir to life inside of her for this man, and her memories hadn't made him more of a monster than he really was. She lifted her chin. "I've come for Rose and my brothers. I'm taking them away from you."

He laughed, and she noticed that most of his teeth were now missing. "Like hell you are. You turn around and leave before I shoot you for trespassing. You have no right to come creeping back here after all this time."

Violet took a step toward him, the rage inside her building. "It must be hard for you to face me . . . Look at me!" she ordered when his gaze lowered. "Look at the daughter, your own flesh and blood, whom you sold to scum for a case of whiskey. A man who beat, raped, and starved me!"

His gaze lifted. He met her eyes. "You didn't just come for them. You came to get even with me. You want to kill me."

Maybe he'd been waiting for her to do just that all this time. Wondering when she'd show up to take her revenge. "I do want to kill you. Getting even was enough until I saw Rose." She nodded at the girl. "I swore if she had bruises on her, I'd kill you."

His smile took her off guard. "Reckon you turned out more like me than I thought you would."

The words cut into her, but didn't deliver the sting he'd hoped. She *hadn't* turned out like him. She knew that now. "At least killing me would have been kinder than what you did. I had to come back. I had to make sure you didn't do the same thing to Rose."

Her father glanced at the girl, frozen by the table, the pan of beans still poised above the plate.

"Hell, I wouldn't do that to Rose. She's the only one I got left to take care of me. The boys, they've all run off. 'Sides, Rose is my own flesh and blood."

"I'm your own flesh and blood, too," she reminded him. "That didn't stop you six years ago."

His smile faded. His eyes turned hard and mean, as they'd been every time he'd looked at her as a child. "You ain't no spawn of mine."

Confusion clouded her mind. What did he mean? He moved toward her, his rifle still aimed at her heart.

"Yeah, you heard me right. Your mama got herself in trouble with some well-to-do young man. One too good for the likes of her. He left her, a baby in her belly, and she got run out of the town where she taught school lessons. She came here when she'd already begun to swell up. Your mama, she was a beautiful woman once. You have her look. Rose, too. But she wasn't too proud after her lover left her, and she wasn't too picky, neither. I knew I'd never have a woman like her unless she had no choice, so I offered to marry her."

Violet had once told Lilla she'd never understood how her educated mother and her no-account father had ever gotten together. Now she knew. As she tried to absorb what he'd told her, she realized she felt no shame. Her heart swelled with joy. Harold Dalton was not her father. His tainted blood did not run in her veins, nor would it run in the veins of her child. Her mother. She had married out of fear of persecution, out of desperation, and found herself strapped to a monster.

"What happened to my mother?" she whispered. "Did you beat her to death?"

He snorted and shook his head. "Didn't have to. After you went off with that Mexican, she just up and died. I think it broke her heart."

The rage came. She knew it would; she'd been holding it inside of her for most of her life, and as with Vega, she allowed it to overtake her. She went for him. He lifted his rifle and hit her with the stock. Violet stumbled back, her jaw throbbing.

"You never did have a lick of sense," he said angrily. "If you meant to kill me, you should have brought along a gun."

"*I* brought a gun."

Violet's head swung toward the door. A man stood there, his gun aimed at the man she was thankful she no longer had to claim as a father. Her heart leaped. Her gaze went to his handsome features. She was never so glad to see anyone in her life.

"Gregory," she whispered.

He didn't look at her, but kept his gaze trained on Harold Dalton. "Put down that rifle," he ordered. "In the time it takes you to turn it around and shoot, you'll be dead."

Dalton lowered the rifle and let it fall to the floor.

"Now kick it over here," Gregory said.

After taking Gregory's measure, Dalton kicked the rifle out of his reach. Gregory walked over and helped Violet rise from the floor. He turned her jaw so he could see it; then his eyes hardened. Violet suspected a bruise had already started to form there. He took her hand and slapped his gun into her palm.

"You want to kill him? I won't stop you."

Her gaze went from the gun in her hand to the man who'd sold her into slavery. His face paled. He swallowed loudly. A bead of sweat trickled down his temple. His hands shook. He fell to his knees. He was right where she had imagined him all these years: down on his knees, begging for mercy.

"I didn't know the Mexican had those plans for you," he said. "He told me you was to work cleaning up in his place. Said he'd pay you, see that you was taken care of."

She shook, too, but not from fear—from anger. "And you took his word?"

"I was drunk," Dalton whined. "I thought maybe with you gone, your ma could get over that other man. But she never did. She loved him till the day she died."

"You beat her," Violet said in a snarl. "You treated her like she was nothing. And you thought she would love you?"

323

He rubbed a hand over his whiskered face. "She was proud, like you. I knew if I didn't keep her in her place, she'd leave me. You see, I had to make her believe she was worth nothing—that no one else would have her."

Tears burned Violet's eyes. He'd made her mother feel the same way he'd made her feel. The same way Violet still might feel today, had Lilla not rescued her from Sally's Saloon, had Miles not shown her love and caring; had Gregory not thawed the ice around her heart. She handed the gun back to Gregory.

"I can't kill him," she said. "He deserves to die, but I don't have the heart of a killer."

"I knew that," Gregory said. "And I knew deep inside that you knew it, too."

She glanced at him. "He's not even my father. I'm a bastard."

His gaze slid toward the man, then back to her. "I'd say you've just improved your pedigree."

"You talk like some fancy dude," Dalton said to Gregory. He looked up at them both with undisguised hatred. "Do you know about Violet? Did she tell you she'd been a man's whore?"

Gregory took a step toward him. "I know all about Violet. I know she's strong and courageous. She could have taken an easy road, one that had been given to her after the hell you put her through, but she chose another path. She chose the hardest one. She's confronted her ghosts. She's come to save her family. Scum like you and me will never measure up to her. She's the definition of the word *lady*."

Violet felt as if she'd been holding her breath for nineteen years and just now had a chance to release it. "You're not scum, Gregory," she said softly. "I knew you'd come for me."

He turned, his eyes meeting hers for half a second. "Then you know me better than I know myself."

She glanced past him at Harold Dalton, still on his knees. "The same as you know me, Gregory."

"I owe you an apology," he said, moving back toward her. A commotion in her peripheral vision distracted her. Harold Dalton dove for the rifle and came up with it. Violet still held Gregory's gun, or else the man would already be dead. She'd hesitated too long.

Gregory placed himself in front of her. "We don't want any trouble," he said. "Just the girl."

"You ain't getting her. Violet, throw down that gun or I'll shoot your man—even if you shoot me."

Violet didn't hesitate. She knew the bastard would make good on his threat.

"Rose takes care of me. Without her, I wouldn't have anyone to clean and cook for me, to chop wood and get dinner. I'd have to—"

"Work?" Gregory interrupted. "That would be a shame. I'll pay you for her."

Dalton's eyes narrowed on him. "Yeah, and when the money runs out, I still ain't got no one to look after me. Just a headache from the whiskey."

"What I have will buy you plenty of whiskey," Gregory assured him. "And someone to take care of you."

The older man squinted at him suspiciously.

"Show me," he ordered. "And don't try nothing funny or I'll shoot you. Or Violet. Hell, she ain't no kin of mine."

When Gregory walked out the door, for a brief moment Violet wondered if he'd walk in again. But her doubt only lasted a second. She trusted him. She *loved* him.

He came back in carrying the flour sacks full of the money they'd taken from the payroll robbery. He moved to the table and dumped the bags' contents.

Harold Dalton sucked in his breath. He walked over and ran his hands through the pile. "Where'd you get it?"

"Does it matter?" Gregory asked dryly.

The man shook his head, his eyes bright with greed. "Don't matter to me."

"Do we have a trade?" Gregory continued.

Dalton didn't even glance at his youngest daughter. His eyes were fixed on the money. "Yeah, take her. Hell, she ain't much good anyway. Always slipping off to sit by her ma's grave or play with Tip. Do whatever you want with her. She's yours."

Gregory, Violet noted, cast her a strange look at the name Tip. She glanced at Rose, who was still frozen, her face a mask of hurt.

"Rose, come here," Violet called.

The girl ignored her. "Pa?" she whispered. "Are you really selling me? Am I really no better than something to trade?"

Violet's heart broke. She knew how Rose felt. The same way she herself had once felt: betrayed.

"Go on with them," Dalton snapped, his gaze still

326

glued to his score. "With this much money, I can finally leave this dump. I can become a man of means, and I ain't spending any of it on you."

"But Pa," Rose whispered. "I thought you at least loved—"

"Get on!" He wheeled around. "Whiskey is what I love. Doing as I please without having to answer to anyone else. You're nothing but trouble. I don't want you, understand?" He raised his hand as if to backhand the girl.

Quick as a cat, Rose grabbed the rifle her father held loosely in his hand and turned it on the man. The weapon discharged. The bullet's impact sent Harold Dalton across the room. Stunned, Violet stared at him as he collapsed to the floor. Her gaze went back to Rose. The color drained from the girl's face, making the bruises on her skin stand out.

"I didn't mean to kill him," she whispered. "I just wanted . . ." the girl crumpled to the floor.

Gregory took the rifle from her hand. Violet hurried over, kneeling beside her. The girl buried her face in her hands. Violet placed an arm around her slender shoulders.

That was how Miles Traften, the sheriff from Topeka, and the ten men who formed a posse found them.

Chapter Twenty-five

"Drop that rifle," the sheriff ordered Gregory.

He did, his gaze meeting Miles's and noting the surprise registered upon the old man's face.

"Who are you?" the sheriff demanded.

Miles rushed forward and threw an arm around him. "This is Gregory Kline. My niece's husband. Good God, man, we thought you were dead." Miles hurried to Violet's side. "Are you all right, dear?"

"Yes." Violet glanced up at him. "But this poor girl is terrified."

The sheriff walked toward Gregory. "You're the missing husband?"

"Yes."

"Well, where in the hell have you been?" His gaze darted toward the dead man, then quickly away. "And who the hell is that?"

Gregory had plotted and planned the whole time he'd raced after Violet, hoping to catch her before she reached Coffeyville. "That is your robber." He nodded toward the money on the table. "As you can plainly see."

"Ted, go take a look at the man. See if he looks like the man who held you up at the swing station," the sheriff said.

A man stepped forward. Gregory recognized him as one of the stagecoach guards. He walked over, stared down at Dalton, and returned. His skin had paled.

"Can't tell," he said in a low voice, glancing toward the women. "He was wearing a bandanna over his face. He's about the same size, though, I guess."

"Where have you been, Mr. Kline?" the sheriff asked.

He'd planned too hard to mess this up. "Tracking the thief," Gregory answered. "I thought he had my wife."

"Tracking him?"

"Gregory's been in Wyoming working for me for three years," Miles spoke up. "Best damn tracker I've ever seen."

"I thought you were shot, or so your wife said."

Gregory pulled his collar aside. "Just nicked me here on the neck. It's already almost healed up. Knocked me out for a while, though. When I came to, I raced after the outlaw because I knew he'd gone after Violet. I figured he meant to make her pay for foiling his robbery attempt in Harvest Grove. The problem was, because of falling from my horse and passing out, I was confused. I rode in the wrong direction for two days before I realized my mistake."

The sheriff still looked suspicious. "Why didn't you come to Topeka and ask for help, or—"

"I thought he had my wife," Gregory snapped. "I wasn't stopping for directions."

The sheriff's gaze went to Violet. "What about you, Mrs. Kline? What are you doing here?"

Gregory hoped Violet's ability to lie hadn't dried up along with her desire for revenge. She rose, staring at the sheriff.

"Looking for Gregory, of course. I realized in my heart he couldn't be dead. I just knew it, and I knew if he wasn't, he'd be looking for me. I remembered what you said about the Daltons being known to hang out around Coffeyville, and that one even lived in the town. I hoped to find Gregory here, searching for me, or at least to uncover the real robber. You haven't been subtle about the fact that you are suspicious of me. I wanted to clear my name."

"But how—"

"Oh, good grief," Miles blustered. "There is your money right there on the table. And there is your robber lying dead on the floor!"

Pushing back his hat, then rubbing his chin, the sheriff said, "I suppose so. But who the hell shot Dalton?"

From the corner of his eye, Gregory saw Violet's sister raise her head. She opened her mouth, but Gregory quickly intervened. "I shot him."

"And I suppose it was self-defense?" He snorted.

Gregory got toe-to-toe with the sheriff. "Yeah, it

was, but even if it weren't, I would have shot him. He abused my wife. Look at her. He gave her that bruised jaw."

Finally the sheriff seemed to soften. He obviously remembered the rumors of the robber's having molested Violet. He lowered his gaze. "Then I don't guess I blame you." He turned to his men. "Get the money gathered up and bring the body along." He turned to Violet and her sister. "You, young miss, who are you?"

Rose looked as if she were afraid to answer. She glanced at her older sister.

"I think she's mute," Violet said. "Obviously she's the dead man's daughter. And if you'll look closely at her, you'll also see she's been beaten, and on more than one occasion."

The sheriff frowned. "A Dalton?"

"A poor, frightened girl," Violet shot back at him, and Gregory had to smile. The sheriff shouldn't get Violet riled.

"She'd best come along with me," the sheriff said. "I'll have to find someone to take her in."

"Who in Coffeyville is going to take a Dalton into their home?" Violet asked. "We'll take her with us."

The sheriff looked at Gregory to see if he'd dispute her decision. "My wife has a soft spot for strays," Gregory said. "I killed the girl's father; I should be responsible for her."

"She'll probably stab you in the back or murder you in your sleep," the sheriff muttered.

"Then that will be my problem, not yours—right, Sheriff?"

The man's attention went to his men, who were carrying out Dalton's body. "Right," he said.

"Are we free to go now?" Miles asked. "We have business waiting for us back in St. Louis."

"I thought Mr. and Mrs. Kline had business here," the sheriff reminded them.

Gregory's and Violet's eyes met. "Our business here is finished," he said. "Right, Violet?"

She nodded.

"I guess I don't see any reason to keep you any longer, then," the sheriff said.

It seemed to Gregory that a collective sigh of relief from everyone in the room followed the lawman's statement. The man walked outside. Gregory watched him mount his horse and ride away, taking the body of the man who'd made Violet's life a living hell—and what he'd once thought was his future, the money—with him.

"Could you both give me a moment with Rose?" Violet asked.

He and Miles nodded and left the shack.

Violet refused to shed one single tear for Harold Dalton, but she did allow Rose to weep.

"I killed him," the girl whispered. "I killed my own pa."

Smoothing Rose's wild hair from her face, Violet said, "It was an accident, Rose. You were defending yourself."

"I didn't mean for that to happen," she cried. "I just wanted to keep him from hitting me." She glanced up, her big blue eyes full of tears. "I'm a killer. I'm like the rest of them."

"No," Violet said sharply. "You're not. And it was an accident. I wanted to kill him, Rose. I've wanted to for a long time. But then I met decent people. I learned how to love, and now I'm trying to learn to love myself, and in time, learn how to forgive. But apparently there is justice in the world, justice that wouldn't let him be spared."

"Will you really let me come with you, Violet? I mean, even after what I've done?"

Her own future wasn't clear, but Violet wasn't about to let go of Rose for any reason. "Yes, you can come with me. And our brothers—do you know where they are?"

Rose nodded. "They ran away. Pa tried to get them to join with some of his kin, but none of them wanted to be bank robbers. They're working a farm not far from here. Sometimes one of them sneaks over and gives me money. They said when they got enough for us to get far away, they'd come for me."

"Well, we're going after them," Violet assured her.

"Then what, Violet?"

It was a good question. Gregory had come back. But had he come back for her? Or simply because his newfound conscience had gotten to him?

"Pack up what little you have, Rose. Meet me outside when you're finished."

Violet helped her sister to rise, then walked outside. It was a good thing she did, because Miles and Gregory looked as if they were going to get in a fight.

"I told you to stay away from her!" Miles nearly shouted.

"And I told you, I don't work for you anymore," Gregory shouted back. "I'll do as I damn well please!"

"You are not going to marry her," Miles said in a snarl. "I'm not having you in my family. If you think you can worm your way in by—"

"Excuse me," Violet interrupted, her hands on her hips. "Are you both deciding my future for me?"

"Violet," Gregory started toward her. "I insist that you marry me."

"She'll do no such thing," Miles bellowed. "I'm not forgetting how he left you to fend for yourself after that robbery. He's probably only decided he'd rather live a more respectable life as a partner in a cattle company than run around as an outlaw."

Gregory turned on him. "And I told you what you could do with your damn partnership!"

"Stop it!" Violet commanded. "You're both behaving like children. Gregory, do you have something to say to me?"

He glared at Miles and stepped toward her. "I'm asking you to marry me."

Although her heart leaped with joy, she tried to display no outward emotion. "Why?"

The man proposing looked at a momentary loss. "Well, for one thing, the baby. I—"

"You told him?" She glanced accusingly at Miles.

Her guardian's face flushed. "I figured if that didn't run him off for good, nothing would."

Violet turned around. "Go away. Both of you. It

may not have occurred to either of you, but I can take care of myself." She stormed toward a broken-down barn, where she'd once spent time with the notorious outlaw, Tip. She'd barely gotten inside when Gregory caught up.

"Violet, listen to reason."

"You know I don't listen to reason."

He took her shoulders and turned her to face him. "I love you, Violet. Yes, I took the money, and yes, I planned to keep going, but I couldn't. I had to make sure you were safe first. Then Miles came and I still didn't go. I had to be certain the two of you left for St. Louis. Then you disappeared and I confronted Miles. He told me about the baby, and then I thought that would make me go for sure. I thought, What kind of example would I be to a child? What kind of husband would I be for you?"

Violet had trouble listening to the voice of reason, but she had no trouble listening to the sound of a man trying to dig himself out of a hole. Especially since she loved this particular man. "And what conclusion did you arrive at?" she asked.

His hazel eyes looked brown in the dimness of the barn. They never wavered while he stared down at her. "I realized that if any woman can make a good father and a good husband out of me, that woman is you. I kept planning this grand life, with all that money at my disposal, and then I realized it wouldn't be anything without you. I realized money can't make the man. Only a man can make the man—or a woman, if she is extraordinary. And you are extraordinary, Violet."

Her insides were in serious jeopardy of melting. "What about my past? You said—"

"I said stupid things, Violet," he interrupted, pulling her closer. "I said things that had been planted in my head, instead of listening to my heart. You're the only person who has ever seen any good in me. You're the only one who has ever made me want to be good. *And I do want to be good.*"

Emotion welled up inside of her. Tears prickled in her eyes, but she turned away from him. She had to make certain he really loved her the way that she loved him. That they had the kind of love that would see them through the good times and the bad. "How do I know you're not asking me to marry you just because you think it's the honorable thing to do?"

He laughed, then turned her to face him again. "Since when has Gregory Kline done anything honorable? I love you, Violet. That's all this can be."

She didn't know how long she'd been waiting to hear those words from him until he said them, and she believed him. "I love you, too," she whispered.

"You're the only woman who would have the courage to," he joked.

Their future looked shaky at best to her. "Will you work for Miles? Take the partnership you've more than earned?"

He shook his head. "No. I won't have him believing I married you for any reason but the true one."

"We're not robbing banks for a living," she warned him.

"No," he agreed. "I've had my fill of that. I've also learned a thing or two about ranching. I thought we might return to Wyoming. Get our own place."

Violet lifted an eyebrow. "You hate Wyoming."

Gregory drew her into his arms. "I only hated it because you weren't there. We can both start over, Violet. Together."

Another problem occurred to her. "Rose told me where my brothers are. They're working a farm not far from here. I'm sorry, Gregory, but to have me, you'll have to take on the rest of my brood."

His lips brushed hers. "I knew that coming here. If we plan to start our own ranch, we'll need the extra help."

The gentle brush of his lips brought passion quickly raging to the surface. She wanted him—now, forever. Violet liked the idea of all of them getting a fresh start in a new territory. "Thinking back to what I said . . . it seems you will have me in your bed, after all, Mr. Kline."

"And the sooner the better," he answered. His voice was husky. He captured her mouth. The kiss had only begun when Gregory jumped and jerked away from her. "What the hell is that?"

Violet reached down and scooped up a large black cat with a white tip on its tail. "This is the outlaw Tip. I guess we ended up ransoming him after all."

"I suppose he'll have to come along?"

She nodded, then smiled. He smiled back, then leaned forward to claim her lips again. A discreet cough had them pulling away from each other.

"Violet, your sister is waiting," Miles said. "She looks at a loss. I think you should come and comfort her."

337

She wondered how she'd break the news to Miles that she would marry Gregory. He seemed dead-set on believing the worst about the man. "You tell him," she decided before walking away.

Gregory found himself in an awkward position. Telling Miles anything didn't seem to do any good. He joined the man outside the barn.

Lips pursed, Miles asked, "How much will it take, Gregory?"

He laughed. "You haven't got enough. I love Violet. I want to marry her, take care of her. You're just going to have to trust me, Miles."

As if it pained him, Traften admitted, "You did come back and do the right thing. If you hadn't given up the money from the robbery, Violet and I might both be in jail now. She told me that you've done some very heroic things on her behalf. She said I had misjudged you." His gaze finally softened. "I guess Wyoming did change you."

Gregory shook his head. "No, Wyoming didn't change me. *Violet* changed me. You were right: it doesn't matter how wealthy you are, or what you manage to achieve in life, without family and loved ones, they mean nothing. Violet taught me that, and it's a lesson I'll never forget again."

Miles slapped him on the back. "I do believe something has turned you around. I'll reinstate your partnership. Love is wonderful, but one must support a wife."

Running a hand over his cheeks, Gregory said, "I'm refusing your offer. Violet and I are going to

Wyoming, along with her sister, her brothers, and an outlaw named Tip. We're going to start our own ranch."

The wind clearly left Miles's sails. "B-but Wyoming is so far away from me." He frowned, then smiled. "I have an idea. Let's see what Violet thinks of it."

Gregory would have liked to see what he himself thought of it first, but Miles marched toward the horses, where Violet and Rose waited.

"Violet, dear, Gregory has just told me the two of you, along with your family, plan to start a ranch in Wyoming. Why Wyoming? Why not Texas? You could be near Lilla, and I'm thinking of moving out there myself now that I'll have grandchildren. I want to be near them."

A sick feeling settled in the pit of Gregory's stomach. His gaze flew to Violet.

Her face lit up. "I would love to be near Lilla. We could raise our children together, but . . ." She frowned. "Everyone there will remember that I once worked . . . Well . . ."

"Oh, pish-posh." Miles waved her worries away. "Nearly the whole town is made up of former prostitutes and their cowboy husbands. Lilla says Texas is a place where a person can find themselves. Can become anything or anyone they choose to be. What do you say?"

"It sounds wonderful," Violet answered. She glanced at him. "Gregory, what do think? Gregory? Are you all right?"

He was not all right. "Texas? With Wade and

Camile Langtry? With Lilla and Grady Finch? There isn't one in the whole lot who wouldn't like to peel my hide off in strips."

She burst into laughter. He didn't see anything funny about the situation. She came to him and threw her arms around his neck.

"You are not a coward, Gregory Kline. You just like to pretend to be one so you don't have to do anything heroic, and you won't mess up your nice suit or your handsome face. I want to go to Texas."

He didn't, but if it made Violet happy, he would. "All right. Texas it is."

She kissed him in front of God and everyone. Not a prude, regardless of what she claimed, he kissed her back, and soundly. She pulled away from him and glanced at her sister. "Rose and I will be with you in a moment."

He stood with Miles as Violet and Rose walked to a small wooden cross. Miles became teary eyed as the sisters prayed over their mother's grave. He placed an arm around Gregory's shoulder. Gregory frowned at him and shrugged it off.

Texas. The place where this had all started for him, with his blackmail scheme so long ago.

The sun shone down on Violet, highlighting the blond in her hair. She looked like an angel to him. But she wasn't a saint. Violet was a flesh-and-blood woman, one with a passion to rival his own. He didn't deserve her, but he'd spend the rest of his life trying to.

After a few moments, the sisters rejoined them. They mounted up, Violet in the saddle with him, since they needed an extra horse, and Rose holding a squirming cat. He hoped that this time when Violet rode away, the ghosts that haunted her life would stay forever buried. A moment later, his worries were laid to rest.

Rose started to glance behind them.

"No, Rose," Violet said. "Don't ever look back. There's nothing there for you. Just keep looking ahead, and sooner or later you'll find your way."

Gregory leaned forward and nuzzled Violet's ear. "Or an angel will come along to guide you."

Epilogue

Violet's younger sister, Rose, had never seen so much chaos beneath one roof in her life. Her brothers were arguing over which of them a pretty rancher's daughter in the area preferred. Lilla Finch's toddler, a sturdy little boy almost two years of age, ran circles around her legs while beating a wooden spoon against an old pot.

She loved the idea of having a close family, but sometimes it was too close. They had guests that afternoon, which was nothing out of the ordinary. Rose just couldn't figure out why her sister and brother-in-law's house had to be the main gathering place, since it was the smallest one of anyone's present. Her "uncle" Miles was present, along with his beautiful daughter, Lilla, and her handsome husband, Grady Finch. Wade and Camile Langtry were also there. Of course they'd brought along their twins, one who was an angel, the other a devil. An old couple named Hank and Margaret Riley added to the house's cramped confines. They were too ancient to have any young kids, thank goodness, but they spoiled everyone else's. Tom Cordell had come along with his daughter, and he'd brought Maria— once his housekeeper, soon to be his wife.

Sometimes Rose felt overwhelmed by so much togetherness, and by the fact that she usually ended up attending to all the children while the parents entertained one another.

She heard her sister laugh at something Camile Langtry said. The women were gathered in the parlor. Knowing Camile, it wasn't anything Violet would deem suitable for Rose's young ears. Lilla Finch said something and the women all burst into laughter again. Rose didn't see why she couldn't be in on the fun. She wasn't a child anymore. In a few months she would be plenty old enough to marry.

A loud curse from Miles drew her attention to a table in the dining room. Miles, Wade, Grady, Tom, Hank, and Gregory were all playing poker.

"I swear you're cheating, Gregory," Miles accused. "How many hands is that he's won?"

"Too many not to be cheating, I'm thinking," Wade Langtry drawled.

Rose's brother-in-law didn't comment. He bounced a baby girl upon his knee, and obviously too hard, because the baby spit up on his leg. As if it were of no consequence, he grabbed the rag from over his shoulder and mopped up the mess.

"I have to cheat," he finally commented. "I want to buy Ryder's bull. I have to build up my herd so I can give Helen a nice inheritance."

Helen had been Rose and Violet's mother's name. Rose felt warm all over when she looked at her niece—who had to be the most beautiful baby in the world. Gregory said so about every five minutes, and Rose put a lot of stock in what her brother-in-law said. Everyone seemed to do the same, although it had taken a few fights for Gregory to earn their respect. Gregory had brains, too, and he'd come up with lots of ways to improve all their ranches.

Most amazing to Rose, though, he never hit her or Violet—although she'd once seen him send Wade Langtry flying. Gregory kept her brothers in line, too, and that in itself was no easy chore.

"I've had my eye on that bull, too," Grady Finch spoke up. "How 'bout I go in halves with you and we share him?"

Gregory nodded. "He's young. I imagine he can do both our herds some good."

"He's an Angus," Tom Cordell pointed out. "I'd think you'd want to stay with Herefords."

"Angus is the way of the future," Gregory argued, then played with one hand, since he held Helen on his lap with the other. The baby had a card in her slobbery fist, Rose noted—no doubt one Gregory might need later.

"If Gregory says so, it's probably true," Miles rejoined the conversation. "He has an uncanny sense about these things."

"An uncanny way of winning every hand at poker,

too," Hank Riley complained again. He threw down his cards. "I ain't been dealt crap for three hands."

"Hank, your language," Gregory warned, then kissed Helen on the top of her blond head.

"Give her to me." Hank held out his arms. "I ain't got to hold her since we arrived. 'Sides, I want to see what card you've slipped her."

A tug on her skirts had Rose glancing down. Cammy—Wade and Camile's little girl, and a hellion if ever one had been born—stared up her. "Clint's tied up on the porch."

"How did your brother get tied up?" she asked.

She shrugged, her devilish eyes suddenly innocent. "Don't know, but he can't get loose."

Rose suspected she knew how Clint had gotten tied up. "Watch young Matthew for me while I go get him untied."

Cammy took the spoon from the toddler's chubby fingers and showed him how to bang the pan louder. On her way to the porch, Rose heard Matthew let out a wail. No doubt Cammy had failed to return the spoon and had wrestled away the pot in the bargain. She'd give Grady Finch all of one second to be on the spot, urging his young son to stand up for himself. And she'd give Wade Langtry all of another second to be there in his daughter's defense.

Clint was indeed tied up on the porch. He didn't look upset, though, only resigned to wait for someone to come along and undo whatever trouble his sister had gotten him into. He had the bluest eyes Rose had ever seen.

"Did Cammy do this?" she asked, just to see what he'd say.

As usual, he said nothing. He only shrugged. She bent and untied him. He awarded her with a quirky little grin she thought would get him out of trouble often in the future. It was his daddy's grin, if everything else about Clint Langtry was his mother's. Once Clint scrambled inside, Rose took a deep breath of clean Texas air and walked around the house.

It wasn't as grand as the Langtrys' place, and not as big as Grady and Lilla's place, but it was cozy and comfortable. Her brothers slept in the bunkhouse with the hired hands and Rose had a room all to herself. They all went to school. Lilla taught them lessons. There had been much debate about what would go up first in Langtry, the school or the church, but since the town seemed to produce children on a grand scale, the school had been decided upon as the first choice. Next spring they would all work together to raise a church, too.

Conversation between the women floated to her when she passed an open window.

"Of course you're not too old to wear white at your wedding," Lilla scoffed.

"*I* wore white," Margaret Riley said.

"You are still pure, aren't you, Maria?" Camile teased the ex-housekeeper.

"Tom's legs may not work, but everything else he has does," Maria answered, and another burst of feminine laughter followed the remark.

"I have a toast," she heard her sister say. "Here's to laundry. May it not be the only thing around your house that is hung."

That really set the women off. Rose shook her head bemusedly and moved on. She'd never seen so many couples so in love with one another . . . or whatever it was that kept them together. She glanced at the sunset. It always took her breath away. A tall figure on a horse moved toward her. Rose quickly smoothed her wild hair. That figure always took her breath away, too.

"Evening, Rose."

Rose stared up at him. Storm Ryder. She'd never heard of a boy having such a name. He'd told her it was taken from the fact that he was born during a raging thunderstorm. His mother was an Indian and believed a child should be given a name that coincided with an event during birth.

"What are you doing here?" she asked, but knew perfectly well the answer. He rode by every Sunday about this time, for it was the time Rose watched the sunset.

"Just enjoying the scenery," he answered, his gaze roaming her.

She pretended not to notice. "It is a nice evening for a ride."

"Company again?" He glanced at all the buggies around the house.

"Always," she answered.

"Want to ride with me, Rose?" he asked.

She opened her mouth to answer, but Gregory appeared.

"You keep hanging around here and I'll have to put you to work," he said to Storm.

"My father sent me over to tell you he'd come down a little on that bull if you're still interested."

"Tell him I'll be around tomorrow to talk to him about it." He stood there, and Rose supposed he would until Storm rode away. To her surprise, the half-Indian boy didn't move on.

"I'd like to call on Rose."

"She's too young."

"I'm nearly sixteen," Rose reminded Gregory, her heart fluttering inside of her chest.

Her brother-in-law glanced at her and frowned. "Well, when you are sixteen, we'll talk about it again." He turned and walked toward the house. "Come on back inside in a minute, Rose."

"He treats me like a child," she fumed, glancing back up at Storm Ryder.

His dark eyes appraised her again. "You're *not* a child."

Her brothers would hit him from here into the next sunset if they'd seen the way Storm had just looked at her. Rose liked it, but she'd never tell him so. Violet had warned her often enough about the danger of a man with charm. And Violet should know: Helen wasn't but a year old and Violet had another baby on the way.

"One of these days, you will climb upon my horse. I'll ride away with you and never bring you back."

She gave him a haughty quirk of her brow, as she'd seen Lilla do often enough when her husband, Grady, got out of line.

"You're full of yourself. My brothers say you're nothing but trouble."

He smiled at her, his teeth a flash of white against his dark skin. "Some girls like trouble."

"I'm not one of them," she assured him, and turned to walk back toward the house.

"I think you are," he called after her.

Her heart beat fast inside of her chest. She didn't look at him again. Some didn't like Storm because of his mixed blood. Some called him a half-breed, said he'd turn wild someday and no telling what he might do. But Rose could hardly be judgmental, given her past. She steered her thoughts from Kansas and what she'd done. Violet had told her never to look back, and she hadn't. She wouldn't. Whoever the beaten girl was who'd accidentally killed her own sorry father, Rose was no longer her.

She was a Kline, not a Dalton. Gregory had given her and her brothers his name. And someday Rose would climb on Storm Ryder's horse and ride away with him. This was Texas, after all, and Lilla said that in Texas, a person could become whoever they chose, do whatever they set their heart on doing. Rose had her heart set on Storm.

Until Gregory realized she was a grown woman, she'd bide her time. She had to help Violet prepare for a visit from Gregory's family next month, anyway. He hadn't seen any of them in a long time, but Violet had kept on him until he'd agreed to invite his parents and his four brothers for a visit. Rose sighed. Now, *that* should be interesting.

Ronda Thompson

Violet said that families should be close, should love one another, should do anything for each another. Rose was glad her sister felt that way. Violet had saved them all. She'd risked her life to do so. Now the roof over Rose's head held a houseful of love inside. Regardless if Gregory didn't get on well with his family, Rose figured they would patch up their differences. Helen, the beautiful blond baby girl with deep violet eyes, would see to that.

"Rose, come inside," Violet shouted from the porch. "We're going to pull taffy."

It was a ritual they all performed when they got together. A way to connect with one another, even if it was sticky work. Once, in what Rose guessed might be a shocking display of bad manners in front of guests, Gregory had licked the gooey mess from Violet's fingers. Rose figured Violet had called him prudish about something again and he'd meant to prove her wrong.

An arm went around her waist. "Isn't the sunset beautiful?" Violet whispered beside her.

"It sure is," Rose answered softly, but she wasn't watching the sun sink. She could still see Storm, his tall, straight silhouette outlined against a fiery backdrop. She put her arm around Violet's still-slim waist and hugged her back. "Thank you, Violet. Thank for giving me this life. Thank you for teaching me about love, and about forgiveness. Our mother would be proud of you."

Her sister's eyes filled with tears. "She'd be proud of you, too, Rose. She'd proud of all of us."

Arms around each another, they walked back to the house. The past became a more distant memory with each new dawn. She and Violet had wrestled their demons, and in the end they had won. The future was a fiery red sunset—a light in the distance, with the strong, solid form of a boy fast approaching manhood.

Violet had found love, a good man, and was happy. Rose knew that. Her sister smiled more than anyone she knew. And if Violet could rise above the wrongs committed against her, if she could be brave, learn to forgive and forget, then so could Rose.

"That Storm Ryder is trouble, you know," Violet commented, her lips stretching into a smile. "It'll take the right woman to tame him."

Rose smiled back. "Some women like trouble. And I might just know who the right woman will be."

Desert Bloom
Ronda Thompson

For Lilla Traften, the Texas Panhandle is nothing but hot cactus and dirt, its inhabitants worse. Grady Finch, the rugged foreman of the WC Ranch may be devastatingly handsome, but he is tactless. Worse, the heat is getting to her; sunstroke is making her dream of Grady's hands upon her, of the sweaty love they might make in the dust. Hardly normal thoughts for a proper miss and charm-school teacher! Still, she can't help wondering what will win the heart of a man like Grady. She'll have to prove she can survive on her own. He'll have to see that not only the land can undergo transformation, but that Lilla, too, can flower in the desert.

___4943-0 $5.99 US/$6.99 CAN

Ronda Thompson

Scandalous

Christine is shocked that she's agreed to marry. Her intended, Gavin Norfork, is a notorious lover, gambler, and duelist. It is rumored he can seduce a woman at twenty paces. The dissolute aristocrat is clearly an unsuitable match for a virtuous orphan who has devoted her life to charity work. But Christine's first attempt to scare him off ends only with mud on her face. And, suddenly finding herself wed to a man she hasn't even met, Christine finds herself questioning her goals. Perhaps it is time to make her entrée into London society, to meet Gavin on his own ground—and challenge him with his own tricks. The unrepentant rake thinks she's gotten dirty before, but he hasn't seen anything yet. Not only her husband can be scandalous—and not only Christine can fall in love.

___4805-1 $5.50 US/$6.50 CAN

COUGAR'S WOMAN Ronda Thompson

On the journey to meet her fiancé in Santa Fe, Melissa Sheffield is captured by Apaches and given to a man known as Cougar. At first, she is relieved to learn that she's been given to a white man, but with one kiss he proves himself more dangerous than the whole tribe. Terrified of her savage captor, she pledges to escape at any price. But while there might be an escape from the Apaches, is there any escape from her heart? Clay Brodie—known as Cougar to the Apaches—is given the fiery Melissa by his chief. He is then ordered to turn the beauty into an obedient slave—or destroy her. But how can he slay a woman who evokes an emotion deeper than he's ever known? And when the time comes to fight, will it be for his tribe or for his woman?

___4524-9 $4.99 US/$5.99 CAN

PRICKLY PEAR

RONDA THOMPSON

Daddy's little girl is no angel. Heck, she hasn't earned the nickname Prickly Pear by being a wallflower. Everyone on the Circle C knows that Camile Cordell can rope her way out of Hell itself—and most of the town thinks the willful beauty will end up there sooner or later. Now, Cam knows that her father is looking for a new foreman for their ranch—and the blond firebrand is pretty sure she knows where to find one. Wade Langtry has just arrived in Texas, but he seems darn sure of himself in trying to take a job that is hers. Cam has to admit, though, that he has what it takes to break stallions. In her braver moments, she even imagines what it might feel like to have the roughrider break her to the saddle—or she him. And she fears that in the days to follow, it won't much matter if she looses her father's ranch—she's already lost her heart.

___4624-5 $4.99 US/$5.99 CAN

In Trouble's Arms — Ronda Thompson

Loreen Matland is very clear. If the man who answers her ad for a husband is ugly as a mud fence, she'll keep him. If not, she'll fill his hide full of buckshot. Unfortunately, Jake Winslow is handsome. Lori knows that good-looking men are trouble, and Jake proves no exception. Of course, she hasn't been entirely honest with him, either. She has difficulties enough to make his flight from the law seem like a ride through the prairie. But the Texas Matlands don't give up, even to dangerous men with whiskey-smooth voices. And yet, in Jake's warm strong arms, Lori knows he is just what she needs—for her farm, her family, and her heart.

Lair of the Wolf

Also includes the sixth installment of *Lair of the Wolf*, a serialized romance set in medieval Wales. Be sure to look for future chapters of this exciting story featured in Leisure books and written by the industry's top authors.

___4716-0 $5.99 US/$6.99 CAN

CALL
OF THE
MOON
RONDA THOMPSON

Jason Donavon walks in darkness, seeking release from his
curse. It has the power to destroy everything—to take his human-
ity. In a world where he no longer belongs, he feels eyes watching him. Something even more sinister than himself stalks the
night.

The woman who materializes to save him from the forces of
darkness holds answers to the questions he's been afraid to ask.
She takes him to her world, to the wilds of the North. Yet in a
place where nature rules supreme, Jason knows danger awaits. He
will be forced to fight his love for a woman forbidden, and dis-
cover whether salvation will come from resisting the seductive
light of the moon—or in surrendering to it.

"A great new voice in the genre!
No one writes sexy werewolves better!"
—USA TODAY BESTSELLING AUTHOR
AMANDA ASHLEY